Evolution

Evolution

Jennifer MacDonald

Writers Club Press
San Jose New York Lincoln Shanghai

Evolution

Writers Club Press
an imprint of iUniverse.com, Inc.

For information address:
iUniverse.com, Inc.
620 North 48th Street, Suite 201
Lincoln, NE 68504-3467
www.iuniverse.com

ISBN: 0-595-13512-9

Printed in the United States of America

For Mark, A.J. and my mother Carol Ayn.
Also in honor of my friends that have passed on,
you all know who you are.

CHAPTER I

It was hard to sit comfortably in the thick, padded chair. My stomach was like a lead weight and my skin was too hot. No part of my body was free from the vibrations of stifled emotions.

The sun shot laser beams through the office window on every inch of my body. I felt the warmth but it wasn't calming like it usually is with me and the sun. It was too hot, it was annoying and I felt my face turning red at its intrusion. I wanted to explode but I never let myself have that kind of freedom. My anger dissolved into depression.

"I understand you Kelly and I really know what your going through but you must understand, you're not the only one. At this stage in your sobriety, this is all very normal. How long has it been? Three years?" asked Jerry Henderson, a calm, middle-aged man who genuinely seemed interested in my pitiful life.

"Four years Jerry. Four God damn years of confusion and turmoil. Isn't it supposed to get better? They say it gets better. I want it to get better! Come on, what's the hold up? Do you know there's a light at the end of the tunnel? Is there a purpose to staying sober?" I thought for a moment that I may explode right there in the head-crackers office. Wouldn't it be the perfect place for an emotional blow-out? He was a therapist, he would know how to handle it.

Something inside me refused the much needed release and once again, I denied myself the right to feel freedom and slid back into my seething mind.

Jerry was trying hard to help me get it all out of my system but when it came right down to it, I didn't trust him enough. He slumped down in his high-backed mahogany chair looking defeated. Some childish part of me felt proud, as if I had won a battle.

"Kelly, I know your hurting but I also know it hasn't been all that bad for you over the last four years. Look at the good things you've done with yourself. That's what I want you to do over the next week. List your assets and your accomplishments since you got sober. We can discuss them next Thursday."

It wasn't hard to tell the session was nearly over. He always gave his "think positively, look on the bright side" spiel and burdened me with homework about three minutes before the little gold buzzer on his desk went off. His timing was remarkably stable.

"I'm not happy. I don't even know what I'm doing anymore. Worst of all, I don't know what I want to do. Don't I have some kind of purpose? I want one, one that I like, something that makes me feel alive, bold, special. I'm sick of wanting to be normal. I've been trying normal for too long. Normal is stupid. Look at all the stupid things normal people do. So much suffering just so they can fit into the grand scheme of things. It's not fair. I wanted to be normal and all I got was alcoholism and now all you can say is that I'm a normal alcoholic. Everything is normal and it still doesn't work. I want to know what's beyond normal, what's…" The tinny buzzer broke my speech and Jerry smiled professionally.

"Twenty years of drinking isn't going to be cleaned up in four years of sobriety. I'm telling you honestly Kelly, every human being is looking for the meaning in their lives. It's just part of the fun of being human." With that he raised himself out of his fancy chair and held out his hand to me. "Let's get you another appointment."

My body shriveled a little with the disappointment of not being allowed to finish my ranting. I needed to do some ranting, I had years of ranting to do but I always let myself get cut off. Truth is, I was always on the edge of a ranting session and it was wearing me down.

We walked out to the carpeted reception area where everything was a quiet shade of green. The blonde lady at the desk matched the surroundings.

"Just set your normal time up with Jesse…Well you know the routine. Remember your list. Goodbye Kelly."

Before I could open my mouth, he whisked a young man into his office and shut the heavy door. I smiled at the older woman behind the desk while deciding whether or not to make an appointment. I wanted to do something different this time. She waited for a moment, looking at me with expectation but finally decided to break the silence with "Same time next week Ms. McGrail?"

"Actually Jesse, no. I'll give ya' a call to make the appointment. I might be busy next week." That was good. It was different. Four years I'd been paying this guy to figure me out and set me straight. I had to have the guts to break the tradition, maybe that would get me out of the slump I was in.

None of this psychological sifting was helping me anymore.

"I'll just wait for your call then, Ms. McGrail." she said with the intention of sounding like a firm goodbye.

"Yea sure, you do that." I smiled at her and thought about saying "So long Jesse, I'm outta here." but knew it was too rude for my usual demeanor. I didn't know what I was doing nor did I think that any of this would help me with my debilitating emotional problems but for the moment it gave me a sense of great power, just to think for myself and act on it without consulting with anyone else.

Though the air was cold, the sun continued to shine with it's full intensity. Stepping out onto the parking lot pavement, I soaked up the energy from above. The sun set off tiny sparkles in the black, ice covered surface making it look more beautiful than it really was. I grabbed for the handle of the door to my rusted out Tempo but before opening it, I pulled back. It didn't seem like it could be my car, I deserved something better. Right there, next to my car sat Jerry Hendersons' six month old Jaguar.

"I paid for that." I said out loud and laughed. I decided to walk home.

After the hour long walk home, I thought it was possible that the heavy burden of my depressed spirit was lifting. I didn't feel entirely stable but I had three and a half days left to my four day holiday. No sense wasting them all on bad moods and dark thoughts. The phone rang as I entered my humble home.

"Hi Kelly. It's Shirley here. Sorry to have to call you at home like this. I know we agreed that you'd have a couple of days off but we just got this big project and we could use your help. Gimme a call as soon as you can, okay? I really appreciate it. Bye-Bye for now." The machine clicked when the message ended.

My face dropped along with the keys that tumbled out of my hand. My stomach bubbled with anxiety. I lunged at the machine, fully willing to smash it to tiny bits, but I stopped myself and stepped back. Wouldn't it be stupid to ruin my stuff because I'm pissed off at her? I erased the message and shut off the machine.

"Sorry Shirley, I didn't get your message until Sunday night and by that time it was too late. So, so sorry." I practiced what I would say to her on Monday morning. Sure, I'd hear about it for weeks but if I went in at that moment I may of given in to the urge to kill her. I figured I'd be better off taking a long, hot bath and forgetting it. My favorite places in the world were my old, claw-foot tub and my bed. I soaked away my cares until the bright sun set behind the distant western mountains and all the windows in my apartment looked like black holes. Perfect, just what I needed to calm my raw nerves and solidify my new found confidence. I went over the decisions I'd made. I wasn't going back to the therapist and when I had a day off then everybody else could kiss my ass. Yes, there's my power. I crawled into bed and turned off the world.

The next morning brought me a positive outlook and a feeling of harmony. I enjoyed the day being relatively free from obsession with my mental state. That evening, Cassie, one of my close friends, and I had been out to a movie. We were walking to her car afterward, mine was still in the parking lot of the Henderson and Croft Counseling Service, and talking about the movie we'd just seen. Suddenly, a tall man cut in front of me. Cassie grabbed my arm pulling on it to prevent a collision. All but his slightly weathered face was hidden under a course, hooded robe. His hazel eyes were focused intently on mine which produced a mesmerizing reaction within me. I swayed and trembled beneath his gaze. A cold gust of wind snapped me back to reality. I shook my head to break the eye contact. He pulled down his hood releasing locks of billowy, golden hair which danced wildly in the wind. After saying hello and flashing a slightly mechanical smile, he turned and walked in the direction from which he came.

"Okay…Whoa, that guy was really weird. Who the hell does he think he is? Did you see those clothes? He's just damn lucky I didn't give him a taste of that women's defense course I'm in. I shoulda set him straight. Sonofabitch, what a weirdo."

"He just said hello, Cassie. You can't beat someone up for saying hello." I felt a little shaky as I watched him walk away.

"Men should know better than to approach women in dark parking lots. Any guy deserves to be beat up if they're going to do things like that." She pulled her coat up around her tiny neck as if to protect herself better.

I looked around at the well lit parking lot and the eighty or more people going to or coming from the theater and shook my head at Cassie.

"Besides, he cut me off in mid-sentence and now I don't remember what I was going to say." she said with a childish whine. I laughed a little but wasn't paying much attention to her self-centered rambling.

The strange man had affected me. I gave my head another shake and shrugged off the preternatural feeling. I looked around the parking lot again but I couldn't see him.

"Kelly?" Cassie nudged me with her elbow. "Are you still with me?"

"Of course Cassie." I turned to her and vowed to myself to forget the whole moment. I needed the social acceptance, so I refrained from talking about how I felt, best that she didn't think I were strange or abnormal.

We went on with the average night out and I went home. By the time I reached my apartment door, I had put away the memory of the robed stranger. After all, vague feelings about meeting a weirdo on the street couldn't be trusted as anything of value. There was millions of weirdos, this one wasn't anyone special. I went to sleep in denial.

With the weekend over, I went to work with as much enthusiasm as I could. I thought about calling my kind therapist but fought the urge. I was addicted to him, I thought. I was going through therapy withdrawals, making up excuses for why I wasn't ready to handle life without those once a week check-ins with the man who could teach me how to behave in the world. It really was time for me to handle life on my own but it seemed so hard.

The dreams started about a week after the encounter with the strange man at the movie theater parking lot.

I left work early and went home deciding that sleep would cure my pains and get the crazy day over with. I found myself praying as I lay in bed, something I did very little of unless I was feeling particularly hopeless. I cringed at the warning signs of another downward emotional spiral coming on, worse than it was before and I couldn't get those positive thinking tapes to reprogram my mind. I tossed around in bed, trying to find a comfortable position. It didn't come quickly but I finally fell to sleep in the darkness of my room.

The large man appeared before me again, the same way that he had in the parking lot. He smiled and put his hand on my shoulder. I brushed it off as defense against feeling his strength.

"My name is Sacro. I look forward to knowing you Kelly McGrail."

That's all there was to it, the dream ended when he said my name. It lasted a minute in total if one can actually put time on a dream. The problem was, it wouldn't stop. It kept on, unfailingly repeating itself.

My body jolted upright with a claustrophobic feeling. Sweat beads dripped from my cheeks as I clawed the bed sheets. The waking relieved some of the anxiety and when I truly realized I had only been dreaming, I laughed at my childishness. Yes, it was just a stupid dream, nothing more.

The dream took over the moment I fell back to sleep. I awoke on several occasions more irritated by the invasion each time my eyes fluttered open.

By morning, I was quite numb. The dream had gotten boring and my memory of it faded steadily the longer I stayed awake.

Going to work was a blessing as I could always find some way to ignore myself in my responsibilities. All I had to do was act normal and everything would be okay.

"Kelly, about last week. Maybe you should think about getting a pager. We really needed you here and that answering machine doesn't do you much good when your out gallivanting around." Shirley had come to offer me business advice. She did it every time she didn't get what she wanted out of me. She babbled on but I heard nothing as I let my mind wonder to images of the dream man.

"Are you listening to me Kelly?" The shrill voice yanked me out of my daydream. Shirley was standing over me with her perfect business suit, matching coffee cup complete with the bright red lipstick ring around the rim and practically shouted into my face.

"What's going on with you Kelly?" She saw that she had my attention and calmed her harsh voice. "You're normally very attentive."

"Normally, I am very attentive to you aren't I?" I asked.

"Yes, very much. Is everything all right? Maybe we should have a talk in my office." Shirley loved talking in her office. Since she didn't actually do any work, she took it upon herself to mold her employees to fit her liking by talking one on one in her grand office. I'd always joked with the others that she was secretly hypnotizing us so we'd do what she wanted more often.

"No Shirley. I don't want to talk in your office. I want you to go away so I can finish my work." It just popped out of my mouth. Judging by the look on her face, she received it like I'd thrown a brick at her rather than an answer to her question.

"Excuse me Kelly. I hear my phone. We will talk about this later." she said, smiling for the rest of the office staff who was undoubtedly looking our way. Her phone wasn't ringing.

My muscles relaxed, my heart sang, I turned to my desk and finished my work. I'd never talked back to that hideous woman, not ever in the five years that I'd worked for her and oh, it felt divine.

Shirley didn't come back but the memory of the dream man did. He popped in and out of my awareness throughout the rest of the afternoon. Being a master of denial and ignorance, I was able to push the dream image farther back each time it appeared. By the end of the work day, I was on automatic pilot.

Go home, go to work, eat, sleep. I barely got through the basics and the sleeping became intolerable due to the continuing dreams. My grasp on sanity was slipping.

Every night the dream went on running through its fixed loop, not a single second of variety to change my focus. It was obvious to others that I wasn't doing to well. I couldn't talk to anyone about my troubles. Jerry Henderson left messages on my answering machine but I didn't dare call him. I was embarrassed that my already dark vision of the world was getting bleaker.

My job was the first thing to go. I made it easy for Shirley to find a reason to fire me. It might have been the time I yelled out a firm "Fuck You" when she asked me if I'd get coffees for her and the division manager before they went into their meeting. I really didn't realize that I'd lost control, I didn't feel a thing. I justified every ignorant action by proclaiming "That asshole deserved it." I wouldn't deny that I was in pain. I knew I was "acting funny", as Cassie had said one evening over the phone. She called to cancel our regular movie night because she couldn't handle my moods.

The dreams continued so I decided I would just stay awake. I passed out a few times much the same way as I did when I was drinking. A drunk never really sleeps, they just pass out when they hit their limit. This was the same thing.

God was punishing me I thought as I looked out my window to the cold, dark streets. I had the heat turned off and all the windows open to let in the minus fifteen-degree Celsius winter air. I could see my breath drift out into the night. No way would I go to sleep. The dreams were part of my punishment and Sacro was the devil coming to take me away. God was testing me. I prayed for another chance. I cried in hopes that doing so would wash away my terrible sins. God had to forgive me. Even though I longed to talk to somebody, I only yelled at those that dared to be concerned. Finally, I had successfully driven away all of my friends. I thought the devil must have won the battle over my soul, how else could a being feel so miserable?

Weeks of this insanity passed through me. Alone in my apartment, I flickered through morbid emotions. I toyed with the idea of putting myself into a psych hospital but couldn't get up the nerve. It would mean talking to people and having to explain myself and what was the point of doing that?

One particularly cold afternoon, after letting the pangs of hunger reach my awareness, I stumbled to the kitchen only to find nothing to eat. The cupboards had been emptied and my hunger overcame fear. I needed to go out and get food. I dressed myself to venture to the corner store, not daring the journey until darkness fell. The bitter, cold wind hit my face as I walked out and oddly enough it felt good. I had never enjoyed the biting air of winter but just then it reminded me that I was alive. After so many long days of numbness had passed over me, I supposed I'd forgotten the refreshing qualities of feeling my own presence.

"Please, let no one see my tonight." I whispered to the frozen air. Sure, I was alive in the world but I didn't care to share that knowledge with anyone. I had treated people so horribly that, on top of the anger, I felt smothered in remorse and shame. How could I explain myself to anyone? I didn't even want to try.

I made my way to the little house-turned store on the corner. The storekeeper greeted me with her usual bright smile. I peered out from beneath my dark hood. She squinted her eyes at me, her smile faded. I knew what she saw, I'd looked at myself before I left my place. My skin was as blank and pale as a sheet of empty paper, a complete contrast to the shadowy rings around my pale blue eyes. My hair spilled out from beneath my hood in dark tangles. I scared her. What a strange pride I took in that. I knew that I looked like a crazed mad woman, it wasn't something I could hide behind my heavy winter coat.

She didn't recognize me at all. Her face contorted in concentration as she tried to figure out if she'd ever seen me before and I watched as it loosened up with the realization that I must have been a stranger. I looked away from her and grabbed a basket. I took whatever was easiest to get at, not too concerned with the quality. My usual health consciousness had gone with my sanity and personal hygiene.

The last of my savings was passed to the nervous storekeeper. She had called someone from the back who was watching me intently while he packed my groceries into bags. I wanted to yell at them, tell them both that they knew me. Yea, I was the lady who came in every evening after work, with my cheerful manner and polite smile. The one who bought fruits and vegetables and whole grain bagels and always had pleasant things to talk about. Ha-Ha-Ha, look at me now!

I grabbed my bags of food, pulled my dark hood over my neck and head and braced myself for the cold, night air. The storekeeper and her companion watched my every move. The door swung open before I reached it, letting a bitter gust of wind and snow hit me dead on. A bold figure stood in the doorway, not moving, not letting me get through. I stood, looking down at the person's shoes and realized this person had no intention of getting out of my way. I looked up toward the face, brimming with anger and ready to yell, "Get the hell out of my way." when I found that I was looking into the eyes of someone familiar.

My hazy brain scrambled for the name or some symbol of recognition. Was it someone from work? No. Someone from an A.A. meeting? Maybe, but no. Then it clicked in.

"You're not supposed to be here." I whispered. My mind began to whirl. I knew the man's face but couldn't accept the reality of it.

"It is all right." he said gently.

Everything around me faded to black. All I could see was his carefully constructed face, that face from my dreams.

"I can't…you're not real…" I stammered. My voice faded out like my vision. I lost my balance and my consciousness.

I dreamed in the blackout, a good dream of complete release. Nothing appeared. There was only great darkness all around me. Warm, comforting darkness. I could see nothing but I felt clear-minded. A serenity I had not felt in months had settled over my heart. Sensations of tremendous peace washed through me. I had never known such tranquillity and I certainly didn't want to ever leave it.

So this is why I had suffered, I thought, just so that I could experience this moment with complete abandon. The blackness swirled around me and I sensed a distinct liquid movement. The braids of black twirled around me. I was pulled toward the center of a large twisting spiral of nothingness. I started to panic but let it go. The pull of the motion was intoxicating, and I let it take me.

The feeling of powerlessness was remarkably invigorating. Such freedom in this utter lack of control, if I stayed in it forever, I would be happy.

Light hit me with incredible force, as if I had been falling from thousands of miles above and suddenly hit water. Light. Great spears of light charged through me. I was in pain. I felt afraid again. The light brought with it all of my own worldly senses. It was cold again and I shivered uncontrollably. My eyes were struggling to focus. Shapes and sounds danced into my awareness. My bedroom took its full shape through the intensity of light.

In my bedroom, laying on my bed, I moaned through the pain in my head. He stood in the doorway.

The man from the store, from my dreams, was in my apartment. He walked slowly to the side of my bed, as if approaching a wild animal. Each step he took echoed through the halls. I could find no words, I was thinking in a language of mortal terror. I hung onto the one word that made sense to me, God. I said it over and over again, God, God, God.

"It is all right. You are safe. I am not here to do you harm." He spoke while looking around my bedroom. I wanted to say something but my voice was gone. I thought about him the way he appeared in my dream. Could I be mistaken? No, it was him. It is him, I thought.

"You did not meet me in your dream." he said, this time looking directly at me.

I convulsed in shock. Had he read my thoughts? My private thoughts!

"We met in a parking lot."

I relaxed a little. That was true, we had met in a parking lot after the movies. I'd forgotten that reality completely.

"What...who...what are you...do...doing here?" I managed to stutter through my shakes.

"I am protecting you, guiding you, changing your life." He said plainly.

We looked at each other in silence. I was dumbfounded by his response. What a strange thing to say. My mind began to flutter and race again but the strange man held onto me with a fixed stare. He entered me through eye contact and comforted my soul. The pain I'd been living with for so long was being lifted out and away from me, released through his stare.

"What are you?" I asked, overwhelmed with his presence. It fell out of my mouth before I could stop it. I felt embarrassed immediately afterwards but he didn't hesitate to answer.

"I am different from you or anyone you know Kelly."

"Yea, I can see that...How do you know my name?"

"Your friend spoke it when we met in the parking lot."

That was normal enough. Yet something about him wasn't real, didn't seem possible.

"My name is Sacro." He said it with the intention to jolt me to complete attention. My heart fell into my stomach. The dream that had driven me to madness formed clearly through my inner vision. I knew, without doubt, that the only place I'd heard that name was in the dream.

Sacro calmed me without my consent. He read my fear and quieted me. I wanted to freak out, charge off my bed and make him go away but I couldn't do anything. I just laid there, certain that my end was near, maybe welcoming it. So take me to Hell, how much worse could it be?

"I am not your devil, Kelly. You have nothing to fear from me."

I knew he was being honest. As afraid as I felt of his being in my house, I knew he was something more spectacular than a devil.

"I will take you from here now. Trust me Kelly. You can feel that I am not a threat to you."

It was true, I could feel his calmness, his sense of balance and love. He moved a little closer to me and smiled. I pulled back.

"I'm not going anywhere." I said and bumped my head on the wall as I retreated.

"I can bring you to a place of usefulness, a place where you can feel courage and comfort. Is that not what you have wanted for so long?"

"Yes, but I don't know you. God! This is crazy. I'd be an idiot to go with you. For all I know you are trying to kill me." I felt dizzy with fear again but, just as before, his simple gaze calmed me.

"You know that I am unable to hurt you. I am sorry that is such a surprise. I will take you from here because you have a need for qualities you cannot find here. I know where you can get what you need. Do not fear this, you can come back if you do not appreciate what you find. You are ready for this Kelly, otherwise I would not have come." His smile widened.

I sat up slowly, feeling his strength encouraging mine. He moved closer. A fierce gust of emotion swept through me. The closer he came, the stronger it got until I fell back, stunned. He reached out and gently touched my hand. I couldn't feel his skin. There was fire in his touch, like I was holding the sun. I was incinerated without pain, pulled into his warmth. The walls of my bedroom fell away. The floor vanished. There was nothing physical supporting me but I felt secure. The heat was so soothing that I didn't care what was happening or where I was going.

Sacro was all around me although I could not see him. He spoke to me, telling me to let go of the world. So I did. I let go of everything that I thought of as mine. I had nothing to lose anyway. Maybe it was the only way I could find my right senses.

I floated in the comfort of being released from the life I'd been tormenting in. I let my body mingle with the loving touch of Sacro's mind.

His words caressed me to restful dreaminess, allowing me to savor each divine moment. I cared nothing of the world I was leaving behind. Oh, sweet bliss, had I been wrong all this time? Had I mistaken this man for a devil when in fact he was really God? Or maybe just an angel? Whatever he was, he could not be bad, not evil. He was too perfect, too kind with his preternatural caresses. An angel had found me and I was going home. I rested on the thought, taken completely by the spiritual quality of it, how I had longed for something to feed my spirit and finally it had come.

CHAPTER 2

I don't know how much time had passed since we left my apartment. When I came to consciousness, the comfort of Sacro's warmth was gone and I was alone, at least I felt alone. My eyes felt heavy and hard to keep open. I fought the urge to drift back into that sweet unconscious state from which I'd just left. The reason I fought was because of the intense beauty all around me. So stunning was the scene that I thought I could not miss it. Shades of red and blue mists circulated in smoke-like swirls enveloping me. I was like a jellyfish controlled by the tides of a vast ocean. Beyond the purple fog, bright white points of light beamed out from every direction. No walls, no floors-just black, endless space filled with a brilliant display of light. Patches of gaseous color hung about in many different spots.

I strained to gain focus hoping to see something solid. It was so abstract that I didn't feel connected to anything. It was only then that I realized I was being moved by the purple mist that surrounded me. The sweet, spiritual feeling I had before I passed out was no longer with me. I'm dead, I thought, dead and gone to some endless purgatory. It was beautiful to see all of that which I could see but it wouldn't take long before I got bored of the vision. How long would I be made to drift in this dance of color? How long would my feeble mind handle the monotony of such a pretty display of nothingness?

My thoughts grew intensely fearful. He had tricked me into believing him. Devils did that sort of thing all the time. I'd fallen for it and now my real body was lying stone cold in my bed. It would be my landlord that would find my stiff corpse since I had driven everyone else away.

Distracted by my fantasies of my own funeral and the reactions of the people who had claimed to know me, I ignored the appearance of a large object in the distance. It wasn't until the object became so large in my view that I took notice that it was moving towards me. It's shape grew and I was concerned that it would smash into me at a very high speed. Dead or not, the thought of colliding with this thing was not appealing.

My eyes picked out details as it approached. Craters marked the surface. It was obvious that it had been struck several times before by objects much larger than myself. I doubted that I would make the slightest dent in it's course gray face. If I'm dead, will this hurt? I thought. There was no real panic on my part, I had no energy for it. I knew there was nothing I could do. With no control over my body and a burning desire to fall back into that spiritual sleep I'd been in, the massive rock had been given complete control of the situation. So be it, I thought, let it have me. I hope it doesn't hurt. I shut my eyes.

Tremors of impact jolted my body and forced me to open my eyes. I watched in amazement as the stunning mass bounced off me, not me rather, the cloudy haze of purple that encased me. I'd felt the collision but no pain, I was being protected, shielded by the curious fog.

I hadn't died, no body was lying, rotted in my bed. All of me was here, body and soul and I was being protected. I made efforts to turn so that I could see the horrid rock but nothing came of it. I was locked in, moving steadily forward. I could witness where I was going but not what was left behind.

I relaxed myself. In the midst of the bizarre scene, I experienced safety. With no preconceived notions of how I should feel or what I should do, freedom welled up inside. Sweet freedom of the kind one might feel as a very young child or very old person. I had not been told what normal was in this situation since no one, to my knowledge, had ever done anything like this. The journey hadn't been mapped out by the older and wiser. I was here to make my own decisions. The acceptance of this gave me more than freedom though, I was for the first time, experiencing the peace of an emptied mind. No thoughts, no fears, no happiness, my mind was clean and clear. How long this lasted, I couldn't tell since I had no conceivable idea of time. Freedom to it's fullest degree.

The emptiness led me into a state of clarity about the purple cloud around me. It was talking to me. Billions of beings lived to make the protective shield, all working together to keep me alive. Their harmony gave them strength, so strong that they could deflect a mega asteroid without losing the life of a single one of them.

The new awareness led me back into the realm of thought and questions. I wasn't ready for the answers though. The questions multiplied and the emptiness vanished but not without leaving me changed. My soul had formed a base in reality for the first time in my life.

My mind exploded with the sound of Sacro's voice. It was so unexpected since I had thought that he'd abandoned me. More voices, discussions circling my thoughts. Sacro wasn't alone, he was talking with others but I could not make out their words. The rambling went on for awhile and I began to doubt that I was actually hearing anyone but my own active imagination. Still, it was comforting, hearing the tones in my mind.

With the same manner of abruptness that his voice had interrupted my thought, a bright vision of him flashed before me. It was an inner vision, not that he was standing in front of me but rather, he was coming out from within me. I wanted to hug him regardless of my doubts about his intentions.

"We have prepared you. All I require from you is trust." he whispered.

"Okay, I guess."

"No Kelly, I need you to do nothing but follow my lead. You cannot guess, do you understand me?" He spoke louder.

"Yes." A lump of fear came up into my throat. I coughed, swallowed and focused on him with all my effort.

"Trust and compliance Kelly, that is what I need from you. Let me do everything. Resistance will cause complete physical disintegration."

"You mean I could die?"

"Yes, but only if you resist."

"I was thinking that I was dead already." I said tempting him to tell me something about what was happening to me.

"You are not dead. Trust me. You will always have life. I am preparing you for landing. Are you ready to follow me?"

"Yes, I am. What do you mean I'll always have..." He cut me off before I could finish the sentence.

"Are you ready now?"

"Yes" I said with conviction. His smile filled my mind.

Rushes of hot and cold flooded over me. I could depend on him but why, I thought, was it so hard to let him do everything? Sacro's words and image caressed my spirit. The veil of sleepiness was lifted off and away from me. My skin and muscle burst alive with intensity and the living mist that had been protecting me gathered and came into me like a deep breath. I could feel it's force in my abdomen. I contained that which had contained me.

My eyes widened at the sight of a planet. Not my planet though, not my Earth home but something new and different. Excitement welled up. My fingers and toes tingled with smooth serge's of blood flow. My head opened up, not literally, it was as though I was separate from my body and could easily fly out through the top and come back again. Sacro urged me to remain calm and do nothing and then I began to drop. Drop. Drop. My scream was choked by a swallowed gush of air. I gasped and stopped abruptly. Many voices entered my panic, soothing and quieting me. Very gently, they eased my heart which was threatening to pop out of my chest.

I hung there for a moment, catching my breath and trying to open my eyes. Once I'd achieved it, I wished silently that I had not. I looked down and immediately felt the urge to throw up. Strange sensations mingled throughout my body and I knew that the mist I'd inhaled was still protecting me, helping me adjust to the external events taking place.

Unseen forces guided me into a horizontal position over the planets surface and again I dropped. It was only for a second. I had no time to panic before I was stopped by an object I'd not noticed before. It was hard to see in the clear skies since it was made from transparent materials. It closed all around me and my positioning returned to that of being perpendicular to the planet. It was like standing in an elevator, quite comfortable and normal except that it wasn't attached to anything. Suddenly, it flipped over so that I was head down to the planet and then I fell with such speed that I had no time to fear any of it. The "elevator" stopped about two feet from the ground and opened. I fell out, stunned but grateful that it happened so fast and that there was solid ground beneath my feet again.

Sacro stood tall and bold beside me. He helped me stand up and handed me a robe. In all my wonder, I hadn't noticed I was completely naked, had been since I left my apartment. I grabbed it and threw it on. He held out his hand, urging me to touch it to satisfy my curiosity. It felt real, fleshy and solid not like in my apartment. The moment I felt his skin, I wanted to hug him but was too shy and self-conscious to do so.

He stepped forward and embraced me. Feelings of his friendship warmed my soul. I wasn't afraid.

"You will meet friends here, many friends." he whispered into my ear. He released me and stepped back. I looked into his eyes and realized that he wasn't human, he really was very different than me or anyone I'd ever met before. His face brightened with amusement as he read my face and my thoughts.

The eye contact was broken and he put his arm around my shoulders. We began to walk. I followed and looked around expecting to find the others I'd heard on the journey to the planet. I felt a distinct presence other than that of Sacro or the beings of the mist in my body but I saw no one else. My attention was taken over by the new surroundings. For God's sake, I was on a different planet! The sky displayed varying shades of green, layers from light to dark. I could see no clouds but a bright sun that appeared to be closer to the planet than Earth was to it's sun. It's rays brought great energy to my body.

There were two moons, one directly above us and the other close to the horizon behind us from the direction in which we were walking.

"You will see another moon as the day moves along." Sacro answered my question before I could ask it. The moon above us looked startlingly close. I imagined it's great mass colliding with the planet causing massive catastrophe. Sacro reacted with laughter and assured me that my fear of the worst had no bearing in reality.

Fragrant trees surrounded us, some with dark blue bark and yellow leaves, some with yellow bark and white leaves. Smaller plants lined the red, dirt pathway that we walked upon. More colors than I've ever seen in one place. It was like a living cartoon.

"This is fucking amazing!" I yelled. My face burned red at the embarrassment of my outburst. Sacro laughed again and patted my back.

"Your actions do not offend us. Do not worry on how you should express yourself. You are full with wonder and the awesome experience of Evolution. Yell again, as much as you want."

I did yell out again. Holding my arms open to the green skies, I yelled in joy and freedom. Happiness dominated me, fully and completely.

And then it appeared. The presence I'd felt was taking shape right before my eyes. A soft, shimmering outline formed out of nothing. I stood still and watched carefully. The inside of the outline sparkled and filled up with a vision of wild beauty.

"This is Dante." said Sacro and nodded politely to the being. I stood, mouth hanging open but silent and stared at the creature. Dante smiled. I was amazed.

"Is it human?" I asked Sacro, still not fully accepting the reality of it's presence.

"I am." said Dante. His voice was smooth and clear. It danced into my ears. I couldn't tell if it was a man or woman which was unnerving. It had such qualities that would serve either sex well. I instinctively looked over it's body to check for any indications.

"I am human. I am male. Does that satisfy you?" he said, a smile formed around his thick lips.

I jumped, embarrassed that he could pick up on what I was looking for.

"I am the future of the human race." He added.

"Future of the human race?" I looked to Sacro then back at Dante, my brow furrowed at the strange statement he had made.

"Let's just say that I have evolved."

That wasn't hard to see. He glowed with living energy. His dark green eyes held all emotions at once. Skin that was smooth like glass, long hair that, despite it's dark color, shone like gold in the sunlight. Subtle features that made him extraordinarily different than any man I'd seen before.

He wore a finely tailored suit that enhanced the powerful aura of his muscular body. Not a modern suit but more of a decadent eighteenth century style, a few frills around the collar and wrists, a suit that displayed a flare and taste for quality. It would have looked strange and out of place had he not exuded such a calm and comfortable manner.

But what did it mean that he was evolved? How could a person evolve more than the rest of us, I wondered. Dante smiled at me.

"It's a long story, kid." He was doing the same thing as Sacro. Reading my thoughts right from my mind. I suddenly felt heavy and confused.

"No Kelly, do not be afraid. Let me show you my home. Do not worry over the strangeness of this experience, please understand, you will learn to adapt." Sacro said.

I leaned into his arm and let him lead me along the path.

Chapter 3

We made our way to a building that Sacro called an uplift. Anyone could use it at anytime to prepare meals and rest, and all for free.

"We've got a lot of these, all over the place. Nobody has to go hungry or tired here." said Dante as we walked through the entranceway. The building itself was a small pyramid. Most of the space inside was taken up by cupboards and coolers where food and tools were kept. I sat down at the simple wooden table in the center of the room while Dante and Sacro prepared our meals.

"Do you eat meat?" asked Dante. He had his back to me so he yelled over his shoulder.

"Yea." I answered.

"That's too bad. We don't eat any meat here." he called out. I wasn't sure how to respond so I didn't say anything and continued to wait, once again, finding it difficult to do nothing while others were so busy.

Dante laid out the meal and began to eat. I waited until Sacro sat down before I picked up my fork and dug into the orange clumps on my plate. It was all vegetable stuff but nothing I could put a name to. The flavors exploded in my mouth, it was fantastic. Never having been a fan of any vegetable but potatoes, I was pleasantly surprised by the unique flavors. My plate looked like a painter's pallet with splotches of bright colors plopped side by side.

We were silent through the meal, to busy eating to do any talking. I felt myself getting sleepy and by the time I slurped in the last bite of the blue noodley stuff, I could barely keep my eyes open. They talked for awhile as I sat back, I was trying to pay attention to their conversation but they both noticed my withdrawal from the activity. I needed rest and without further hesitation they cleared up the remainder of our meal and led me outside. We walked a short distance, which used up most of my remaining energy and arrived at a gray, stone house.

Dante said goodbye as we approached the door.

"You'll be seeing me again soon. Bye." he said as he walked off in the direction we had come. My vision blurred and he got dimmer with each step. He turned and smiled just before he disappeared completely. Sacro waved.

"Do you see him?" I asked.

"Yes, but I know what to look for." With a gentle nudge, Sacro led me through the doorway of the house.

"This is for you Kelly."

"What?" I was sure I didn't hear him correctly.

"This house is for you. Resting here should be pleasing."

"No way. You're not serious…are you?" I looked around the front room scanning the place for some sign of other occupants.

"Is there someone else here? Who owns this house, really?" I sputtered out my questions without breathing. I just couldn't accept what I heard.

"This is your home. It was made for you. You can have it for your own personal use for as long as you see fit. I sensed that you wanted to be alone, is that correct?".

"Yea, I want to go to sleep, I can barely stand up but I don't under-stand, you can't mean this is my house. You're just letting me sleep here right? Someone else really owns this place, right? Oh, I get it, it's your house, you said you wanted to show me your home. This is your place." I thought I'd figured it out.

"When I stated that I wanted to show you my home, I meant all of this. Everything you have seen today is part of my home. Kelly, it is simple. I have no other way to explain. This building is yours to have, to use in any way you see fit, until you decide that you do not want it. I understand your lack of acceptance since you are a human being from Earth. It is hard to accept this when you come from a place of struggle and hard work but there is no need of that method here. Just for this moment, forget what you understand of working hard for your rewards and take this home as a gift, a thing that you deserve to have regardless of the work you do or do not do. You have this house because you are alive and need shelter to sleep peacefully." said Sacro.

The society in me couldn't believe it, could barely even comprehend a gift of such magnitude without expecting to owe something that I could never repay. No one, alien or not, gives a house away for nothing, I thought. What could they want from me?

I looked at him. Tried to look into him as I knew he could do with me. It's too much, I thought, he's too kind. He held my stare and drew my gaze into his. We stood there, looking at each other, I felt stupid and embarrassed that he would know that I doubted his motives. He didn't let up at all and with his gaze he showed me his truth, let me see into his mind. He was indeed very honest about his motive for giving me the house. He offered it because I needed it. In one eye to eye moment, I was able to let down my defenses and allow Sacro's generosity to get straight into my heart. My socially conditioned mind still screamed out doubt and suspicion but it wasn't as loud as my heart's song of acceptance.

"This is not the world that you have always known. Remember that fact every time that you doubt. Enjoy this place. I will come back when the timing is right for us." and with that he left.

The door clicked shut. I stared at it for awhile, confused, wondering if I should run after him. I had wanted to be alone, to sleep but when he left I thought sleeping to be an absurd idea. How would I sleep alone, in a strange house, where when I looked out the window, I saw green skies?

I started for the door, ready to yell for him to come back but suddenly stopped as I looked around the large room. My house, I should at least investigate it. I let my sense of adventure gain control. Slowly and carefully, I looked around the room. The first things to get my attention were the doors. Four of them on the opposite wall from which I entered. I let my gaze wander over the rest of the room momentarily blocking out the possibilities of what lay behind those doors.

Two arched windows, one on each side of the front entrance, let alien sun beams shine into the room. They were both equipped with elegant shutters in case I didn't want the company of the light. I ran my fingers over the smooth wood from which they were made. Or was it wood? I wasn't really sure.

The whole room was elegant yet still comfortable to be in. On the left, as I still faced the front doorway, a couch, along with a grouping of chairs and a coffee table sat looking ready for a friendly gathering. I touched the smooth fringe on the back of the chair closest to me. My chair. My chair? It didn't seem real. I'd never had anything so nice, so expensive looking. It felt expensive. I got goose-bumps from touching the velvety fabric. I sat down on the edge of the couch. Slowly, I inched back into it's heavenly comfort and within seconds was fighting the urge to pull up my feet and go to sleep. No, keep exploring, I said to myself, there's got to be a bed somewhere. I made a mental note of examining the beautiful display of artwork on the walls and various tables after I'd gotten some rest, and moved deliberately to the farthest door to my left with my back to the front entrance. After turning the knob slowly, I peered in expecting to see someone, the real homeowner, reading a book or something. No one was there. The room was full of equipment, none of which I recognized except for the one large screen and seven t.v. monitors that circled it. Little lights flashed silently on long consoles full with knobs, buttons and faders. It looked like a spaceship's computer room. I left the room feeling somewhat intimidated by the complicated arrangement of gad-getry and wondering why Sacro would equip my house with things I knew nothing about.

"Whatever" I said out loud and moved on to the next door to my right.

"Oh my God." I said, again out loud. There it was in all it's magnifi-cence, my claw-foot bathtub, at least it looked the same. It even had the same little white daisies I'd painted around the outside of the tub with one difference, there were no chips or flaws anywhere, it was brand new. I longed to run the warm water and crawl into it's deep basin to soak my cares away. Not now, I thought.

The rest of the bathroom was new and shiny clean. I used the toilet and moved on entering the front room again and walking to my right to open the next door. I steeped into a large, bright kitchen, painted in vibrant yellows that glowed with the sunlight coming in through tall french doors. It looked like a normal kitchen-fridge, stove, even a dish-washer and lots of cupboards and shelves. There was a big, white table in one corner with eight beautifully carved, white chairs around it. I looked out the french doors to a round patio that held a smaller table with simple, heavy looking chairs, also painted white. I continued to look beyond the patio to which I was quickly reminded how far from home I really was. All I saw were alien trees and plants that shimmered with energy. Two moons glowed with a purple hue, one just above the treetops and the other, nearly out of site behind them. I peered out as far as I could without opening the doors, looking for signs of other people but I saw none.

Drawing my attention back to the kitchen, I looked over it again but lost interest in favor of finding a place to sleep. Once I was back in the front room, I faced the last door and opened it. Yes, a bed but not just any bed, it was my bed. I ran over to it not noticing much of anything else in the room and jumped on the soft mattress. Yes, yes, yes! It felt like my bed, even had my oversized comforter draped over it. It was so exciting, I was like a child who just found a favorite teddy bear she'd thought she lost forever.

I sat in the middle of my double bed and looked over the rest of the room. Another doorway with it's door wide open stood in the corner. I fumbled with the robe I was wearing so that I might get up to explore the room but my body wouldn't let me go.

"Oh, I'll see it later." I sighed and fell back into my bed. Even though there were two large windows on each side of me, the room was getting darker. It made my quest for sleep impossible to put off any longer. I got up to pull the course robe over my head and threw it in a clump beside the bed. Then, sliding under the comforter and in between the crisp, white sheets, I stretched out to my full extent and relaxed completely. I opened my eyes for one last moment, just long enough to catch a glimpse of the darkening green sky. I fell to sleep believing I was in a dream.

Sometime in the night, I woke up. My eyes blinked wide open and I stared up at the ceiling for a moment trying to figure out where I was. I sat up quickly with panic clouding my thoughts.

"Is someone there?" I called out. I thought I'd heard something. It was very dark in the room with the only light coming from the moons' reflections through the windows. I pulled the sheet up to cover my bare chest and peered out the window. Points of light glittered in the sky. Stars of many colors, not just the white bits I'd grown used to from Earth's point of view. This could be heaven, I thought, it was beautiful enough to fit the descriptions I'd heard.

Suddenly, I felt the presence I thought I'd heard before. It made me jump back into bed in fear. I sat frozen, listening for disturbance in the house. My quiet concentration led me inward, where I discovered the source of the commotion. It was the beings of the purple mist settling into my body. I was feeling their tremendous energies mixing with my own. Tingling sensations again in my fingers and toes along with a cool, flowing motion up through my legs, abdomen, chest and throat. I was sharing my body with these microscopic entities and I wasn't afraid of them at all. They were helping me to adjust, guiding me to be peaceful and strong.

Easing back down into the soft mattress, I stretched out again, relaxed and closed my eyes. All of my fears, worries and cares evaporated into the still night allowing sound, dreamless sleep to regenerate my body and soul.

CHAPTER 4

This was a new life. The light of the new sun shone through my window and bathed my room in radiant energy. I put my feet to the floor and reached up as far as I could. The old aches and pains of my usual morning stretch were gone, my body had no struggle with my intent. The simple robe I had worn laid in a clump on the floor. I threw it on and went out, through the front-room and into the kitchen. I could hear a faint beeping sound as soon as I entered. I stopped to focus on its location. I followed the sound out of the kitchen and back into the front room. I could hear it coming from the equipment room, the place that housed all that high tech stuff. I went in and located the source of the intermittent tone. A little blue box sat alone on a small, round table. There were three buttons, none of which had labels, and two light panels. One of the light panels was flashing in sync with the beeping sounds. I stared at it for awhile wondering how to deal with it. Hundreds of dreadful fantasies went off in my mind, about the possibilities of what could happen if I pressed the wrong button. In my imagination, I went from simply stopping the noise to creating mass planetary destruction as possible consequences to my actions. I supposed that one could call that extreme thinking but I was on a different planet, looking at a contraption that I wasn't even remotely familiar with, anything was possible. The beeping was getting quite annoying so I made a choice based on intuition and hopefulness. My faith in the power of luck. I pressed the button closest to the flashing light. The beep turned into a long steady hum and the blinking light just stopped and remained dark. The other panel flashed on. I waited for several minutes to see if anything else would happen. Nothing. I pressed the next button, the one in the middle. The humming stopped. Something inside the device made a click followed by a soft whirring noise. I jumped back. Both lights were on but when the whirring stopped there was nothing, no sound, no light.

I went to the bathroom. There was nothing else to do really. With no annoying beeps, I figured I could just ignore it, get it right out of my mind. That idea lasted about thirty seconds after I'd finished in the bathroom. I went back and quickly pressed the remaining button. I winced at my action. A very loud bloop came out of the little blue box and I almost hit the ceiling. Both light panels flashed and I thought of running away but quite suddenly, I heard the soothing tones of Sacro's voice. I moved closer to the machine to make sure I was hearing correctly. Yes, it was Sacro's voice and it was coming from the little blue box. It was an answering machine. I laughed at myself as I listened to Sacro speak of meeting with me. I welcomed the idea of his company. The message ended and I realized that I had no idea of how I would reach him. The silent machine began beeping as it had before. I pressed the button that had produced Sacro's message. His voice came through again.

"I will be there when you indicate that you are ready. Check your rooms. There is an appropriate supply of nutrients for you in the kitchen. We will find clothing for you very soon. You will not have to wear the robe much longer. Send your thoughts when you are ready for me.".

That answered my question about what the telephone might look like, they didn't need phones they just send their thoughts around. I was probably the only one that needed this answering machine. Send my thoughts? My stomach knotted up. Can he hear everything that I think?

The knot tightened and I had to sit down. I felt angry at the whole idea that Sacro and whoever else might be around could read my mind. Can everyone do this trick here? They get to analyze my mind while I have to stay locked up in it? That's not right. My stomach churned and I clenched my fists in anger at the thought of such violation. I wanted to hit something, just freak right out and tear out my hair, tell them all to leave me alone but before I could take any action on those feelings my stomach began to tingle. It felt like a breeze inside my body, blowing out the knot and releasing the swelling of resentment. The sensation drained me for a moment, I was empty of all feeling. Then a surge of energy blasted through me and quite suddenly, I felt calm. No knot, no burning, just relief and confidence. The whole thing was a roller coaster ride. I could go from tremendous, dizzying fear to deep, quiet serenity in a matter of seconds. Whirling spins of dizzying questions to complete ease and trust. Up, down, fast, slow. All I could do for the moment was shake my head and breathe deeply. My greatest desire was to get off the roller coaster. The peace and confidence highs were fine but the fear and insecurity parts were way too hard for me to handle. Just how does an average human go about living normally after being whisked off to some unknown planet by an alien? I already loved the place, it was absolutely incredible, so leaving here and forgetting about it wasn't an option. The new world was so full with radiance. The sights and sounds were so intense and deep. I could see bright fields of energy that heightened my awareness of life. The sounds brought me pleasure. It all came so easily too. The planet gave me its gifts to cherish. I never felt that on Earth, there was always so much work to do. There would be no way for me to deny this place. The only way I could stop the roller coaster was to find out more about what was really going on. Why me?

My breakfast was simple. Sacro and his friends must have done some very detailed research when they picked me up. The kitchen was stocked with foods to my liking. I had bran cereal with fresh milk and orange juice. The kind of thing I ate when I wasn't being self-destructive. Only one problem, no coffee. I always had coffee. Other than that, it was very normal. I pictured Sacro wandering around a grocery store doing my shopping. No one had ever done anything like that for me. I always had to do those things for myself.

I cleaned up my stuff and within seconds after washing up, there was a knock on my door. I knew it was Sacro because of the effort I had made to talk to him, to tell him I was ready. I opened the door and welcomed him in. I was shocked at the sight of him though. He wore a dress-like thing that looked like something more suited for a woman. I made an effort to hide my shock but I couldn't resist looking him over from head to toe.

"You have many different cultures on Earth." he said.

My head tilted involuntarily and an unsure expression washed over my face, I said "Huh"

"I see you look on me with such a narrow vision but even your own home world has room for diversity."

"What?" I asked. I still didn't understand what he was talking about.

"My choice of dress is rather unsettling to you and I am telling you that it is stranger to me to be limited in my choice of clothing. There are cultures on your own world that would make my dress appear plain. I want you to open your eyes."

"Well where I live men don't wear dresses unless they're some kinda weird." I blurted out. I couldn't believe that I had been so rude and only to defend a belief that I didn't actually believe in. I judged Sacro on his appearance based on standards I had thought of as ridiculous.

"I do not take offense. It is natural to defend your traditional beliefs. I do not expect you would choose to do anything other than follow what you have been taught, it is the human way." said Sacro.

I felt ashamed of myself anyway, not because I'd criticized Sacro but because I hadn't stood by my true point of view. But then again, maybe

I had. He was right, I was just following the path of the normal that I grew up with and rarely did anyone challenge the norm in my society. He understood me and all the pressure of trying to hide the truth was gone. He just knew.

"Are you God?" I asked sincerely.

"No." I expected him to offer more but we both stood there in silence for a moment. Then he stepped close to me and hugged me. My body tightened up under his embrace. I filled up with emotion. A simple hug had me paralyzed and I realized that I had needed it more than I knew.

"Let us go for a walk now. I want to show you Evolution."

"You want to show me evolution?" I asked after he released me from the hug. "How can you show me evolution?"

"It is all of this." He waved his hands around in every direction.

"So you call this planet Evolution like the way I call my planet Earth?".

"Yes and it is our way of living also. Evolution is a conscious effort" answered Sacro.

My robe tangled up beneath my feet as I walked. I tugged and stumbled over the cloth.

"Can I get something else to wear? This thing is driving me nuts." I asked through my frustration at the obstacle course that I was wearing on my body. He nodded in affirmation. He stopped and looked around. A smile washed over his face and he looked more human than usual. I turned to look in the same direction since he appeared to be focused on something in the distance. Nothing except land and sky, alien land and sky. Sacro stood waiting. I squinted my eyes and looked around but still I saw nothing to wait for. Sacro could sense my impatience. I wanted to keep moving, get my clothes and get some answers. I felt like a child waiting for a grown-up to get it together before going to the circus. Let's go, I whined in my thoughts. I kicked a stone that was lying in the path. It shimmered with bright energy, I could see faint fields of color being emitted from the stone. As it settled, the ripples of color faded. I could definitely see patterns of energy emanating from what I thought was a lifeless stone. It was dazzling and it held my attention while I waited for Sacro to do whatever he was doing. Plants gave off sparks and little living creatures roamed around large trees surrounded by cool fields of blues or reds or yellows.

"He is there." Sacro said and pointed in the direction of the rising sun.

I looked up and saw a bright and intense flash of light. The light faded and a figure appeared from it. There was Dante walking toward us.

"Would you mind if Dante joined us?" Sacro asked politely.

"No, I don't mind." I felt thrilled that he would join us, his presence was invigorating. As I answered him, I felt a twinge of anger. Why does he ask me if he knows what I'm thinking? What kind of games is he playing?

"I am not able to hear everything that goes on in your mind. I only hear what you offer to me. It is released in the thoughts that you desire to share. Because you have no experience, you lack control. There are some parts of your thought patterns that are hidden and unavailable to me. The questions you have are often the first thoughts to be released. I ask you questions because I respect your form of communication, even though I may know the answer, it is important you respond with your words. You will learn other methods to communicate soon enough."

"So I do have some control over what I think to you?" I asked.

"Indeed you do and as I stated there is much you must learn. Your inexperience does leave you vulnerable. I do not think that you are aware of much that you want to share. You will get to know your mind far better than I ever will. Then you will control your messages with ease."

"That's good to hear because ya' know what? I don't like people reading my mind."

"What? You do not like for others to know you?" Sacro asked with a faint smile playing across his lips.

"It's not that so much as it is that I don't know anything about you or him." Dante was close to us and I wanted to end the conversation before he reached us. Of course, I knew that Sacro knew that.

"Oh you will learn" said Sacro.

Dante reached us and smiled. A dazzling effect like the colors and energy patterns of the environment. He was so vibrant, his presence so strong, nearly overwhelming. A light breeze teased his hair creating more charm to his image.

"I'm so happy to join you. Thank you for accepting me." Even his voice was exceptional.

"Are you sure you're human?" I asked and immediately felt stupid.

"Absolutely. I'm completely and fully human. Every single cell in my body is human, just like you." He flashed another wonderful smile and took a deep breath like he was enjoying the fresh air.

"Not like me, you are not like me. I can't do that disappearing thing you do" I said.

"I'm not disappearing." said Dante. "I just move very quickly, my friend."

"God knows I have no idea what your talking about." It was starting to give me a headache trying to figure out all these odd things. It was like I was trying to solve a mystery but without really knowing the whole story. I asked questions but the answers just created more questions. I liked Dante and Sacro but I couldn't grasp what they were about. Sacro put his hand on my shoulder and we began to walk again. Dante danced around us. I thought he looked silly but he seemed so happy doing it. He certainly wasn't bound by any social expectations that I had known from my own world. He looked like a child as he pranced lightly about us. Jumping around to a shallow tune that he hummed. How does one go from appearing so charming and sophisticated to childish and trivial in a matter of seconds?

"It's a matter of wholeness." said Dante.

"Oh, and would you look at that, pulling the thoughts right outta my head, eh?"

"I didn't do anything with your thoughts." He looked over to Sacro. "I thought you would have explained all that."

"Yes well, give the young one a chance to adjust Dante. Do you forget yourself?"

"Sometimes I guess I do Sacro, sometimes I want to forget everything that's behind me."

"Fair enough. I understand your regrets but I need your experience to help me with this one. I value your ability."

"There were no humans here to help you with me and I'd say you did a very fine job of it." said Dante. They continued to talk back and forth to each other. I withdrew myself from the conversation and walked along beside them.

I daydreamed of a normal day at home. Normal days used to be boring, especially when there was no work. I used to dream of adventures like the one I was having. I used the idea of a normal life to victimize myself, never giving in to appreciating quiet moments or utilizing present moment awareness. As I walked along with these strangers, I realized how destructive life can be, to do what everyone expects while dreaming of something else. My most normal days were only normal because I knew what to expect by doing what everyone else expected. I had a place to be and a job to do and I wanted that back because it was familiar. There I was, in the middle of an alien adventure and I was dreaming of being back at home doing my normal things in the middle of my normal days on Earth. Maybe it would be more fun to pay all my bills and all those other more mundane things about living life on Earth. These people were too confusing and the skies were green and I felt afraid.

I looked down at the stones in the pathway as I shuffled along. Suddenly I noticed a lack of presence and the conversational voices of Sacro and Dante were gone. Thoughts of normalcy broke apart and I looked up to see that Sacro and Dante were no longer talking to each other and they were not walking with me. They had stopped and were watching me, both with the same look of compassion in their faces.

"What is it? What have I done?" I felt defensive and guarded myself from them. I wanted to keep my fears a secret.

"I understand your pain and your fears." was all Dante said and I exploded into tears. I felt my body cave in under the tremendous pressure of sadness and I collapsed to the ground. They were both with me before I actually hit it. I leaned into Sacro's supportive hold. There was no strength in me at all. I was a dead leaf, wilted over Sacro's shoulder. I cried while they held me. Whispers of comfort too soft for me to understand, came from both of them. I cried for fear of unknown things and for the sadness of losses I had suffered. I cried with no control and my new friends just sat with me and held me, telling me that I was safe. I embraced the safety even through my heartache which made it easier to cry.

Eventually, my sobs quieted and I looked up through tear-blurred eyes, saw the beautiful green skies and bellowed out in fear again.

"I want...want to...go...go home!" I screamed out. I didn't even believe it. I was speaking from a place of panic. A clinging part of me, the part of me that was inordinately attached to my world.

Sacro raised himself and brought me up along with him. I managed to stand on my feet. Dante rubbed the wetness off my face with his shirt sleeve. There was only enough strength in my legs to allow me to stand, I didn't even try to walk. The two men supported me firmly and lovingly. We stood on the path together. I let their warmth and love penetrate me and with their strength the sadness lifted off of me gently. There was still a lingering fear of the strangeness of the matter. How was I really supposed to cope with any of this? All things that were normal to me were out of my reach, all things around me were altered and extraordinary. My legs buckled at the thought. Sacro held me close while Dante rested his hand on my shoulder and touched my brown hair. He gave me a look of such compassion.

"I know what you believe, but your world isn't lost to you. We want to help you make it more wonderful, to give you the tools that you need to add to the beauty and depth of it. Tools that you wouldn't be able to find by yourself and I'll tell ya' it's an awesome set of tools. Earth is a little bit stuck so we get up and push it along to keep it growing. It's an honor to the highest degree you know, to be the key to evolution on one's own planet. That's what you are now Kelly, a key." Dante spoke with passion. I was moved by his feelings but I had no idea how he could perceive me to be a key to anyone's evolution. I leaned against him.

"Let us do one thing at a time. You need your own clothes. Let us go. We will find something you are comfortable wearing." said Sacro. They helped me along with my weak body, such patience they both had. The sadness crept back into me and stayed with me as I walked but I felt my strength increasing despite my mood. It was not long before I could walk on my own. Sacro helped me to breathe, to make the most out of the clean, fresh air. The deep breathing eased my pain and calmed my soul. Each breath brought a greater sense of lightness as my tight muscles relaxed and the heavy weights of fear dissolved. Walking and breathing, breathing and walking, thank God for simple things.

We came upon a compound of some sort. There was movement which meant more people or whatever. I didn't want to meet anyone new. Walking, breathing, walking, breathing. I reminded myself to stay focused. There was a large building, not very high but broad and stretched out. A tall antennae was sticking out from the corner farthest from our approach. Something was coming toward us. It looked like a floating car, like one of those sci-fi hovercrafts I'd seen in space movies. The vehicle came closer and I noticed details quite shocking. There was no sign of a driver. It traveled above the ground, at least a foot and a half and it was fast.

"You are about to meet my good friend Renfrew." said Dante.

"Oh yea, it must be another one of you invisible people, right?" I asked, thinking that I understood why I couldn't see anyone in the car.

"No, Renfrew is alone today, she's out here by herself." said Dante. He appeared very cheerful about seeing this Renfrew person. I watched. As the vehicle came closer, I focused on the details and realized that what Dante was referring to was the vehicle itself. It was a living thing. It drifted up alongside Sacro who had gone out ahead of Dante and me. Sacro laid his hand over what I would call the hood of the car. It was shaped in much the same manner as a convertible car but there were some fascinating differences, one being that it was very much alive. It had no wheels, it was covered in rough, thick skin and it had hair, very sparse, like an elephant. Sacro made some strange noises and Renfrew joined him with similar clicking and humming sounds. Dante and I moved closer, I moved much slower than he did. Renfrew brought four large, powerful legs out from underneath her and rested on them. Dante held my hand to lead me toward her. I saw her look at me with eyes that stood atop stalky appendages positioned at her front. Only one eye turned toward me. I jumped back when I realized she was looking at me. We had eye contact. I could see life in her eye. I moaned. She was fascinating, odd yet beautiful. Dante pulled me even closer.

"Nothing to fear, let Renfrew say her greetings." Dante slapped a hand on her and she made a noise that I could never imitate. Dante made the same sound with some slight variations. He told me to touch her.

"Touch her? Isn't that rude or something?" I didn't really want to touch her but she turned both of her eyes on me and made a sound that answered my question. I touched. I felt her warm skin and the motion of her breathing. She clicked at me.

"Renfrew says hello and welcome." said Sacro. Dante pulled me back from her and turned me around to face him. With a grin that seemed too big for his face, he told me to get in.

"Oh you are enjoying this aren't you?" I asked feeling comfortable enough for a little sarcasm.

"Well you know what? I am, I really am. I'm enjoying every bit of it and you know why?" He cut me off before I could get my response out. "No, you don't know why, but I'll tell ya', I know exactly what your going through. I've been where your at. I get to watch you go through everything I went through and I like it a lot. I know your gonna be alright, all this is good for your soul. It's helping you and your really handling it quite well."

"Great, you get in first and show me the way." I said. Dante got into Renfrew easily and nuzzled himself into a corner of her body. Sacro came up behind me and offered a firm hand of support and guidance. I climbed in and sat down next to Dante. Renfrew's body cavity was unlike any car I'd ever sat in. It was smooth, there were no actual seats but the way her body was formed provided comfortable positioning nonetheless. Sacro came in after me and sat in the corner opposite us in the square-ish cavity. The area was spacious, I could see that five or six more people could have joined us without being squished in. Renfrew's body began to vibrate and hum with an energy that emanated from deep within her. We lifted off the ground as she folded her legs in underneath her massive body. I felt the sensations of floating. She seemed as light as a feather while she moved forward. She turned herself around to face the building from which she had come. The vibration grew stronger and she moved faster until all I could hear was the wind.

"She's showing off for you." Dante yelled out. He lovingly patted the side of her body. I took the beauty of the moment inside myself. Here I sat, in a living hover car with a human being that was evolved so far beyond me that I could barely see him as the same species and a glorious alien that I thought could surely be an angel. The absurdity of all this couldn't keep me from appreciating the love around us. These creatures acted as if they'd known me all my life and still liked me anyway. I looked up at the green layered sky and its pale yellow clouds and accepted it all. What else could I do. I suppose I could have gone on fearing everything but it was all too exciting, too wonderful to waste on worry. There was no other logical way to cope with being so far from home. It was during that ride with Renfrew and the others that I gave up a huge chunk of my fear and let the whole experience thrill me.

CHAPTER 5

Dante and I sat on a long bench in the sprawled out building. Sacro told us to wait while he prepared the three of us for entry into Sowthren Court. The air in the large room was thick with coldness and it took me a few minutes to get comfortable with my breathing. Renfrew and Dante talked for awhile, then she looked to me, smiled with her lobster-like eyes and walked away. With her departure, Dante and I were alone. We sat in silence for a long time, so many questions running around in my brain that I couldn't focus on one long enough to actually ask one.

"We can eat when we get inside." said Dante.

"Did I send you that thought?"

"Yea, you sure did but it wasn't coming from your mind. Your stomach is growling louder than your thoughts."

I hadn't noticed due to all of the distractions. Dante's awareness of me made me aware of myself.

"What's in this place, Sowthren Court?" I asked, getting the focus off of my stomach.

"It's basically a city, a place where we can get together, work, create, make progress. Only six places like it on all of Evolution. The only thing about Sowthren Court is that we can't live inside the Dome, it's too complicated. There are some species that do well in it's system, they can stay day or night but most of us are outta there by sundown. The Dome keeps everything under control." He knew he left me with more questions and looked at me expectantly.

"O.K., what is the Dome?" I asked obediently.

"Ah yes, the Dome. Let me tell you about the Dome. It regulates the gravity pocket on the inside. There are a few of these gravity wells on Evolution. These are places that have a higher concentration of gravitational pull. If you were to enter one of these areas without protection you'd be squashed in seconds." he slapped his hands together creating a hard smacking sound that made me jump. "It would be like jumping off of a high cliff minus the fall. Just splat. There is this one creature that can control the wells, in fact their survival depends on it. They place themselves over top of the area and gain energy by resisting the pull. This action creates a nice little pocket of space for us to be in. It takes a little extra environment manipulation for these spots to be comfortable for us, but it works out pretty well. We call the helpful creatures Domes."

I sat like a kid listening to a fairy tale.

"Why not just go somewhere else where the gravity is easier to deal with?"

"In this case, Sowthren Court was built up before the gravity shifts. It would have been harder to relocate than it is to make a deal with a Dome, all they ask is that you don't poke at them. Anyhow, the gravity wells fluctuate, there are three other places built on g-wells like Sowthren Court but there used to be more. The wells shift and move to other locations and generally the Domes go with it and leave whatever is inside to deal with itself. The pressure at Sowthren Court hasn't changed for a long time and there is no indication that it will leave. We have reliable ways to monitor the activity and since everyone that goes inside is happy with the set up, we just enjoy it."

"Will I feel any different when I go in there?" I asked.

"Probably, yea I imagine you will, the air is thicker, that's the only way I can explain it, but it's fresh. It's quite a complex development if your thinking from an Earthly point of view. Do you feel the difference here?" he waved his hand, stirring up the air around us.

I nodded.

"This is an adjustment bay, a place where those who need to can adjust to the changes. If your body was to have any adverse reactions, you would have felt it by now. Not everyone can get into Sowthren Court because of their body structure or individual conditions."

I sat quietly for a moment. My body felt quite good. I concentrated on myself. The air was noticeably different, thicker and colder than outside, but it wasn't intolerable.

"There is another reason for this adjustment bay." There was a mischievous tone to his voice, adding some drama to what he was saying.

"It's also for security. There are some ghastly creatures that we must keep out of Sowthren Court." Dante shifted his focus from me to a doorway on our left. I looked along with him expecting to see some ghastly creature but what I saw was Sacro.

"I'll tell ya' all about them later. Let's go. Looks like things are set up for our entry to Sowthren Court." In a flash he was up and prancing over to meet Sacro, leaving me behind to wonder, once again, what he was talking about.

Sacro motioned to me, indicating that I could join them. I gathered the gauche robe around my legs with some hope that I would soon be changing into something comfortable. We walked together through two enormous doors that led to an equally enormous tunnel. I looked around to see if Renfrew had come back to carry us through but she was no where to be seen. Walking no longer felt very good. I was hungry and tired of the fight I was having with my clothes. I wanted to sit back and relax. We walked through in silence. Dante was doing his child dance again, around Sacro and I like a quiet fairy, all the way to the other end of the tunnel.

"Wait here." Sacro said as he walked to a small panel on the left side of the wall. Sacro talked to it with words I didn't understand. It blinked a few times and the great wall began to shimmer. Sacro motioned to Dante. He went to the panel and talked into it. The wall waved and lost its illusive density. I could see through it. Sacro looked at me and nodded, I followed his direction.

"Repeat what I say to you as precisely as you can." I was a kid about to take a math exam but never studied a single formula. Dante smiled a charming if not somewhat mischievous smile at me.

"Opkey mon dezrite, les dawn armkey bonthwanee." said Sacro.

"Ahh…Opkey man de…rite, lee…" I said. I had completely mixed up the words in my head. Sacro repeated them slowly. I finally got it right on the fourth attack. The shimmering, wavy wall disappeared.

"Our entry is acceptable. What is your first desire?" asked Sacro.

"Oh man, am I ever hungry." I said without delay.

"So am I. Shall we engage in the finest cuisine of Sowthren Court?" said Dante in the accent of a high class Englishman. I gave him an odd look.

"You coulda been rich on Earth." I said.

"And why do you say that?" asked Dante.

"You could be a great actor, you seem to have a particular talent for performance."

"It's funny you say that Kelly, I tried for years in that industry, nothing came of it."

I thought he was joking at first but as I watched I noticed the change behind his incredible green eyes. It brought him down for a minute but only for a minute.

"Everybody is acting on Earth. All the time, playing roles." said Dante giving me a hearty slap on the back.

"What do you mean?" I knew what he meant.

"You know what I mean. You go one place and you act all happy and carefree and you move on to some business meeting and act all tough and aggressive. From there you shake it off, go out with your friends and act like some big shot of the popularity scene. You keep playing those roles turning yourself into whatever gets the best reactions. You have to if you want the big rewards. Always have to play the big game. I don't have that here. No one to please, no money to make, no cares about how to make a living. I've already made it by being here, I am living, really living. I have more wealth than you can possibly imagine by having none." His eyes sparkled again. I was excited by his talk of such freedom. I'd quickly given up freedom in my early teens. There was no room for dreams in the world I lived in. My family's most profound motto was-get a job that pays the bills and don't complain. No room for childish singing and dancing or ideas for beautiful paintings and stories, they weren't practical or useful. How could people be allowed this freedom on Evolution? I wondered.

"So you're happier here?" I asked.

"I get homesick, I was born on Earth and lived there for thirty years, a person gets attached even if it's not good for you, but yes, I'm much happier here."

"You haven't been here long if you left there when you were thirty." I looked over his youthful appearance with admiration. He just smiled.

We continued on through the open space where the wall had vanished right before my eyes. I turned after we passed through to watch it manifest itself into an impenetrable, solid mass. Dante pulled on my sleeve to keep me moving along with Sacro and him. The appearance of the great city overwhelmed my senses. Sowthren Court sparkled in a field of yellow light. The Dome that Dante had talked of looked like an energy shield. I could see beyond it to the green skies of Evolution. The mixture of color was dazzling and perfect. Although it was a little cold for my comfort, there were so many things to charge up my senses that I barely noticed. Sowthren Court was a wonderful balance of beautiful nature and the convenience of a city. It looked harmonious not rushed like I had expected. I had assumed that I would see some kind of earth-type city, an alien New York or Vancouver. I was surprised and delighted at my error. There was a lake to my left and I could see vessels of some sort on the water. The water itself was stunningly clear. No pollution. The air was as pure as it was outside of the Dome. Dante explained that there was a circulation system for the air inside the Dome, a complex system of organic material that worked with the Dome's respiratory system to create and recreate healthy, clean air.

We walked on toward a marketplace. I saw sections, like store fronts with things on display. Odd pieces of artwork and clothing. I wanted to get closer but Sacro put his hand on my shoulder and led me onto another place. I could smell the food before we entered the building. Heavenly scents to a hungry child. Everything was exciting and wonderful. I felt giddy and I glanced over to Dante to see if he was doing his child dance. He was not. He looked sophisticated, even a little arrogant. I wondered if I could make up my own child dance. Not a chance, I was too shy to express myself so boldly. As I looked around the room, I noticed that I could not identify one single creature. My stomach turned at the sights and sounds of so many different beings. Someone approached us and led us to a table. Sacro had to physically support me all the way to my seat. I was mesmerized at the appearance of life that of which I had never seen before. I thought of the arrogance of humans. My whole perception of being changed at the sight of such diversity. How could anyone cope with this? People had a hard enough time with the differences in humans. Skin color, gender, even religion spread us apart but all of these drastically different beings remained here together seemingly in a state of peace. Earth seemed like such an ignorant place. How long has there been such an incredible abundance of life forms in this Universe? I held onto Sacro's arm desperately.

"Quite remarkable, is it not?" asked Dante. It wasn't really a question. I just gazed with my mouth hanging open. Then I noticed another human. She sat with four others, one of them so small that it had to sit on top of their table to carry on conversation. Sacro pushed me along whispering something about eating first. He helped me to sit down and as I did, a silver cube was placed in front of me. Both Sacro and Dante received their own cubes.

"Stick your finger in it." said Dante. I watched Dante work with his cube and I did the same. The cubes hummed and beeped the same as Sacro and Dante. I felt my finger being pulled in slightly and squeezed, then released. The violet skinned being who gave us the cubes came back and took them without saying a word.

It seemed like a normal everyday restaurant except for the aliens. I saw trays of food being brought to different tables. I waited for our menus. It occurred to me that I had no money or even had any idea what money was in this place. I was hoping, almost knowing that Sacro was aware of this fact and would take care of my meal. I continued to wait for the menu. Dante broke into my thoughts.

"They already gave you the menu."

"Oh…did I miss something?" I was pretty sure I hadn't made any choices, not even in my mind.

"It's all in that silver device you stuck your finger into, it took your order."

"But I didn't even know what choices I had, I didn't decide on anything."

"It's your body that made the choice. The pressure on your finger made the choice. The quarzer, that cube, took a reading of your body chemistry as it is right now. Our host has taken it to the prep room where the quarzer loads the information into a system that can use it to prepare exactly what you need from fresh, nourishing foods. The information that your body gave to the quarzer is what you need for health and well-being."

"That's not good, what if I don't like it?" I said desperately.

"You need not worry about that." said Sacro.

"He's not kidding, this place is one hundred percent satisfaction guaranteed." said Dante, some of his childlike enthusiasm was resurfacing.

"There is someone I want you to meet after our meal. You have noticed her already. I think it is best that you meet her as soon as possible." said Sacro taking my attention away from the meal issue.

"Are you talking about the other human over there?" I pointed to the tall woman I'd seen. I was glad for the interruption from the conversation of quarzers, I couldn't hope to understand that kind of technology on an empty stomach.

"Yes, she knows we are to meet with her but she is extremely cautious with other humans. Please make sure you are aware of that when I introduce you. Her name is Donally. She does a very important job here on Evolution. Yet we must wait until after the food." said Sacro. I glanced over to Donally just as she turned and looked at me. She was almost as exquisite a human as Dante, but with a mean edge. She raised her glass to me and looked away.

The meal was a fantastic assortment of foods, none of which I could identify but so well prepared that I didn't much care. Dante and Sacro explained the preparation of the meal with more depth. They explained the point of eating as a means to provide my biological system with what it needed to function to support my inner potential. The quarzer was designed to determine precisely what I needed at the moment of use. It would even detect food allergies and intolerance's. I understood them, to a point. It made sense to me but as they became more technical about exactly how the quarzer worked, I found my attention shrivel to nothing. My awareness however, seemed to expand and my energy level soared. I felt great. I felt perfect. The meal had definitely increased the level of output in my system. I could feel the nutrients working in my body. My companions, who both took the hint that my interest in quarzer technology had dissolved, focused their attention on each other, leaving me off the hook. Not that I wasn't interested in learning the incredible marvels of this new world but that too much information was sending me into overload.

I sat back comfortably and took in the incredible view. There were glorious examples of artwork all around us. Paintings of alien land-scapes and a magnificent statue of a gazelle standing gracefully in the center of the room. I smiled at the sight of it. The artwork couldn't keep my gaze from wondering back to the living creatures that shared the room with me and my friends. Everyone looked so easy-going. Through the tones of the many languages being spoken, a harmonious music wafted around the tables.

I glanced at the dark woman who had been pointed out to me, Donally. She looked over at me with great suspicion in her manner. She was obviously untrusting of me as Sacro had explained. It was an intriguing situation. I wanted to hear her story. Her brown eyes met mine with intensity. I thought she would look away once she noticed that I was watching her too but she didn't, she looked deeper into my eyes like a probe scanning me for something. I broke the contact. I felt intimidated and turned away in fear. I needed the friendly faces of Sacro and Dante. Donally's gaze wore at my back.

"She is scaring me, Sacro." I said. He looked at Dante with what appeared to be amusement.

"She is doing a good job then." he said smoothly. Dante peered around me to catch sight of her. He waved and produced one of his charming smiles.

"She'll be over shortly. The four of us will take a walk together." He wasn't afraid of her at all. I wondered if he was as courageous when he first arrived. Some, almost human looking creature, came by to clear away the mess we made from our meal. I thought he was human until four long arms unfolded from behind his back, two of which had grasping fingers all the way along them. I tried not to show my revulsion at the sight of the oddity. The being cleared away everything in one swipe and left us again.

"You know Sacro, I don't have any money to pay for this." I said. He laughed out loud and Dante joined him. I felt humiliated.

"Why are you laughing at me?" I felt a surge of anger as I spoke.

"It is just that your worries are amusing at times. We have no money. We do not pay for the things we need with papers or metals. There is no obligation to pay for your needs. Food is here because we all need it." said Sacro.

What questions that raised in me. How the hell does any society exist without money or obligation to pay? Money served my world like a false god, sometimes it seemed like the highest power on Earth. I was shocked by the progress of such an idea, such an ideal idea. But it wasn't an idea here, it was real. Of course nothing like this could work on Earth.

It wasn't long before my heightened sense of skepticism crept in and overtook me with the thought that there had to be a catch to this utopian-like situation. There must be something equal to the idea of money, some method of payment for products and services. Nobody does good things without expecting something…right?

"No, there is nothing like it. Believe it or not this world functions on a better system than finances. Money means nothing here, you couldn't give it away." said Dante. He could better understand my shock having lived with the rules of money himself at one time.

"Did I let my thoughts out again?" I asked.

"Yea well, it's pretty hard to hide that kind of shock but your getting good at keeping your thoughts from us. Don't get too good at it though or something else might get them." said Dante as he looked up over my shoulder and focused on something behind me. A shadow crossed over me. I turned to face the shadow maker. Donally stood close behind me, she was smiling at Sacro and Dante. Her smile faded when I looked up at her. I felt a chill from her presence.

"You better watch yourself around me." she said and sat down uncomfortably close to me. I felt her power inside my head as if she were scanning my mind, my whole body, for thoughts. I shook in my seat. I hated the lack of control and I did not want her to know anything about me.

"If you ever learn how to control your little thoughts, you'd better make sure you don't learn how to hide them from me or I will make you dead." she gritted her teeth as she spoke to me. I felt my face burn with embarrassment and anger.

"I don't know who you are but you can't talk to me like that." I stammered, looking to Dante and Sacro for support.

"It's her job to be cautious." said Dante.

"If you are trustworthy, she will not harm you. Do as she recommends and be open, give her your thoughts. It matters not if you like her yet, she does not take offense to your judgments, just be aware that she must know you, perhaps better than I." said Sacro. Dante put his arm up across my shoulders in a show of friendship.

"I say this kid's alright. I'm no expert but I really think we got a winner here." He smiled a big, exaggerated smile. Donally seemed to soften a little.

"So how are you two anyway? It's been awhile." she said, pulling her chair closer to the table. I sat in silence while they caught up on things the way friends will when they think they're missing something. I was like a little kid again but it didn't feel so great this time. I was afraid and unsure of myself. Far more vulnerable than I ever thought I could feel. This person had just threatened me in a manner that I was not used to dealing with. She said she'd kill me if I did something that she didn't want me to do and I wasn't even really sure what that meant. There sat the two others who had supported and protected me, talking to her with great enthusiasm and joy. They were like the best of friends and I was a child fearing for my life again. I trembled in my seat, quite a contrast to the easy going, relaxed feelings I'd had just moments before. Swoosh on the roller coaster. Donally looked at me every once in awhile during her happy conversation with Sacro and Dante but not once did she speak to me and I was O.K. with that. Obedient and patient was I, there was no courage in me for any sort of confrontation with this woman.

I noticed changes outside. I could see out from the windows and doors of the place, colors shifting and moving. Just the progression of the day I supposed. I detached myself from the group. Daydreams wafted around inside me, a simple escape from the new person or better yet, from my fear of her. Uncontrolled images floated in and out of my consciousness. I had no desire to control them or clear them away. I needed the freedom of unhindered thought. I found more than just thoughts however, there were memories surfacing too. Memories of things I'd lost. Loved pets that had long since died or been taken away from me. Friends that I had learned things from or taught things to. Family faces that brought with them feelings of warmth and safety and then some that terrified me at their sight. My own personal memories gave me a sense of stability even in this place that was so bizarre to all of my senses. I still knew myself. What I was remembering was mine and I had learned many valuable things from it. Many people had treated me like shit before but I dealt with it, I grew out of the hurt. Lots of people didn't like me or consider me with respect, so what?

My memories brought me right back to where I was, even though I had been trying to use them for escape. Donally wasn't the worst person that I'd ever met. So far, she was all talk. My own past was guiding me to treat her differently from the people I had feared before. I would not repeat my mistakes. Sacro's words came to me. There was something he'd said to me before they started their friendly conversation.

I would have nothing to fear if I was trustworthy.

Was I worthy of their trust? Could I be open and honest with them? I felt hot breath against the side of my face. I turned toward it and met Dante not more than an inch from me.

"Don't let us down Kelly McGrail."

CHAPTER 6

We walked together for a long time. Donally continued to direct her conversation to Sacro and Dante but she did show some respect for me. She was good with my friends. She listened to them and spoke with much affection and consideration. I was aware of the communication that went on between them that I couldn't hear. Sacro assured me that they were not being secretive, only utilizing a form of communication that I couldn't understand yet.

"I will teach you." he promised. I trusted him. I trusted Dante. I even liked Donally although I was still scared of her. Suddenly, she turned to me.

"You need some clothes, let's go and get you something comfortable to walk around in." She smiled showing brilliant, white teeth that contrasted her dark skin and hair.

"O.K." I said. It was all I could spit out beyond the shock of having her address me directly. I still felt like a little kid and besides that, last time she said something to me, it had regarded killing me.

"We are going to spend some time together. We are going to get to know each other. I hope you have good taste in clothes." said Donally. Her hard edge had softened quite considerably.

"That would be great, this robe itches in all the wrong places." I spoke nervously.

"Look, I really don't think I'll have to hurt you. I am the one who is going to have to prepare you for some of the not so nice aspects of being a human here on Evolution. I have to be a hard-ass Kelly, people are dangerous here. I don't want to lose you like I lost the others, I don't like the way people go sometimes and I don't want to see you get sucked into it. You have been very open through your fear, that's a good sign."

"You see, you just gotta listen to me. I was right, this one's gonna make it." said Dante seemingly proud of himself.

"Yes, perhaps, but it's only the beginning. They tend to crack when the pressure starts." said Donally. She was looking at me while she said it.

"I'm sorry, I guess I really don't understand what I'm doing here. This is overwhelming to say the least, but I trust you. You have been so kind to me, all of you. I miss my home but I do feel happier here maybe even safer so, Donally, I'll just do whatever I have to do to be open with you. I'm not even sure what that means entirely but maybe you would teach me. I'm still afraid of you but I'll just get over it." I said as calmly as I could. My insides felt frozen.

"And you'll fear me for awhile yet. Just listen to these two." she said flicking a thumb toward Dante and Sacro. "If you accept what they tell you and make it your own I will trust you and you'll have nothing to fear. It's worth it, the learning and the struggle to understand, that's the hardest part. I hope you make it." She smiled again, this time showing a little compassion.

I felt the strength of the group. Dante had faith in me. Sacro was willing to teach me and I felt that at some point, Donally would be willing to protect me, but from what I wasn't sure. They talked about battles of some kind. Would I meet some evil, monstrous aliens that wanted to destroy all good things?

We walked on and entered one of the small buildings. I saw humans, not many though. Human presence seemed very limited. It felt good to see the familiar body types.

"Don't be so comforted by the sight of humans." Donally's voice was frightfully firm.

"Why? What's wrong with it? I'm human, your human. They're normal to me. Is that bad?"

"Yes, it could be very bad for your health."

"Hey, hey, hey…let's just take it easy here. Donally, we'll take the kid and get some clothes, nice clothes. There is no danger in here. Knock off the serious, foreboding crap. I feel like having some fun." said Dante. Sacro nodded to him and Donally.

"Fine, we get the clothes and I'll lay off for awhile, I need the break anyway." She looked at me with that intensity that was so intimidating. "Then we can sit down and explain a few things."

Sacro sat patiently while the rest of us milled around the shop. I mingled with rack upon rack of fine clothing the likes of which I had never seen. Dante and Donally brought out articles that they thought might appeal to me. Dante's choices showed his eccentric style. He would have me dress like a princess with elaborate lacing and flowing silk garments. Donally was altogether different, more practical. She choose clothes of sturdy fabrics and clean cuts, things I wouldn't be afraid to get dirty in. My tastes lay somewhere in between and as they came to me with their discoveries, I piled each article, one on top of the other until I had a stack of clothes as high as I am tall. Five feet and three inches worth of clothing, all for me. I asked Sacro for his input but he graciously declined involving himself in the activities.

I tried each thing on and relished in the praise that was given as I stepped out of the dressing room. Most of it came from Dante but Donally and Sacro both added their nods of approval when they'd seen something they liked. Dante picked out clothing for himself as well and he had a silk shirt packaged to be sent to someone I didn't know.

We left the clothing shop with each one of us carrying more bags than I thought possible to carry, most of them mine. I was thrilled to have such an experience of freedom. To dress in any style I choose based only on my taste not in my wallets contents. I would have paid thousands of dollars for the clothing I had picked out but after changing into a short, silky dress and picking up all the bags I could carry, we walked out of the shop without paying a dime, signing a statement or swiping a card, the shop keeper even wished us well.

"This is unbelievable!" I said, my face beaming with the joy of freedom.

"It's just the plain old realities of Evolution Kelly, the longer you're here the more you'll come to appreciate it." said Dante.

"So let's get this stuff to your house and get on with business. Everybody into that?" Donally looked to each of us but rested her eyes on Sacro.

"Yes, that is a good suggestion. We will talk at Kelly's house, is that acceptable to you Kelly?" he asked me.

"Of course." I answered as I fumbled with my bags.

We walked through the clean city streets back to the compound where Renfrew had left us earlier. Another creature, similar to her, took us all the way home. It was a less friendly ride than we had experienced from Renfrew. This creature was not warm to any of us and was far less concerned with communication or introduction. It was a quiet ride. We arrived at my house and the living transport left us without hesitation. I waved to it thinking the polite gesture may count for something but it didn't look back to us, not even to Sacro.

"The home owner must enter first." said Sacro. "Please, place your hand on the door handle and wait until the vibration stops."

I did what he asked and the grand door opened easily.

"Wow, this is really my house, isn't it? Let me guess, the door handle is some sort of special device that scans my hand for a chemical analysis and matches it with a preprogrammed signature designed to open only when I touch it. Am I close?"

"Well, check out the whiz over here. Yea, that's close Kelly but don't get too cocky." said Dante. Donally looked to Sacro with question and of course, concern.

"No need for worry, I assure you Donally, we are safe. They could place explosives outside this door and we would not feel the vibration on a physical level. Let us go in and talk in peace." Sacro used his remarkable abilities to bring calmness to each of us. Donally's expression loosened up but she still made the extra effort to make sure the door was closed firmly behind us.

I carried my bag of clothing to the closet and put each article away with great satisfaction. It was so incredibly exciting to be in my own home. I enjoyed the chance to make the place comfortable for all of us to talk and get to know each other. They all waited patiently in the luxury of the front room. I offered the others refreshments, Dante accepted a glass of water and then we began to talk. With my own glass of the most refreshing water I'd ever had, I sat down with my guests.

"We have been trying to work with humans for most of your existence." said Sacro.

"That's not very long." I said stupidly.

"No, that is not what I meant Kelly." he said. Dante snickered.

"He means human beings, not just you. These people have been working with human beings from the beginning of our time on Earth." said Donally. She got up as she spoke, to look out the window. Her long, braided hair glistened in the light.

"It is more accurate to say that we have been with Earth before the rise of the human species, in fact we are responsible for much of your progress. You know what the term 'evolution' means, we have already discussed that. It is no coincidence that the name of this planet is Evolution. This planet is the origin of the word that you use on Earth, your people just do not realize the realities of Evolution. We are the creators of progress on Earth and with many other planetary communities as well. What we have done is created situations that have allowed you the opportunity to be involved and eventually, to take over the process of evolving. We make suggestions but we do not control the outcomes or actions. That is left up to you as we must consider certain laws of nature and spirit. You must see to your own cause and effect, be accountable to your own choices. There are those who will listen, most often the creatures that you term as lower life forms the animals, follow our guidance and with some exceptions, they embrace our pathways. They develop on trust and take pleasure in allowing us to guide them on their journeys of growth. Humans however, do not take to this trust so easily. As I have said, we do not take command or control, so we have watched as humans have taken some bad falls in the process of evolving. The pitfalls in evolution have not all been because of humankind but it does manifest in human form"

Donally and Dante both nodded their heads in agreement.

"So, are you what we have always called God? If you created us then I guess you must be." I said.

"No, I am not God. Listen carefully here. We create growth and progress. We nurture already existing life forms and give them options for their journeys. Creating life has never been our responsibility. There is the God, as you call it, but it has even greater depth to it than we know. Evolution deals with life after it is created, we take care of the living, God deals with everything else. We work together but it is not my right to explain God to anyone. My purpose is to tell you of your purpose here if you will accept it. We would like your help. It is not as if you are the only hope but you do have qualities within you that can aid us in changing some very adverse conditions on Earth. You are a valuable asset to your planet." explained Sacro.

Noises from the other room interrupted him. Donally jumped at the sound and hurried to the equipment room. Sacro followed her with a greater sense of control and serenity than she had displayed. Dante just sat and looked at me, he smiled. I tried to talk to him with my mind, thinking that maybe I had a better handle on the telepathy thing. Talk to him I did, he could hear my thoughts but I couldn't hear anything from him. He broke my concentration with words.

"I can hear you. It takes more than a little concentration to receive though. Giving thoughts is the easy part, receiving them is a bit of a trick." said Dante.

"Fine, whatever, I just thought I'd try it." He caught the coldness in my voice.

"What do you expect? This ain't magic, buddy. Everything you have seen here has formed out of dedication and talent. You haven't been here long enough to even know what's going on let alone to master the art of thought transmission. Expectations can kill you so save yourself a few migraine headaches and a heart attack and take it easy."

"I just wanted to try it. What's the big deal?" I asked with all of my impatience in tact.

"It's no deal at all. I'm telling you that I know your getting all wound up because of your expectations. Trying is one thing, expecting to do it right all the time is something else. You're expecting, not trying. You expect to be like me. I've been here a lot longer than you and I'm way ahead of you. I've learned things, taken the time to learn. Do you understand? Learning comes before doing."

"Dante, I don't want a purpose here. Sacro is going to come back in here and give me some huge job that I can't do. I knew this was going to happen, I knew all this wasn't really for free. I can't pull this off. Why me? I have nothing to offer. I just wanted a normal life. This isn't normal Dante, not my kinda normal. He's talking about all these big things that he wants help with, he's talking about evolution. I can't help you with evolution, I'm barely sane. Maybe I'm not sane at all…" I was definitely panicking.

"Kelly, your overdoing it. He's only asked you to listen. Just listen. He hasn't told you to save the planet single handedly before next June. Give yourself the serenity to listen and learn from Sacro. Then you can start to think about it."

I had no defensive reaction, no way to justify my fear, he was right. Sacro and Donally returned from the other room. Dante got up and stretched out with the grace and beauty of a perfect cat.

"What's in there? What's all that stuff for?" I asked.

"Most of it monitors the movement of the humans on this planet. That's part of my job, to know exactly where every human is all the time." said Donally.

"Before we can explain the need for the equipment, I want to explain more about why you are here." said Sacro. He sat down close to me. He closed his eyes and remained silent for a moment.

"I was telling you of your potential to help your people. You are not the only one, as you can see there are other humans that have been brought here to develop skills for evolution. Some take these skills back to Earth to show others. We hope that for each person that learns here, thousands will be guided on Earth. The progress in most of your peoples is very profound. We have returned people with physical and mental advantages as well as some with developed spiritual and emotional advancements that have gone on to lead others to higher levels of life experience. Some of these changes would have occurred without our help because of the natural attraction to grow but there are many blocks that you needed help to get over. Some of your dark times in history would have lasted longer and been far more painful if there had been no aid from us. We would like to see the human race and the other animals on Earth reach states of enlightenment. I know you think you have reached great heights as a species but there is so much more. Do you understand what I am saying Kelly?" said Sacro.

"This sounds so unreal, so unbelievable, I mean…yea, I understand but why me? I don't see what I have to offer. I can't even take care of myself and your talking about using me to teach others about growth and enlightenment? I gotta say it's a little weird."

Sacro was quiet for a short time. I used the silence to try to connect with myself. I needed to be grounded. It seemed more like a dream than ever before. It would have been easier to believe that I was just nuts, the only problem was that I knew the truth. I was sane and it was all real. Before me, sat the secrets of evolution. Questions being answered that millions of people spent their entire lives searching and dying for. Just the simple fact that Sacro confirmed the idea that there really is a God was an absolutely stunning bit of information since I was never entirely sure about that.

"It is good for you to have a hard time with this. The information is much for you. Think on these ideas and decide for yourself how or if you want to be part of your world's evolution. We would be cautious if you did not question and discuss with us anything you do not understand." said Sacro.

"Wait just a moment here. I'm still cautious of this one. Promising potential? Yes, I see it too, but many promising people have turned on us. I still don't have enough reason to trust Kelly." said Donally.

"I'm willing. I see a lot of reason." said Dante. He smiled at me.

"What is all this danger about? What are you not telling me? Donally, what have I been doing that you can't get along with me? I've been open to you, haven't I?" I asked.

"Open? Yes, you've been open. You have some great qualities about you. As a person, I think you're a lot of fun but I've seen too many great people make stupid choices, so I need more than a few fine qualities to go by." said Donally.

"Her caution is justified. We have brought many humans here. In fact, we have brought many of everything here. You have noticed the diversity in life. The problem is that we have not encountered such a self-defeating type as humans. There is a basic trust that we have developed with all of the other species from all over the Universe but we are having a problem with humans. We are welcomed and accepted by all with this one exception. Some of your kind do not trust and will even destroy our messengers believing that they are protecting themselves. Some of these people are here on Evolution. They have no intentions toward friendship. They kill and destroy their own people and have no regard for the lives of other species. Many of the Sitrans were kidnapped and beaten at the hands of these enemy humans. They saw what the Sitran can do and wanted their services. They saw them as a resource but instead of respecting them, the humans wanted mindless slaves. The Sitrans are the beings that help us ease our traveling burdens. Renfrew is Sitran. They have always been very gentle and kind, they had no chance against the brutality that the enemy humans imposed. There is no war for a Sitran so they were easily exploited. The enemy humans are the only real danger. Everyone has come here with equal potential for improving the quality of life on Earth. Some have indeed nurtured that but the few that are not are destroying much of the progress that we have worked toward. You may have noticed the silence and withdrawal of the Sitran that brought us here." said Sacro.

"I noticed." I replied.

"He was tortured in a way I care not to discuss. He was tortured because he refused to aid the violent humans in their war against us. He was unaccustomed to the trappings of fear. Now he fears all humans and will not offer a bridge to your people. His silence to you is his way of hoping that you will all go away. He wants peace again, the peace he had before the humans came here."

"I've known Buzzell for a long time. He was one of the first that I met here and nothing, not one word has he spoken to me, he won't even look in my direction." said Dante with sadness. I assumed Buzzell was the name of the Sitran that brought us to my house. Dante looked as if he carried the burden of Buzzell's pain.

"What can I do?" I asked. I put my hand on Dante's shoulder as a gesture of concern and compassion. There was no way I would ever want to be an enemy to these wonderful beings. How could any human be so negative?

A breeze of freshness in my heart, to feel that I really wanted to be a part of a great purpose. Sure, I could help end the pain caused by these bitter humans. But I still didn't have any details. All I knew of was the general injustice of their brutality.

An odd thought broke through my feelings. I didn't see anything besides the loading bay when we were going to Sowthren Court. There was no dome or city to be seen from the outside.

"That's one of our methods of defense. They can't get into our major centers if they can't find them. We've got many mindbodies working together to distract the enemy. The Dome is only slightly detectable from the outside. It combines reflections with it's own intelligence to camouflage the city. Because the Dome is an entirely living organism, it has control over it's own energy system which it uses to create images that mimic or add to the surrounding landscape. One of the enemy groups did come across the edge of the Dome, but it's smart. It can expand and contract to keep the outsiders confused of the actual boundary. Each day, the Dome will change in diameter, it's very effective." Donally answered my question.

"The hostile humans haven't even found the doorway into the loading compound. They're far from being a threat to the cities." said Dante.

"You can't be too cautious though, you know that Dante. Strange things have happened with this insane group, don't be so foolish to think they may not fluke out some how and get into the cities, then we'd be fu…" Dante cut Donally off.

"I'm cautious, I'm always cautious, as much as I can be but I think that they're weak and ignorant people. They destroy themselves with fear. They work against each other. If we ignored them, they'd just wear themselves out, fight each other and defeat their own armies. I don't fear them the way you do Donally. You give them way too much credit."

"Talk to Buzzell about fear, ask him if the caution I have is exaggerated." Donally said intensely. Dante said no more and again we sat in silence. Donally's words cut through Dante's optimism. Donally moved closer to him and looked into his eyes. Realizing that she'd hurt him, Donally put a hand on his shoulder to express her compassion and regret.

"We do not want war. Evolution will not look to senseless killing and fighting as a means to stop these humans. We cannot speak out about growth if we choose to kill everyone that opposes us. It leaves us with a complicated challenge. How do we prove to them that we will not harm them? That is why they fear us, they see us as a threat but in what way? We do not have an understanding of the beliefs that control their decisions to hate. I have no experience with such hatred. Some of the helpful people say that we represent a threat to the very thing most Earth societies are based on. Our way of living is too fair, some humans with financial power would not accept our moneyless way of being but even our human friends do not understand the levels of hate and violence these people exhibit." said Sacro.

"Humans don't need much reason to be hateful. Look at Earth, really take a look at it, it's easy to see that we take the place for granted. We go ahead and destroy the very planet we live on. It doesn't make any sense but it's common where I come from. My world has never been free from war. There's always some fight going on somewhere." I said.

I never did have much faith in mankind but this made it even more difficult. To find out there was a place in the Universe where peace was a reality and the only things screwing it up were power hungry humans was a hard blow. In fact, I thought it impossible. How could we be the only ones? I watched the suffering on my own planet and grew used to it. Destruction, hate and violence was just part of being alive and we all had to deal with it, that was the Earth way but to see that hateful force of human aggression spread out through the Cosmos was too much for me. I had no other solution for them except to gather them all up, send them back to Earth and forget about the whole planet, let it deal with itself. Dante cued in on my thought.

"We can't just send them back unless they're willing to go. If we try to force them through time and space, they will die. Our means of space travel depends on the willingness of the traveler. That willingness creates the needed energy flow to encourage movement. None of these barbaric humans are willing to leave."

"I don't get it. Why do they want to stay here if they hate you and are afraid of you?" I asked.

"To turn Evolution into Earth Two." said Donally.

"They are thinking profit and power. Look at this place Kelly, this planet is paradise compared to Earth. It's full of fantastic things that could make a lot of money. Nobody living here has any desire to market, advertise and put ownership on the treasures of Evolution. This planet is a goldmine. A big investment haven to those of greed. What they innocently call business is really an exploitation of resources and people. I've met with some of these humans, they talk well of the good of all but they don't have vision. To them it's about quick cash. Small minded people, all of them and what they see is a way to keep their interests taken care of while they lay waste to the rest" said Dante.

"They have no idea how this all works. Evolution advances because of the cooperation, not the competition of living things. We're not creating tools that we use and control. Even our machinery has living components. Everything runs on living energy, life converted to power not the other way around." said Donally.

"These humans are full of greed and they cannot understand our world. They demand to have access to our technology but they have no knowledge of our society. We have no secrets. The value of life is based on the quality and care that we put into living. Money has no quality on it's own. The enemy humans have placed their value on profit and when profit is the only goal, there must be secrets. They think in terms of secrets and conspiracy because, for whatever reason, that is all they know." said Sacro.

"They go on and on about making deals with us. They say that if we give them use of our planet, then they can sell its resources to the people back on Earth. They make promises of great wealth for us. Oh yea, we can share in the big fortune, what a prize. We have more than they do already. One guy tried to show me an economic chart forecasting the enormous profits people like Sacro and I would receive on his offer. Of course this left many more people with nothing but he went on about free business opportunities and everybody gets their chance to make a living. I mean you couldn't be more stupid. None of that fiscal garbage matters. Everybody here lives beyond wealth of the monetary kind. They just don't understand." said Dante, his passion was definitely sparked and he was very enthusiastic.

"Take, for example, the vehicle that brought you to Evolution." said Sacro. I nodded remembering the mist that I had floated in as I flew through space. The mist that supported me. The mist that was now with me, inside my body.

"The life that exists there is not some thing that we can manufacture in a laboratory. It just is what it is. I did not create it. I do not have the knowledge of why and how it is willing to serve us. It just does because it chooses to. It does what it does because it likes to do it. There is no ownership, no contracts and no payments, the rewards are beyond price. It lives by symbiosis. There is give and take for all involved. It is for health not money. These humans of war want to make deals and bargain with us. They want us to sell workers to them. They say they will stop the fighting if we would only cooperate in business plans." said Sacro.

I sensed a profound mixture of energy coming from Sacro as he spoke. He stood up slowly. His image changed, shimmered as if unstable. He walked over to the front door and held onto the frame to steady himself. The temperature in the room turned uncomfortably warm.

"Take a break, he's getting mad." said Dante. It scared me. I was never too comfortable with anger.

"This is mad? Is anything bad gonna happen? Should we leave him alone?" I asked.

"No, as if it would be like that. Sacro just spent time explaining peace to you. You think he's gonna blow up in your face now? No. He's just different. Not the same level of emotional energy. Sometimes you can see it. Little sparks around his body. Just don't try to console him right now. I can't even touch him in this state, way too much power. Still you don't have to fear him, not ever. Sacro would never hurt anyone." Dante folded his arms across his lap.

"Trust what he says Kelly. Dante's right. I tried to touch him once when he was like this. It was like getting a blast from a wicked bolt of lightening. We just aren't built for that kind of power." said Donally. She shuttered at the memory.

"Sacro calls this active detachment. Releasing his energy and his desires together to solve the problems of Evolution. He trusts that while letting go of the problems, one can create higher opportunity. Trying to solve problems all the time is wasted effort and becomes a joyless set of tasks. Sometimes one has to make a conscious effort to rid oneself of the need to solve everything that appears to be a problem. He gets that way with the enemy humans because it's so senseless, such a mass of ill thinking coming from the humans. I'm beginning to understand how he does it. I've been practicing this myself. Sometimes I just want to take on everything right away, get it over with and move on but I listen to him, I stay close and I watch. Look at him." said Dante.

I did. I looked at Sacro. I could see his energy dancing around his body. He had that angelic look again. This being dealt with the most aggressive of his emotions in an awesome and captivating way.

Noises came from the equipment room and Donally ran to it as if it called her name. Dante guided me away from watching Sacro and talked

to me about the equipment. He explained it was used for tracking pur-
poses, to monitor the enemy humans. We needed to know where they
were and how they were grouping together. Dante went on about how I
would become part of the team and learn how to use the equipment to
aid in protecting others. He said I was very unique and valuable.

Did I believe him? Not entirely. Having no experience in self trust, I
had learned to give up. I was well practiced at ignoring my uniqueness.
My soul cried out, 'Go for it Kelly!' and I always replied with, 'Can't do
it, sorry'. My inner voice had become a barely audible static fuzz in my
mind. At that moment though, I heard it very clearly. My little spirit had
broken through the wall I'd built up and encouraged me. I looked
around feeling like I had just woken up after a very long sleep but I still
felt nervous and doubtful of my ability.

"Dante…, I would like, well, what I mean is, I want to…" I stammered
with insecurity. Fighting back the urge to squash my intuition with
doubt, I finally managed to say "I want to help you."

"What was that? Can't hear you. What do you want?" he asked me
teasingly. I took a few deep breaths. I glanced around the room. Sacro
was pulling his strength back into his body. I could see Donally
through the doorway, working with the equipment. And then I looked
back to Dante.

"I want to be part of the team. How can I be of service?" I said with
bold conviction. I had made my first real commitment to Evolution.

Chapter 7

After what seemed like hours of talk, I began to feel the drowsy cloud of my diminishing attention span. I simply could no longer listen to the incredible information my three friends passionately gave to me. Before I got to this point I learned many things about myself and my shallow understanding of life. Simple things had eluded me, the basic arrangement of humanity and my purpose, the one I'd been so desperately searching for were shown to me in a clear and concise way. I had not had any understanding of humility in all of my life and without that, purpose meant absolutely nothing. We talked about my options and unlearning what I had spent thirty-some-odd-years learning. In fact, most of those years I'd spent learning what not to do to be a happy, healthy individual. Moments in the conversation I felt the weight of wasted years and began to think of myself as having no good qualities but Sacro cheered me up by discussing abilities that he had witnessed in me that I never knew I had. He talked about my great communication abilities. I laughed out loud thinking he was joking. Nobody else laughed. Sacro was serious about me.

Great communication ability? Me? I couldn't see it. When I left Earth, I was lonely and afraid of people. I made small talk well enough but I was never bursting with expression, not in public anyway. Most of my efforts were in trying to keep people away but Sacro persisted in telling me I had the gift of reaching out and touching others, all I needed was direction and practice, then I would be free to use the gift.

Donally excused herself to go home and rest. Before she left, she told me that she hoped everything would work out with me.

"It just means I'm beginning to trust you, which is far more important than having my approval. Well, it's been a day. See ya' later." she said on her way out. I felt honored and relieved by her new confidence. She opened the door and I could see one of the Sitran waiting outside, ready to take her home.

I caught the door before it closed all the way and looked out into the night. It was a colorful darkness, even the shadows were bright. The wholeness of Evolution was breathtaking. Every taste of the air was clean and warm. Why would any human being want to refuse the wisdom it offered? How stupid does one need to be to see that a price couldn't be placed on this planet, this society? Evolution was complete. Everyone had whatever they wanted and needed. I couldn't even imagine the kind of thinking that these hostile people engaged in.

Sacro and Dante joined me outside with some chairs and we sat quietly together gazing at the brilliant, shining stars. My two friends fit into the scenery so well, they belonged to the planet and the beauty of its environment. I didn't feel as connected as they looked. I wasn't part of this yet, still only an observer. There were moments in the day that I thought I was watching a movie. Seeing the story unfold before me but not being able to factor my self into it. I wanted to live where they lived, in the truth of Evolution.

"Alright then, I shall be on my way." said Dante. My stomach took a little flip. I didn't want him to go.

"Why? There's so much I still don't understand." I was trying to hang onto the moment even though I knew it was time to stop.

"Yea, your right about that. There's an immeasurable amount of information you don't comprehend but I'm still going home." With very little effort, he picked up his and Sacro's chairs and went inside.

"I must go as well." said Sacro. My stomach knotted up.

"Wait, I don't want to be alone right now."

"I want to go home. We all need time without the outer influences even if they are good ones. We can join again when we are fit and rested. Use your inner wisdom to guide you. Kelly, you have many decisions to make, you need silence too. Defeat the fear of being alone with yourself."

"Do you feel afraid?"

"No." I waited for a moment because I thought Sacro was going to offer more, some tasty bit of wisdom to help me deal with fear, but he didn't. Regardless of my own anxiety, I had to let them go. Dante put away all of the chairs, kissed me gently on the cheek and disappeared into the night.

"When will we see each other again?" I asked Sacro nervously.

"No plans, just relax. We will be together soon. Trust what you hear in the silence and leave the rest of us to our own solitude."

I felt his warmth again. A wonderful wave of comfort washed over from him into me. My fear drifted away easily.

"Thank you." I said and smiled at him in hopes that he understood that I truly received his kindness.

He turned and walked away into the enchanting darkness. I shut my door and began walking to the kitchen. Sounds beamed out from the equipment room. It startled me but I went to the call of the noises anyway. Just the sight of all the high tech stuff was intimidating since I didn't understand any of it. There was one very large screen with all kinds of symbols and designs, which I didn't recognize, surrounding its frame. The inner part of the monitor showed a map with little dots moving around it. I watched as some familiar scenes formed. Pathways, hills, even trees showed up. I saw my own house. The rotating image changed to focus on another area that I couldn't identify, and then another. It was running through a series of focal points. Words appeared along the bottom of the image. They were english looking but were moving by so fast I couldn't actually read any sense into them. I wondered if Dante and Donally could read the words that fast. I looked at the console of buttons, keys and levers beneath the screen checking to see if there were any labels or instructions attached. Nothing. One simple button probably would have slowed the streaming words down but which one. It was too scary. I didn't want to be responsible for some kind of system failure.

Moving images appeared on the screen again. They were clear, not just little dots like before, but shadows, outlines of actual things. They were human outlines that were gathering together near a building. I knew this building. I had seen it's distinct shape on my way to Sowthren Court and from what I remembered this place was very close to my house. These people were the enemies, I was sure of it. I was watching them moving together, probably to plan some horrible invasion. I felt angry. Bold ideas grew in my mind. Ideas of going out into the night and sneaking up on them and then…what? These people were violent and destructive. They'd probably kill me right on the spot. I continued to watch. I counted one hundred and thirty-one people gathering together just a stone's throw from my home. One hundred and thirty-one very mean people gathering together just outside my house. Anger turned to fright as I realized I could've seen the whole thing from my bedroom window, they were that close. The equipment room had no windows. I imagined these people getting together and storming my house. Throwing rocks at my windows, coming in with guns and grenades to blow me apart. Maybe I could lock myself up in the room so they couldn't see me.

The little answering machine box startled me with its beeps. I pressed the buttons as I had before and heard the voice of Sacro.

"Close the blinds on your windows. They cannot get at you while you are in your home, and please Kelly, get some rest."

The machine switched off. My fears had reached him. I wondered if he could turn off his awareness of the voices calling out to him or was he so strong that he didn't have to turn them off? I did what he asked of me. I closed all the blinds with tremendous anxiety as I expected to see a psycho-killer standing near every window, just waiting for me to get close enough. No one appeared. I made it to my bedroom window and looked out. I saw the people going into the Quonset type building. They had built a fire just outside the front entrance. Some of them were standing around it laughing and talking with each other. They were greeting each other with handshakes and hugs. It looked like an old fashioned town hall meeting. I turned off the light in my room and watched them. They looked friendly and happy, not the picture I had formed in my head of crazed-maniac people bent on destruction. I could see some of the faces quite clearly. Two of them stood out, the fire seemed to spotlight their faces for me. A tall, clean looking woman with short, blonde hair and a shorter, handsome man. He had a warm smile on his face as he talked with another man beside him, making gestures of compassion and understanding. She also smiled as she talked with another couple. Sometimes they would look to each other and moved closer together. She put her arm around him and seemed to lead him into the building. The rest of the people followed. They left the fire blazing as they closed the broad doors. I stood back from the window.

What had I just witnessed? It looked like a happy backyard barbecue, everyone that I saw looked clean and polished and politically correct. Big, smiley faces and friendly gestures. It didn't fit with my picture of the enemy. I wanted to see dirty people wearing old army fatigues. I moved back to the window and saw two people come out of the building by a small side door. One of them pointed right to my house and I crouched down to avoid being seen. My heart raced. I waited nervously, knowing they were coming for me. I waited some more. No need to panic I thought, Sacro said they couldn't get in here. I peeked out the window but saw no one. I reached up for the release and the blind dropped over the window. Sounds from the equipment room called out for attention. I ran to the room to see if I could make it stop. Entering the room, I could see the screen displaying my own house. I was looking at my front door. To my intense horror, there was a large, bulky shadow looming across my door. I froze. I felt like I was playing a video game without the right controls and I wouldn't be able to hit the reset button if I thought I was gonna lose. A very light, steady rap on my front door caused my blood to turn ice cold. The screen flashed out a very readable message,'DO NOT APPROACH FRONT ACCESS ROUTE'. I heard the knock again, this time with more force put into it. I backed out of the equipment room and closed its door. I walked backward to my bedroom, keeping my eyes on the front door and fighting the tricks of my imagination that flashed the scenes of a splintering door flying all over the room. The knocking continued. I ran to my room, jumped to my bed and like a frightened child, hid under my covers until the knocking stopped.

I was up for most of the night. I didn't get out of bed save for the one time when I had to go to the bathroom. I ran out and back as fast as I could, dashing under the covers again as if that made me invisible to anyone who may come in and try to kill me. I managed to calm myself by believing what Sacro had told me about no one being able to get in. I repeated that to myself like a monk chants a mantra, 'no one can get in, no one can get in'. The trust I had for Sacro kept me from going insane from fear. I believed in him and if he said no one could get in then no one could. The fear had more to do with the fact that these insolent people knew I was here. I had no idea why they would want to see me, it was their intentions that gave me the feeling of dread or what I imagined their intentions to be. The will these people must have to want to exploit this near perfect world.

As the colors shifted outside from darkness to daylight, I dozed in dreamy fear and looked forward to the safety and comfort of being with Sacro again.

CHAPTER 8

"You want me to do what? Are you kidding? I can't do that!" My shouting contrasted the laid back design of the room.

"I know it sounds like hard work but it would be fun. You'll meet lots of people and get to travel a lot." said Dante.

"That's precisely why I don't want to do this. My God, Dante! I don't want to meet a lot of people. It's all too important, too political, too many rules that don't make any sense. People are impossible to deal with you know?"

"Yea but we aren't talking about your typical earth-bound politics." said Donally as she inspected some small piece of equipment she'd taken from a nearby closet.

"No, no, no. I can't do it. The very thought of all that confrontation makes me feel sick. They would think I'm nuts. God, I don't even want to go back to Earth, there's got to be something else I can do. I thought that I could just stay here."

"We want someone who can work between Earth and Evolution. It will soon be time to make our presence known to Earth. We need a spokesperson." said Sacro. He was dressed in very common looking trousers with a light shirt which made him appear more human to me than he had ever looked before.

"Your gonna tell everybody on Earth about this place? Are you nuts? Haven't you heard about the Roswell thing? This alien stuff freaks them out, no one can handle it, especially the politicians. They'd just as soon have us all killed, don't you watch t.v.?"

"No, they won't, not if we do it slowly and carefully. It's time we took some bigger risks with Earth, before they destroy it." said Dante. "Kelly, you'd make a perfect liaison between the two worlds. Think of it, with our training you will be unstoppable, my friend."

We were all sitting in a common room in a small building in Sowthren Court. Even after a sleepless night I was stunned to wakefulness when they presented me with this absurdity. A diplomat. They wanted me to carry out diplomatic assignments to build a symbolic bridge between the two worlds. I was not the right person for the job. Why didn't they know that? I was never one for the formalities of true diplomacy or any kind of politics and I had no patience with people. Maybe they weren't as perceptive as I thought them to be, to mistake my abilities so much to think that I could ever learn the art of diplomacy was really quite a huge miscalculation of my potential.

"Let's get off this for awhile. We're scaring her." said Donally as she got up to look out of the window.

"No way, I want to talk about this. Why would you think this is a job I would want or could do? I don't think I've shown any signs of being entirely stable enough for a job this big." Some part of me was trying to work out the possibilities, maybe entertaining the whole idea, hoping they could actually give one good reason why they thought I was capable of this.

"You need a great change in order to progress in your own evolution. You care about Earth and you are honest. Your only real defect is your attention to the things that discourage you. You let the circumstances of a troubled world take your courage and then you cease to believe in better things. You could do this job. You have the belief that things can be better, it is still alive in you. With our help and encouragement you could counsel the people of Earth. You would have all the support you need. Have you ever had all the support you need? No need to answer Kelly, I already know." said Sacro.

"There are too many greedy, mean, people on Earth, like the one's that are fighting you here." I said, defending my inner doubt.

"So what are you saying Kelly that we just shouldn't try?" asked Dante. He reached out and touched my shoulder which sent a charge through my body.

"Well, no. It's just that I'm not the right person. I mean, why not you Dante? You'd be perfect, with all your charms."

"I already have my jobs. I don't want to do everything." said Dante.

"Well, there's got to be other people here who could do this, who would…" Dante cut me off.

"Yea, there are other people here who could do it but we are asking you Kelly. We think you would be the most successful. Why are you so quick to decide you can't? You're not even sure of what we're asking."

"Yes, your asking me to be a representative of something great and beautiful and I can't do that. I don't even know what I stand for. I don't know enough about anything to represent a single point of view, not to mention a whole planet. I'm telling you, I can't do it."

"Alright everyone, there is no need to make this hard. It is, after all, your choice Kelly. There are enough things for us to do, we can find something else if you are not attracted to this type of work. I do ask that you read this before you settle on your decision." said Sacro handing me a thick textbook. I took it and agreed to read it. Dante had his arms crossed over his chest looking uncharacteristically defensive.

"I'm sorry Dante, I didn't mean to yell." I said.

"It's O.K. Kelly. It's hard to be nice when you don't believe in yourself. I understand."

I had nothing more to say to him. I felt angry at his sarcasm.

"I'd love to stay and listen to the two of you go at each other but there seems to be a bit of a problem at the third Dome. I can't make out what they're saying here." said Donally looking at some other gadget she held in her hand, "I'll meet up with you later."

"Wait. I'll come with you." said Dante and they both left.

"What did I do to deserve that?" I asked Sacro. "Why is he so crabby?"

"He believes that you can do this and he is upset that you do not. If you embraced this job, you and he would be working closely. He was looking forward to that."

"I'm sorry. It just looks too complicated for me."

"I suggest that you make no decision until you have read the outline in this text. Our definition of politics may be quite different from what you understand it to be. Remind yourself that there is no money to lose or gain. You will always have everything that you need. Let us go now and put our attention to other things."

"What things? Where?" I tucked the book under my arm and followed Sacro down a long, narrow hallway that led to a huge lobby. It was crowded with people and other things. Something flew over my head and landed in front of Sacro. It was a hideous looking creature but Sacro showed no disdain. He talked with it for awhile as I stood a few feet away gazing at the aliens milling around, talking, flying, slithering or walking.

"Kelly, I would be grateful if you took a walk to familiarize yourself with Sowthren Court. I would really like to talk with Debinar for awhile and I think you may find the walk more exciting."

Warning bells went off in my head even though no danger existed.

"I will find you when I am finished. Go wherever you want." he said.

Sacro and the flying beast walked away together and I was left standing in a crowded room of non-humans. It was all too sudden, nobody warned me that I'd have to be alone. Something brushed by me and smiled, at least it looked like a smile. I smiled back and made a break for the door. There was less activity outside. I stopped to catch my breath and calm my nerves. I looked around at the smooth walkways. The streets shone. No garbage, no cars, no loud machines. It wasn't hard to find inner peace when the outer environment was so serene. The book fell from under my arm and hit the ground, reminding me that I had been carrying it. I picked it up and looked around. I had a goal. I could just read the book, which would keep me occupied until Sacro could come and find me. I walked a short distance toward the lake and found a comfortable spot to begin my study.

The surroundings made it difficult to get focused. The whole area was so intensely beautiful. I watched the glittering aura of the Dome that surrounded us, protected us and I marveled at its strength. I shook my head and concentrated on the words of the book. It was an instruction manual, instructions on interplanetary diplomacy. I laughed out loud, how could they see me doing this job? Me, the one with the history of alcoholism and drug abuse. Me, with my extreme moods and fears. Could I really learn how to deal with people in a tactful and tasteful manner enough to persuade powerful people to unite with alien cultures from other planets, other galaxies? I'd seen all those movies and t.v. shows on Earth, the ones that told stories of monstrous creatures waiting in dark corners of the Universe for an opportunity to rip peoples brains out and take over their bodies so they could breed and dominate the world. There were a variety of fear-based beliefs about aliens. The thought of sticking my neck out on Earth to speak out for aliens of more than just one type, was a bit numbing. I knew the way Earth worked, well not Earth so much as its people. They would lock me up or ignore me, call me crazy. I couldn't swagger around with government officials and tell them to trust me on this one, the aliens are our friends. They'd just check their almighty database, see the various de-tox centers I'd been to, bust me for the eight hundred dollars I owed in taxes and ship me off to an institute of their choosing.

The book was beautiful in its concepts. The job, as it was described in the manual, looked like something worth doing. It was a job of peace and well-being, a job of great purpose. There were many different aspects to the work, things that I could see myself doing and being happy with. There was the research and travel, planning and organizing and working closely with Dante. What bothered me was the amount of courage it would take for me to work with people. Sacro wasn't human, he was easy to work with, he had all the answers and I could trust him. Dante was human but he was beyond the small minds of Earth politicians and their kind of greed. Donally was extremely honest and straightforward and she didn't have anything to gain by hurting me, at least not now anyway. Even if Donally's appreciation wasn't directed toward me, I could see that she loved the ways of life on this planet. The millions of humans on Earth were all together different, most of them anyway. Especially the kind of people I'd be dealing with, the ones that were already powerful with money and media. How much would they warm up to the idea of life without need for money? Life based on desires to unite and share love with ALL creatures. Was it even possible? That was the whole problem for me. I didn't believe in this way of life for my world. I had grown so rigid in the ways of Earth societies. To meet with prime ministers and presidents and others of power, and persuade them to give up weapons, territories, wars, economies and allow integration with other planets was far fetched. Earth wasn't a fast changing place, people had to take their time and much of the time change was associated with suffering. The world I left was divided by beliefs, cultures, money and society, it was hard enough just to get along. Most of the time we didn't even bother to try to love and nurture each other, not when there was so much work to do, money to make and ladders to climb.

I read on through the book and thought of the billions who would benefit from the implementation of the incredibly progressive ideas. If even one little country believed in Evolution it may save them from the horrors of poverty, starvation and war. Just one country could decide to join with Evolution and save themselves the hassles of closed mindedness. I could think of a number of places that had nothing to lose by dropping repressive governments and giving their trust to Evolution. The problem was in the highly established systems, they would certainly oppose me because they seemed to have more to lose. The ones that took pride in the wars they had won or were controlled by their economy wouldn't see fit to give up everything they'd fought and worked so hard for, even if it meant a better life for everyone. We could have used this intervention a long time ago.

I grew closer with the idea until it seemed like it was a possible plan for me. I turned the pages and became more intrigued by the nature of the job of representing Evolution. My parents would be so proud, if they could stop fighting each other long enough to notice. Kelly McGrail-Interplanetary Diplomat for the Unity of All Species. I liked the importance it imbued, such honest ideals and positive goals.

Who was I kidding? Even my parents would think I was nuts. Oddly enough though, I wanted the job, the type of challenge I'd never known. If I could bring the kind of peace that Evolution had brought me, to one tiny nation on Earth, I would be successful.

The clouds in my mind cleared out. I felt a knowing of how this world could be so successful without the use of money. I had wondered what the catch was. The catch was that when everything was given so freely like my house, my food and clothing, I felt grateful and able to give something back. I wasn't obligated to do anything but I wanted to. My motivation for giving wasn't to make money, it had grown into something deeper.

"Spirit is always grateful." said Sacro from behind me.

"I can see how this might work Sacro, I really can!" I felt the excitement of discovery. I remembered learning that the Earth moved around the sun, not the other way around. It seemed important to me when I was five because the knowledge made me feel stronger and more independent.

"Understand this Kelly, you are not obligated to do this job because you feel that you have to pay us back somehow. That is not the case. We only desire that you contribute in ways that are suitable to your individual nature. I choose this position because I thought it would suit you. You are free to disagree and explore other options." I stood up to walk with him.

"I still need time to think about this Sacro. I haven't even finished the book yet, but it sounds amazing. I just don't think I have the courage to pull this off by myself."

"Did anyone say you would do this alone? If someone told you that they were mistaken. This one job requires great teamwork. No one individual does all the work. Even the Lone Ranger had a helper, he just would not give him as much credit."

I laughed at his reference. The Spirit of Evolution, watching old Lone Ranger episodes? Sacro laughed along with me. The point was made and I did realize that my thoughts of aloneness ended with me. I had more help and guidance than I knew what to do with. I could no longer use the excuse that no one cared about me and my contributions.

CHAPTER 9

"There is a breach in Well Dome Three. It has been injured, infected with a virus and the whole system is breaking down. It's all gotta be moved Sacro, or we'll end up losing everything. I can't do anything to stop this, the rupture where the virus was entered has increased by thirty percent in the last twenty minutes, the whole membrane is decaying. It's now or never." said Donally in an uncharacteristic panic.

Sacro and I spent the afternoon at my house pouring over the technology in the equipment room. I was fascinated and so eager to learn. My mind was clear and concentration so intensely focused that I thought I could've listened to him into the wee hours of the next morning.

Dante and Donally had called out to Sacro though, who advised them to come to us immediately. They were both wide-eyed and flushed with activity.

"These fucken humans! They're a damn plague and they're adapting to some of our defenses. God Sacro! Nobody even knew they were there before it was too late. Nobody had a clue that they even knew about Dome Three. They've found ways to shield themselves and infiltrate our defenses. We should just kill them all, get it over with. I'll even do it myself! They are killing innocents and they don't care. None of them deserve life!" yelled Donally.

"No, that would make our position weaker than it needs to be. Do you have any details that you wish to share? We will need to revise our systems again." said Sacro. He showed strain from the news. Dante sat next to me. I could feel his exhaustion.

"If we could keep those two apart somehow, the rest of them would be easy to handle." said Donally, "But first, we have to move everything out of Well Dome Three or we'll lose a lot of our resources.

I asked a few questions after the intensity of the panic died down. Dome Three was one of the other stable gravity wells where a Dome had established itself. They used the area for supply and food storage. Some beings worked in the Dome by day, just as it was in Sowthren Court. There seemed to be no indication that the enemy humans knew it was there.

"No way to stabilize Dome Three, she's dying Sacro. It's a new disease that's been introduced to her and we have no cure." said Dante.

"This is most unfortunate. Have those that are willing, begin the evacuation. We must remain here to figure out a way to break down this deadly partnership between Raleigh and Slater." said Sacro.

"Already started the evacuation. If anything remains after Dome Three is gone, members of the Sitran are willing to go in and get whatever they can. They'll be able to deal with the gravity increase better than anyone." said Donally.

"We need a team for reestablishing another Dome." said Sacro.

"No, we can't put another Dome there, not yet anyway. We don't really know what's killing this one, if we put another in place to soon, it might get the same infection. We have to be sure that the area has not been permanently contaminated." said Donally.

"That is true. Have an inanimate shield put in place or we will have the sky falling in." said Sacro.

"What!?" I asked.

"The moons Kelly, will fall on our heads if we let that well stay open to long. We happen to like those moons where they are." said Dante. I wasn't sure if he was joking about the moons but Donally left quickly to put the shield in place.

"I guess I underestimated their forces." said Dante putting his head in his hand. He looked defeated and overwhelmed. I was uncomfortable with his sorrow. Dante was supposed to be my source of strength. I felt bad about the argument we had earlier.

"I'm sick of this fight Sacro. We don't need to save these people. How many more do we sacrifice for them?" asked Dante.

"We brought them here. I brought you here. I will not discard the ones that do not believe in me or Evolution. There is some possibility that they may reinvent themselves."

"And how many will die before Raleigh sees the light? I don't have your compassion anymore Sacro. I just don't value the lives of people who choose this war. I think they should all be sent back whether they are willing or not. Evolution is suffering from the choices of a few greedy, thoughtless people, why support them? Why let them go on living here? They are beginning to think that we are weak. This compassion is going to be the end of Evolution Sacro, then who are we going to help?" The anger Dante expressed dominated my house. I could feel the pain of his words vibrate through my whole body. Dante cared about Evolution so much that he was willing to defend it to the death. It was disturbing.

"Those creatures of Earth fear their death and have no regard for the lives of others. I share your discomfort of their presence here but I will not be responsible for sending them to Hell. If they die by our actions now, they will die in fear. That fear will keep them in death. Dome Three does not fear death." said Sacro.

"She's dying in pain Sacro, even I can hear her cry." Dante began to cry.

"Yes, but she is aware Dante. She knows that the pain is a stepping stone. I have been through such pain, she will be released. She welcomes her transition."

"What do you mean?…you have been through such pain?" I asked.

"Kelly, I have died more than one biological death. It is part of life. Each journey that I make is more fulfilling than the last as long as I trust the process. I have felt great pain and no longer fear it. Now, I am beyond the confines of biology. I am whole but I continue to grow."

I was a child again, shocked by what I had just heard. It was a good feeling, to hear that death is a transition and not an end. I'd heard it before but never really believed it. Somehow, Sacro made it real for me. Dante sensed my wave of elation. He got up from his chair, walked over and embraced me. I supported him. I hugged him with my complete attention. He broke the hold and left, closing the door behind him. I went to run after him, hoping to bring him back.

"Leave him Kelly. He needs this moment to himself. He will be alright. I would like your help in developing an effective way to trace these humans. I do not want this to happen again."

"I don't even know what you were doing to track them before." I said evenly, ready and willing to do whatever I could to help.

"How did you get here Kelly?"

"I'm not sure Sacro, there was heat and the mist and my body was all weird."

"The mist, what do you remember about the mist?"

"It stayed with me, it protected me. It's here with me now."

"That is it. The mist, we call them Devids or Devid Communities. They remain in the human body. They help it to adapt to new environments and they allow us to locate and identify the human that they are working with. Their consciousness is linked to the equipment in this house. Somehow there is interference, their intelligence is not reaching our system. Raleigh and Slater must have found something out about their Devids."

"Can they hurt me? I mean by being in my body."

"Yes, oh yes, the Devids could hurt you but they will not. In fact, they bring with them a certain element of healing to your body-mind."

"What about these people you talk about? Who are they?"

"Raleigh and Slater. They are the greatest set back to our growth and peace with most of the other humans. Raleigh wants power and Slater wants her approval."

"So what makes them so hard to deal with?"

"Each other. They feed off of each other. When they combine their intelligence it multiplies. Together they organize their attacks on us. If we could separate them, most of their plans would be incomplete and unworkable. There is however, another factor involved."

"I think I've seen them. Outside my house at that thing over there." I pointed to the direction of the building where I'd witnessed the gathering of the humans.

"Yes, they usually act as leaders for the human groups that are not so dedicated to taking over Evolution. There are some of the enemy humans that will not follow them but they will not be with us either. The majority of them stay under the Raleigh wing. They are willing to listen to her, so they meet at different buildings away from the main compound."

"What do we do now? Can you see where they are? Do you think they killed the Devids?"

"We will find these things out." He sat down in front of the tracking controls. Images came up on a large screen. Two smaller monitors lit up with scenes that were not familiar to me.

"They have affected all of them. Not one of them is showing on our system."

"This is bad! This is really bad! They could be anywhere. We gotta do something."

"We are doing something. We can use the implants. It appears that the Devids have been removed from their bodies. I do not wish to put them at risk any longer. The Seletzium implants are our best alternative. Kelly, you contact Dante and let him know that we will need his aid. Tell him that we are putting the Seletzium in place. I will contact Coalamine to assist us."

I affirmed his request, not really knowing how I would carry it out. I waited, thinking on how I could locate Dante. I didn't know where he was or how to find him.

"What is it?" Sacro broke into my ignorance as I sat in silence beside him.

"How am I supposed to find Dante?"

"Use your thoughts, he can hear you. Your intention will find him."

"Oh yea, I forgot that he can hear me." Walking out into the front room. I sat down and focused my thoughts. I cleared my mind with deep breathing. I pictured myself calling out to Dante slowly, steadily, repeating his name to be sure he could hear me. Sacro broke my concentration when he entered the room.

"Kelly, you need not be so rigid. Your preparation is too fancy and frustrating. Just talk to him as though he were here with us. Do not wait for a response because you are still unable to hear him, you have not yet learned to receive, but be sure that he can hear you. Now go ahead."

"Why don't you call him?" I said angrily and a little startled by my lack of tolerance for being told what to do.

"You can do it Kelly. I asked you and you agreed." he said calmly and went back into the equipment room.

Dante joined us just after I had finished eating. Donally had called in to let us know that the evacuation was close to completion and the shield was in place. She agreed to helping us with the implant mission and told us she would be with us as soon as she was sure that everyone was out and the shield was sealed. Sacro left Dante and I to get the Seletzium chips that were to be implanted in the enemy humans.

I felt funny. This was big mission stuff and I was never much of a big mission kinda person. It seemed like a huge weight had been dropped on my shoulders and I wasn't strong enough to hold it up. Dante told me to go to bed for awhile, sleep until we had gathered our resources for the mission.

I laid in my bed and cried. Part of me still wanted nothing more than to go home and forget about this whole Evolution place. The problems I'd dealt with on Earth weren't a big deal, they were just my problems, just problems that I needed to worry over to make myself feel something. They were never as serious as I made them out to be and rarely ever affected much of the rest of the world. My cries reached deep into me. I was afraid of how important I had become, how these others depended on my help. I didn't want to fail them.

Dante knocked on my door and I grunted out an invitation to come in.

"I can hear you. Sure this is important Kelly, but we can still have fun. Get some sleep. We don't need you right now. Take it easy, all things are just the way they need to be right now."

"What the hell does that mean? Why do things need to be this way? It seems pretty fucken stupid." I stammered through scared tears.

"I don't know, it's just something Sacro says to me when I feel like crap but I trust him. I've come to learn that I can trust him and I know that you can to." He pulled the blanket from around my shoulders and rubbed gently, healingly and I slipped away into a sound, dreamless sleep.

CHAPTER 10

All of us were eager to begin the mission, the task of implanting Seletzium into the two hundred and forty-two people that lived in the Raleigh/Slater colony.

There were the others that we had no way of locating. Small groups of renegades that showed loyalty to no one but themselves. They did however, meet with Raleigh and Slater and as our system showed, performed the same procedures that the others did to remove the Devids.

"Damn it, we gotta start this thing. Where's Coalamine?" Donally yelled impatiently. She stood over the console in the equipment room preparing it for me. Her dark face glowed with energy and passion and for a moment, I envied her incredible strength and fearlessness.

"Relax Donally, you gotta show Kelly a few things anyway. Now's your chance unless you want to stay here and do it yourself." said Dante.

All at once the three of them, Sacro had been sitting quietly near Donally, looked at me. I smiled but not as a reaction to happiness or amusement but of nervous energy. Donally patted the seat of the chair beside hers indicating that my part in the mission had begun.

"I gotta go to the bathroom first." I tried to say it gracefully but knew everyone could hear the uneasy wobble in my voice. I walked quickly to the bathroom and shut the door. I was panicked, overwhelmed. My face felt hot and beads of sweat formed on my forehead.

What am I doing? I thought as I ran cool water over my hands, face and neck. My hands shook hard making it difficult to cup the water to my face. I caught sight of myself in the mirror, a sight that startled me. There I was, bright-eyed and healthy looking. My blue eyes were clear despite the tension I harbored behind them, there were no dark circles. My skin was silked with perfect color. My hair flowed down over my shoulders—God, I looked beautiful! It was comforting, soothing to be so overjoyed with my own face, like looking at an old friend or sister. This is what Evolution was doing to me, giving me room to grow into the person I'd always wanted to be.

The nervousness that accompanied me into the bathroom had vanished, it had been replaced with a great sense of courage, similar to what I'd been envying in Donally. Only seconds before I'd wanted to escape this mission. I told them I wanted to help but I didn't, not really. Now I did, I desired nothing more than to help them. Offering myself to Evolution was the only thing I wanted to do and it gave me such a great sense of purpose of a kind that I'd never before felt. This world was a reality of ideals. If I could help bring harmony back to Evolution, I would do anything they asked of me. And hadn't it been my species that was responsible for tipping the scales of harmony?

I toweled off the water that dripped from my face and went back to the equipment room. Donally pulled the chair back and I sat down quickly trying to show her my new found eagerness to be involved. Only moments later, Coalamine finally arrived.

I gasped involuntarily, as she entered the room. She stood about seven or eight feet tall. I looked up slowly, my eyes taking in the alien's profoundly disturbing qualities. Her long neck extended to a bald, oblong head and as I stared, she coiled her thick tail around her torso.

"Hello." she said and held out a long, spindly hand. The claws on the ends of her fingers looked deadly. I stood, frozen in place, by my fear.

"Coalamine, this is Kelly McGrail of Earth." Dante said casually. He supported me with his hand, gently pushing me forward. I moved the chair back and stood to greet her.

Coalamine smiled revealing large, sharp teeth. I had no voice, my courage was gone. Dante shoved me toward her and I managed to take her hand. She clasped on and lowered her head until her face was level with mine. I did nothing but stand rigid in my spot, frozen like a deer in the glare of threatening headlights. With a gentle tug Coalamine pulled me close to her until we were cheek to cheek. The mouth full of teeth, positioned right next to my ear, made a long, breathy, hissing noise. I felt her breath, it was cool and almost soothing. She moved to the other ear and did the same.

"A Kivian greeting, Kelly McGrail." said Coalamine. I held onto her hand and stared, mesmerized by her presence.

"Let go, Kelly." Dante said and pulled me back.

"What? Oh yea…Sorry, I'm sorry." My embarrassment turned my face hot but I did manage to let go of the Kivian's hand. A definite smile washed over her face and my first impression of her changed. Her eyes were warm and soft which counteracted the fierce look the rest of her features carried.

"Okay people, let's get this thing happening." yelled out Donally. Each one of us prepared for our part. I would be staying in the equipment room with Sacro. Dante and Coalamine would be doing the dangerous work of entering the colony and implanting the humans. The seletzium chips were microscopic and were contained in small vials, one for each colonist. Dante and Coalamine were equipped with vapor syringes, when they plugged the chosen vial into the syringe, they could activate the tool by pressing lightly onto the skin of the target, usually in a soft area like the neck or underarm. The chip would be transferred into the body from the syringe by passing through a laser leaving the delivery painless and undetectable.

Donally would be watching the perimeter of the colony to make sure Dante and Coalamine went about their business unnoticed. She and three others would be watching over the grounds of the whole colony in case anyone should be lurking around.

Everyone involved, except for me, were telepathically linked. Sacro would give me the details as he received the information through the others. My job was to record the events on our system and receive the Seletzium implant codes once they were inserted in the body. It was more of a training exercise for me. Sacro could've done the job alone. I knew that, but they wanted to include me and the job, with Sacro's guidance was almost risk free. If I screwed up, Sacro was there to bail me out.

Donally gave me a few final tips before they left. Standing silently next to each other, Dante, Coalamine and Donally held each other's hands and lifted their heads to face skyward. Each one hummed softly while Sacro pushed me to join in the circle. Together we held each other in hand and voice. The activity connected us for and just one moment I was more than myself, I was part of what they were, the glory of Evolution. The strength of the vibrations subsided and each of us broke away from the bond.

"We are outta here, now." said Donally opening the door. Dante and Coalamine said nothing and they all walked out into the dark of Evolution's night. I said a silent prayer for their success, our success.

Once back in the equipment room, Sacro and I went over the details again. He was much quieter than usual, he appeared distraught which worried me immensely.

"What's wrong?" I asked.

"I am not sure. It is as though I have overlooked some important detail about this mission and something is preventing me from embracing the solution." he sat back in his chair and took a deep breath.

"Should I call them back? Maybe it's a bad omen or something, you know? Maybe you should call them." My voice rose to relay my discomfort.

"No, it is not for them that I am concerned. What they are doing now is good and well-planned, very good judgment. No, it is the colonists, I fear I have missed something very important. I must put this aside for now though, they will be ready for us soon."

I watched over the monitors to ready myself for the first successful implant. I could see the outline of Dante and Donally and one of her perimeter guards who was also human. Their Devid's continued to transmit information about location and even body functions. Both Coalamine and Dante could increase their vibratory nature making it appear that they had disappeared when in fact their molecular structure was just moving at an extremely accelerated pace, too fast for humans to detect. This trick allowed them both to move freely through the colony unless there was a need to come into contact with something solid. A need to open a door or touch another person would slow them down making them visible again.

Sacro relayed the events to me as Dante and Coalamine prepared to enter the first and largest of the buildings on the enemy compound. We'd gone over structural plans of the buildings, five of them in all. We had a grand advantage since the area had already been mapped out before the Devid's were disabled. Raleigh and Slater ran the place like a military base and routines were adhered to with the strictest order. All would or should be sleeping at the hour of Dante's arrival. They would be able to move about freely with caution, at least that is what we hoped for.

"They have found the workers housing." said Sacro.

Information came pouring into the system as each implanted Seletzium chip was injected into the bodies of the sleeping enemy. It was like tagging wild animals only easier. Once the chip was inside the body, It would attach itself to DNA strands and transmit a unique color pattern for each individual, no two were alike.

One hundred and fifty of them were housed in the first building, none of which had their own rooms. It was a communal arrangement with sleeping mats being only three feet apart and showers and toilets out in the open. Dante's physical reading had changed markedly as he made his way through the two story building. Sacro explained the disgust and anger Dante felt at the sight of the living conditions which the enemies endured. Only victims lived in such a manner and there was no need of victims on Evolution. Dante sensed the spread of disease among them and thick was the air, of the smell of mold and decay. Dante and Coalamine did their job and moved out of the filth quickly and quietly.

The other ninety people had divided up in two separate buildings and the remaining two, Raleigh and Slater, granted themselves the most refined and luxurious, private building. It was strange that no one objected to this arrangement but for whatever reason that I did not understand, Raleigh and Slater were accepted as the royalty of the tribe. No one ever challenged their authority.

The last of the five buildings sat empty in the dark of night, only to be used by day as a food storage and supply house. Dante and Coalamine passed by it and entered the next structure on their chosen path. It took much longer to implant the forty-six people in the smaller building since each had their own private room. Most of them had no locks to hinder quick entry but the few that did had to be carefully maneuvered so that no evidence of the intruder's actions were left behind.

As they left the building, Coalamine noticed the grand, white house where Raleigh and Slater reigned. A light was on in the top, right corner and a figure stood in the window. Coalamine crouched back and pushed Dante into the shadows. They both watched the window intently from behind a sheltered bench.

"Why doesn't that freak just go to bed already?" I said through clenched teeth.

Dante had relayed that it was the figure of Margaret Raleigh that stood in and paced back and forth in front of the window and that he would not move until he knew she had gone to bed.

An hour passed by and we all waited to hear the news that Dante and Coalamine were back at it. I grew more impatient with each passing minute. I hadn't realized how agitated I'd become until Sacro stopped my nervous drumming on the console and told me to go stretch my legs.

I went out into the cool, comfortable night and stood, stretching in front of the doorway. Suddenly, the hairs on the back of my neck stood up and gave me a tingling sensation. I felt unsafe as I realized those humans could be out there, watching me. I ran back in and slammed my door.

"It is not usually like that here. One day you will know the true peace of Evolution. That is my wish for all humans, to know that we are meant to feel safety and security and that it is our birthright to know the undying love of the Universe." Sacro had followed me to the front room and after he spoke, he went back to the equipment room leaving me standing there alone. I sat down and reflected on his words. What a beautiful statement but something of which I'd never experienced. Undying love was not within my understanding but I knew that I wanted to feel it and that if I ever did it would be beyond incredible.

I went to the kitchen and made a small meal to keep my stomach from growling and my mind from stewing over my impatience with the lack of activity. Halfway through it though, Sacro called out to me. I bounded into the equipment room and took my place beside him. They were at it again, already in the third building and planting the Seletzium. I went right to work receiving the patterns and putting them into recognizable files. Sacro joined in as I couldn't keep up with the speed at which Dante and Coalamine worked.

Suddenly, Dante's readings changed to express a high level of adrenaline shooting through his body. Sacro reacted to the reading by connecting with Dante, helping him to calm down and relay his fear to us. Someone had been awake and as they entered one of the rooms, startled them. The lone man was sitting in a chair by a window. The room was dark except for the reflected light of the moons. He turned to face the intruders with more shock and fear than Dante could ever feel. The man looked ill. Dante described the pale, blank face that looked back at him, it was thin and drawn, his eyes wide with fear but also lacking energy. As Dante moved in, he noticed the man was actually drooling.

Coalamine stepped in front of Dante and placed her large, spindly hand over the sick man's face. He quietly slumped over in his chair and seconds later I received the data from his new Seletzium implant. One of Coalamine's strengths was her mesmeric powers. Just by touch, she could put another being into a light trance or a heavy sleep, depending on what was required at the time. As Sacro explained this to me, I remembered shaking her hand. I'd felt her power then.

Dante's readings went back to normal when they left the room. Within half an hour, I had two hundred and forty signals to organize. Sacro and I worked speedily, assigning proper names to their colorful Seletzium signatures.

Dante and Coalamine had yet to face the hardest part of the mission, that of implanting Margaret Raleigh and Jacob Slater. With only one hour before the light of the sun alerted the colony to daybreak, they moved in quickly.

Donally and her crew moved in closer and focused their attention on the elegant house. To my surprise Dante and Coalamine walked away from the house, passed it's well kept yard and to a large tree-like plant about 200 feet away from the back of the house. Both of them proceeded to uncover a hidden hole in the ground at the base of the tree.

"They are going underground." Sacro said as he received the images from Dante's mind. "They are going to use the tunnels that the Nashkins built."

"Okay…what?" I asked, thinking I must have missed something.

"Nashkin Roadens, the former occupants of the house. Peace-loving people and underground dwellers."

"Underground? What, they lived in the ground? Like gophers?"

"Yes, I suppose you could make that comparison. Nashkins have evolved further than gophers but similar tunneling abilities."

"And they lived in that house, the one Raleigh lives in now?" I asked.

"That is correct. They came here to experience a different way of living. The tunnels were made by the children, mostly for play but their parents wanted them to keep their skills active for their return home. They encouraged extensive tunneling under and around the home. They have been gone for quite some time but the tunnels haven't eroded in the least."

"How are they going to get in the house?"

"Dante spent a great deal of time with the family that occupied that house. He played with the children for hours at a time, around the house and in the tunnels. There are three entrances opening into the house, all of them in the cellar below the basement. The current occupants don't know about the cellar." Sacro stopped and was silent for a moment.

Dante's thoughts were active in Sacro's mind. They communicated together intensely which left me out of the action for a minute. I tried to concentrate, gain access to theirs thoughts but nothing outside of myself stirred in my mind.

"They are in Kelly. You will receive the signals soon." said Sacro.

I looked to my screen and within minutes the bright patterns of the living enemy came through finally, Raleigh and Slater were traceable again.

We worked piecing the colony together as the rest of the crew made their way home. Daylight was breaking all around us and I, more than anyone, needed rest, sweet sleep.

"Are they coming back here?" I asked Sacro of Dante and the others.

"No, they will each go to their homes. All of us need a break, a time to rest." he answered.

"So, what is it Sacro, you still look bothered, do you know what it is yet?" I asked impatiently. Seeing him with a worried look was extremely troubling to me as he was usually so strong and sure of everything.

"I fear I have missed something that will profoundly affect these people. There is something missing." he rubbed his brow in an unaccustomed gesture of frustration.

"You care for these people, don't you? After all the chaos they've caused, you still care about them."

"I have no hate for them. I brought them here. What I wanted for them then is the same as what I want for them now, to heal. Their refusal to co-operate disappoints me but I still find it of great value to treat them with respect. I do not want to fail them if I can aid in their recovery but now, I think I have."

"Is there anything I can do?"

"No, not now, Kelly. Go and rest. I will do the same. Rest and meditation will bring me the answers, not this worry. Worry is of no use to us."

CHAPTER 11

Many days had passed since the Seletzium mission had been completed. I managed to learn a great deal about tracking the humans with the implants. I had all the files set up and traced each person thoroughly. I knew when they were going to the bathroom. Sacro had left the rest of the job up to me after the night of the mission but I didn't work alone. Dante stayed with me, taught me things about Evolution. I was in a state of constant fascination while Dante expressed his love and experience.

"They are going to die." said Sacro. It wasn't until strange readings started coming from some of the humans that Dante called Sacro in to figure out the cause of the changes and that's when we found out the mission hadn't gone as well as we thought.

"So let nature take its course. They did this to themselves. What about all that 'what you sow is what you reap' rubbish? They have caused more pain here than we've ever known. It's not our job to protect those people. They don't care how they hurt Evolution or Earth, what do they care for anything except their financial status? Sacro, let it go." said Dante. His mood seemed to be much darker since the mission. As much as he didn't like these humans before, he was even more disgusted by them and their choices after having been in such close contact.

"I must not let them all die. Some of them do not understand who they are yet. There is the unborn among them." said Sacro. The mission had brought up new issues as we found that six of the women were pregnant.

"Yea and you know the nature in that. They all made the choice to be there, unborn or not."

"One of those children could be their undoing. One of those unborn may be there to assist us so we can escape the deaths of the many ignorant people that will perish without meaning. I do hold the responsibility, to bring them back to themselves so they can see who they are before they make the choice to die."

"You weren't so close to them, you couldn't hear their dreams while they slept. They're all dark inside. They live without purpose, why not let them go without it. Sacro, they dream in hell and they will not let go of their greedy motivations, not ever. They guard themselves and not even you can hear them anymore but we got close enough to see inside their minds, all we found was bitter, cold hatred. What about the ones they've murdered? It wasn't fair. Good, innocent beings have died without design. What does it take for you to see?"

"Dante, all those that the enemies have murdered, expired with their integrity and their devotion to Evolution completely intact. They will not have to repeat this sort of victimization again. If I can help these enemies, then I will. It is important for the well being of your species that I do the best that I can to help these people learn to accept the beauty that is life."

"Your stubborn, God, you are stubborn! But I trust you and I'll do my best too, just don't expect me to get so close to them again, my tolerance for their existence is weak."

"So, why are they dying?" I asked, still amazed by Dante's courage to argue with Sacro.

"With the Devids gone, their biological functioning is beginning to break down. The Devids are filters for the human body. They go inside and attach to your circulatory and nervous systems, move through your organs to aid your body in adapting to the environment of our Evolution. You would die Kelly, without your Devids. They convert gases that you cannot use into oxygen. It is only a subtle difference but with no protection the human immune system begins to fall apart. The Seletzium can not take the place of the Devids the way I thought it could. Seletzium is just a mineral, it can only illuminate the human DNA signatures. It is strange, I expected more from the seletzium. This is an unfortunate mistake on my part. This is the troubled feeling that nagged me through the whole event and now it appears that I have realized too late what the consequences were to be. I do not know how I missed this but it has happened and it must be dealt with."

"Maybe you should just tell them their all gonna die unless they listen to us. We could help them if they agreed, right?" I said.

"They don't trust us, Kelly. What do you think Raleigh would do if I walked in there and said 'alright folks, if you don't listen to me, your all gonna die'. Do you think she'd be into it? She'd send a mob of her slaves after me." said Dante.

"Yea maybe, but there's got to be at least a couple of people that might listen. If one person heard what we had to say, they would come running when the sickness started to show. It's not ideal, a few people may die before they will trust us but it's worth the effort."

"The illness will spread quickly once it starts. I do not know yet, if the Devid Communities would agree to protecting them again." said Sacro.

"Have you contacted their system yet Sacro?" asked Dante.

"No, but I will do that now. There is no other way that I know of to keep those people safe while they remain on Evolution. And there is certainly no alternative to transporting them back to their home world. The Devids are essential to their survival. It is my impression that the Devids were not harmed in the process that pushed them out of the human system but I am not certain their Communities would give them another chance. I will go and speak with their Council, inform them of this situation. You two can figure out how to communicate with those people. Do not jeopardize yourselves though, we are not risking our own health." He left without hesitation.

"So, do you have radios, phones, fax machines? How do we talk to these people?" I asked Dante.

"No phones or fax machines. Generally, we all work with telepathy. Even you are linked. I know you can't hear us yet but we can hear you, that's how the connection starts. Eventually you'll be able to pick up messages sent to you. It's just a matter of practice and knowing what to listen for. These lunatics aren't linked. They've successfully blocked themselves off of our system. They don't give and they don't receive."

"What about that thing there?" I asked pointing to the answering machine that Sacro had used to reach me.

"Those are great for newcomers but the colonists don't have any. Raleigh made everyone get rid of any connection they had to us. I guess she figured she couldn't dominate them effectively if we kept leaving them little hints as to how asinine they're all being."

"What about radio or t.v., computers, what about the Internet?"

"There are musical broadcasts and broad information networks but they are dependent on equipment also. Raleigh tolerates no outside influence. If those people caught sight of the good things going on out here, they'd leave her. She's accepted nothing, they have no receivers of any kind. I know we aren't supposed to be going in there, but I don't see any way of getting to them without Raleigh being aware of it."

"So, your saying that they are completely isolated?"

"Yes, I believe that is what I am saying."

"Why were they at that other building just over there?" I asked pointing toward the Quonset that sat not far from my house.

"There are some people that live outside the colony that meet with Raleigh's group regularly. They are the kinda people that don't want to take sides. They won't trust anybody but a few select people who feel the same way they do. They live in these little groups, usually four or five of them. The meetings used to be closer to the colony but when Slater got word that you had arrived, they moved so they could get closer to you. All sides agreed. They're trying to get close to you. They do it to all new arrivals. They want to persuade you to join them. Raleigh knows your watching, she knows your curious. She's making it look good for you."

"O.K., we can't get close to them but they want to get close to us or at least me anyway." I said thoughtfully. "They want to get close to me."

"Where are you going with this Kelly?"

"I can let a couple of them get close to me and then tell them what's going on." I said excitedly.

"I don't think that's wise, you don't know what your dealing with here."

"Why not? They don't want to hurt me yet, right? They want to convert me. If I give them my interest for a few minutes, give them the impression I don't know much about anything, they'll trust me to a certain point. They want me to see their good side." I felt brilliant.

"And then you just casually mention that they are all going to die because they were mean to their Devids? I don't think so Kelly."

"No, I don't even have to address the issue directly. The other night, two of them came to my door and knocked. I was so scared, I hide under the covers in bed but had I known they didn't want to harm me, I could have let them in and had a friendly chat. They want me on their side right? So I imagine they'll be open to a little conversation. They'll want to know about me and they'll want me to know something about them."

"They will want you to know their lies." cut in Dante.

"Yea, well that doesn't matter, it's not like I care what they want to say really. I can work the Devids into the conversation. I'll just talk about how glad I am to have the protection of the Devids without dwelling on it too much. They were all informed of the Devids when they got here right?"

"Yes. They all had questions about how they got here so we told them. The Devids transformed their physical structure to withstand space travel, time shifts and all that but none of them stuck around to ask what the Devids were doing inside their bodies once they got here. Slater figured it out that we could track them through the Devids and he's the only one that asked questions of the scientific nature when he first arrived. The man has a scientific mind, that's why we brought him here. He used that information against us when he started building up the enemy colony."

"It'll make them curious when I start talking about how important the Devids are now that I'm here, don't you think?"

"Possibly, if you can do it in a way that doesn't cause suspicion. It might work. You have to tell Sacro and Donally though."

"Why do I have to tell Donally?" My breath caught in my throat. The thought of having to run this by Donally made me want to forget the whole thing. With her being suspicious of me I didn't think she'd relish the thought of me wanting to meet with the enemy, even if it was to help our cause. And she was so loud when she protested something.

"Because she has to know everything that's going on with them, especially if one of us is involved. If your going to invite these creatures into your home, she has to know and she's got to know why. Remember what she said about keeping stuff from her? It still applies, it always will."

"And do you think she'll approve?"

"I don't know if she'll actually approve, she'd be fine with letting them die. She's not much like Sacro, Donally is even less compassionate towards them than I am." I followed him into my kitchen as he spoke.

"Can you talk to her from here?"

"You mean telepathically?" Dante nodded and stood silently for a moment. "No, she must be inside one of the Domes. I can talk to Sacro though and he can reach her. He's better at it than I am. Why?"

"I thought maybe we could ask her to come over so I could tell her about my plan."

"It's better to wait until he gets back. You can explain the whole thing to him first, see what he says, then we'll talk to Donally. It's easier to talk to her if Sacro's already in favor"

We both considered the possibilities of a meeting with the enemy while Dante prepared a meal for the both of us.

It was a perfect way for me to test myself. I would face these people and help them, maybe turn them toward us. If I wanted to take on this task of going to Earth and handling diplomatic relations between Evolution and Earth then I had to face a few challenges here first. I needed to learn the art of conversation. What better way to practice than with hostile people who didn't trust me. That's what most of the people on Earth would be like. If I could talk to them in a way that didn't show my dislike for what they stood for, then maybe I could learn how to talk to all the people on Earth about the reality of Evolution without sounding too unbalanced.

"If Sacro agrees to this, I want to be here, you'll need some kind of back up in case they get weird on you." Dante said between slurps of a tasty broth he had made.

"I was hoping the three of you would be here. I don't know if I could do this alone."

"I can't see Donally agreeing to this unless she had some control over the situation so I'm sure she'll want to be here. We can watch from the tracking room. That is, we'll watch from there if Sacro and Donally agree to this. I've got my doubts.

"What do you think of it Dante? Do you think I can do this?"

"Yea, I think you can and I think it's a good idea considering the circumstances. If it works out, I think Donally would be able to put her reservations about you aside. Yea, it's a great idea and I hope it works out." His eyes sparkled at me from across the table.

My body loosened up with his praise of my idea. It gave me a feeling of confidence and courage to be supported by Dante. I knew right then that I would be able to do anything I wanted if he was around to back me up.

CHAPTER 12

"Are we all set?" I asked.

"We're all set, but are you? I'd be jittering right outta my seat if I was the one meeting with these self-centered lunatics." he spoke with a smile across his lips that indicated to me that he was teasing. "Ah, you'll do just fine though."

"Oh I know. I'm sure about this. I'm doing it for good reasons." I said with an amazing sense of confidence.

"I still like Dante's idea, let them all die. I don't know why I go through this shit with these people, I don't know why." said Donally.

The three of us had been watching their activities over a few days. I monitored their movements and recorded activities that led them away from the colony. Small groups of four or five were sent out after darkness fell to raid the uplifts that were near to the colony grounds. The little buildings were used by anyone who needed them to replenish food and supplies or to simply just stop and take a break from a long walk or journey. They were like little grocery stores with out the need for money. Everything was offered freely but the colonists believed they weren't welcome to take what they needed so they did so in the spirit of stealing. They'd sneak around in dark clothes and sacks, take all they could carry and go home. The supplies were used not only to nourish the members of the group but also to control them. No one was allowed access to food, clothing or provisions unless they worked for it. They ran the colony much the same way as it would be on Earth, with no understanding of the options they had.

Dante and Donally both had experienced a rapid evolution that removed them from the trappings of Earth's social systems, something they promised I would go through if I was willing. I wasn't yet evolved though. I wasn't as appalled by the human colonists as the other long term humans were. These people were disgusting to me but I was still used to their hostility and negativity. Earth was just like that. The greedy, power hungry people of Earth were just part of the normal functions of daily living. News programs and daily gossip was full of the stupid things people did and the myriad of ways we all took advantage of each other. It was commonplace to hear that someone shot someone else for twenty bucks and a pack of smokes. It wasn't that the sane, evolved people that lived on Evolution had forgotten the dark side of their origins, it was just that they had outgrown it. I was beginning to grow out of it too. What was happening to these others that they could completely avoid the positive effects of Evolution? We all lived with tremors of fear and worry, Dante had his dark times when he would much rather let the enemy die, maybe even dream about killing them all himself but his motivation was different than the others. He didn't harm others, he didn't seek out profit while disregarding the suffering it may cause. He'd been working long and hard with Donally and Sacro and the teams of other beings that enjoyed Evolution, to provide these sad humans with options to their undying greed. Dante's moments of darkness came from being sick of dealing with the persistent greed and hatred of the enemy, it was not so much born inside of him as it was a result of dealing with the outer darkness on a continuing basis. This was the case for many of the other inhabitants of Evolution. Any inner desire for hate, fear, greed and the desperate struggle of selfishness had been lifted out of them. I was feeling those inner failings being slowly lifted out of me as well. It was effortless to let the darkness go even though it tugged at my soul, almost begging for me to keep it's place in my heart, it would've been a greater fight to hang onto the pain. I could easily feel trust and respect and did not fear for my well being in terms of getting my needs met. It was amazing what a little free love could do. Of course, I did count the giving of shelter, food, clothing and companionship as loving actions. When I was a child, my parents told me they loved me, quite often in fact, but nothing came to me without a price. By the time I was ten they started telling me how expensive it was to raise a child. I got my first job when I was eleven and I bought my own clothes and sometimes if I wanted something special at the grocery store, I would have to buy it myself. They said they were helping me build a solid character. My character was burnt out by the time I was seventeen. All that hard work and saving money got me a nice little bank account that I could use while I was in the hospital having a nervous breakdown. True character building came from support and sharing, not to get ahead but to just be happy. On Evolution, happiness went beyond money and power over others. It would be impossible to understand that from Earth's social point of view. The cloud of personal gain permeated every person that ever lived there, that's how we all survived. Even the God-loving Christians had their personal agendas for helping the underprivileged as they call them. Pain and suffering builds character. God has his reasons for it the missionaries say, but I know it's not true now that I live here on Evolution. It's not the pain that is the destructive factor in all of this, it's the inane suffering that doesn't make sense. Pain is a simple feeling, suffering is a personal choice.

Would I want to kill these people when they came to my house? No, I couldn't actually kill anyone myself but I could choose to let them die. I questioned myself more than once on my motives for giving them this chance. I shared the feelings that Dante and Donally expressed. I thought it would be natural justice to let them die. They created their own problems. It was their own fearful nature that led them into this outcome, why not let nature take its course?

Sacro had a different point of view. It was something about the potential of the situation and of the people involved. Potential on Evolution is everything, the biggest crime here was to waste potential. I was used to that as well, we did it every day in billions of ways on Earth and most people didn't think twice about it.

Sacros' point of view was very important to me though, more important than my own point of view when it came to matters of Evolution. I trusted his vision, his awareness and his sense of growth. He knew more about being happy than anyone I'd ever known. I could set aside my prejudice toward these people because Sacro inspired me to do so. I could offer them this bit of information so that they could make their choices. Maybe they would die anyway, helping them didn't mean we could save them.

I had all the support that I needed. Donally, Dante and Sacro were in my house, listening from the equipment room, making sure that I could not be harmed. All I had to do was talk to these people, show them some kind of interest and act like I didn't know anything about anyone.

It was dark outside but I saw no signs of the gathering. I paced my front room and made myself crazy with doubt. This was the night they were supposed to be gathering. Sacro came out, gave me a hug and helped me slip into a peaceful state of mind. As he returned to the equipment room, I looked over a shelf of books that I hadn't paid any attention to before. I saw a couple of familiar Earth novels, classics I guess they're called, and a few books I had read before. One large book caught my attention, 'Leo Densworth Died Here' by J.P. Riggs. I was intrigued by the lifelike quality of the picture on the front cover. I sat down with the book and stared at the man who I assumed was Leo Densworth. The picture had a hypnotic quality to it. I felt like I was going somewhere when I looked at his face, going wherever he was. He called me into the book, his book, his story. I began to read and within seconds I forgot where I was or what I was worried about. I expected that was really what a good book was supposed to do

A loud rapping on my front door startled me back to my reality. I felt a subtle resistance to embrace my awareness, I would have rather stayed within the safety of the book. A great wave of anxiety washed over me. I stood up, took a deep breath and released my terror. I set the fine book down and answered my front door. Two people greeted me with bright, shiny smiles and sweet hellos. I smiled back. We stared at each other for a few seconds.

"It's so good to see some humans." I said as nicely as I could. "It's been so long. My name is Kelly, Kelly McGrail."

"Oh, hi Kelly, my name is Sherman Castledown and this is my…associate." said the tall man. He looked over me as if he was checking me out in a bar. I shuttered but kept myself composed. We didn't make eye contact, so I focused on the other man.

"And my name is Jacob Slater." said the other man. I felt a little shocked that they would send such a high-ranking scum-ball to my door. I was careful not to show any recognition to his name or the surprise at his presence.

"Well Sherman, Jacob, please come in if you like. I haven't seen a friendly human since I got here."

"That's odd, they usually send them in quickly." said Jacob as they entered the front room. He looked around with noticeable admiration of the furniture and design of the room.

"I did have some visitors here on a few occasions but I haven't let anybody in. This is all terrifying to me, you know we are on a different planet."

"Oh yes, I'm sorry. Has there been no one to help you adjust to all of this?" asked Jacob, his dark brown eyes locked onto mine. He didn't look crazy or bad or mean. He looked calm and trusting, almost compassionate to my supposed suffering.

I held my hands together to stop the trembling.

"There was a man with me at first but I told him to leave me alone. I didn't really trust him. He took me right out of my home while I was sleeping and brought me here against my will. He told me I could stay here, in this house. I won't let him in here now. He comes by every once in awhile, knocks on the door but I ignore him. I don't know what he wants but I know he's not human." I answered.

"The man your talking about is Sacro and he's no man. He brought us all here. You say you won't speak with him, why is that Kelly? Did he do something to you?" asked Sherman. He spoke loud and with false concern. Where Jacob was sincere in his expression and manner, Sherman was noticeably ego-driven. His eyes ran over everything quickly like he was making assessments of the contents of the room, even I seemed nothing more to him than an object that could be of some value to him, or maybe not.

"Well should I? I dunno, this is all new to me. I could tell he wasn't human when I first met him. He's got spooky eyes you know, freaks me out. I just stay away, how can anybody trust an alien? God, it's all so crazy!" I led them to the sofa where I motioned them to sit down.

"No Kelly. It is Kelly, right? No, your damn smart not to talk to that evil thing. Your instincts are serving you well. Those eyes of his can get right into your mind and screw around with your thinking." said Sherman.

"Do you talk to him?" I asked.

"At one time, we tried to negotiate with him and his colleges. The effort was a waste, they wanted everything their way with no compromises. Oh, how we tried, spent hours talking but nothing worked, they didn't bring us here because they wanted to be our friends. Not him or the sad few that follow him. I am sorry to say that there are humans that have chosen to stay with him and help him bring us down. They fight us to support the alien. It's a dismal scene really. I'm considering that they may have been taken over by the alien, brainwashed. They use mind tricks to control people. It's a horrible predicament Kelly." said Jacob

Slater. He spoke softly with a warm, sympathetic tone in his voice. I nodded trying my best to appear innocent and amazed by his speech.

"Maybe that's what he's trying to do…" I said conjuring up my best distant thoughtful expression. They both reacted to my apparent realization.

"What Kelly, what did he do?" asked Sherman.

I had them. I could see they were eager for anything I could tell them.

"He had his chance to talk to me when I first got here. I was stunned, shocked, I don't remember everything that he said but I do remember him talking about some things that went into my body. I saw them when I landed here. He said these things, I don't know what he called them, would have to stay in my body or I wouldn't be able to stay here. I told him I didn't want to stay here but he wasn't listening to me. He said I wouldn't notice anything different but if I didn't have these things I would die. I remember thinking he was just trying to scare me so I wouldn't try to fight him, you know, a sort of cooperate or we'll kill you kinda thing. I don't remember what he called them but he did have a name for them. Do you know anything about this?"

Sherman sat back slowly with a dazed look, he didn't say anything but his face drained of all color. Jacob Slater looked at me intensely, obviously not expecting me to bring the Devid's into the conversation. I squirmed in my seat a little under his scrutinizing stare, praying that I hadn't blown it by being to obvious or anxious.

"That is what he was trying to do Kelly." Jacob said sternly. He was making an effort not to notice Sherman's reaction to my information. "That alien was trying to intimidate you, he's done it to all of us at one time or another. He wants us to depend on him but I assure you Kelly, there's nothing to worry about."

"Have you ever talked to him? Do you know what he was talking about? What are these things he talked about? God, I'm sorry, I didn't realize how much I missed being able to talk to someone. There's no one else that I can ask these questions." I said enthusiastically.

"Yes I have spoken to the alien, as well as some of the humans that are controlled by his powers. He talked of these things to me as well but there is no validity to his claims. I am a scientist, a doctor actually, what he talked of was impossible and ridiculous."

"He didn't talk to me about this." said Sherman with a distant, almost shocked glaze over his deep set eyes.

"So what are these things? Are they real?" I asked. I was really hoping to get him believing that I was trusting his information and that he would be intrigued with my curiosity.

"It's a long story Kelly, long and technical. The truth is the alien implants us when he picks us up. He says it's to protect us from the stresses of space travel but I know the truth of it. The truth is Kelly, these particles are meant to keep track of us and keep us under his control. He can see where we are, what we're doing and I believe he can read our minds with the aid of these implanted gadgets."

"You can't be serious!? Read our minds? God, that's terrible!" I said dramatically. Jacob Slater nodded.

"Please Kelly, could I have some water?" he asked calmly.

"Oh, sure, no problem. How about you Sherman?"

"No thanks Kelly." he said politely, still with the color of shock on his face. I went to the kitchen knowing full well that Slater just wanted a moment to ease Sherman Castledown and assure him nothing was wrong. I took my time and wondered if what Slater said was what he really believed or if he was good at covering his own fear. If he really believed that Sacro had used the Devids to intimidate him or to create a false dependence, then Slater wouldn't consider the danger to himself and his people until he saw definite signs of illness. Or maybe he was so sure of his science that he wouldn't ever consider that he was wrong.

"Here you are Jacob." I said holding out his glass of water.

"Thank you Kelly."

We sat in silence for moment. Sherman looked a little brighter, but not much.

"Kelly, we have discovered a way to remove the alien devices from our bodies. There is no pain, we can remove them from your body too. Nothing bad has happened to us, so it's quite obvious that Sacro was lying about the true nature of these devices. This alien has control over you even if you don't feel it. As long as these things remain in your system you are at risk of being taken over. We can help you with that." said Slater.

"You could really do that? Are you sure it won't hurt? Do you mean right now?" My questions spewed out in a twinge of real panic.

"No, not this evening. You would have to come to our facility for the procedure. We have established an entirely human base where we are able to live while we figure out how to gain our freedom back from these devious aliens." said Slater "Perhaps in the next daylight after a good rest. We can show you around."

My heart raced. If I agreed to it they would be back here and I would have to deal with them again. If I didn't agree, they would be skeptical of me. I couldn't put myself at that kind of a risk though, not myself or the Devids that lived within me.

"Are you sure the alien was lying about these things? You say that it's only so that he can read our minds and watch what we do and he says it's to keep us alive on this planet, like some kind of inner space suit. I just don't know what to believe anymore!" I threw up my hands in a gesture of total exasperation. I thought if I played the confused victim a little bit longer I could get myself a few cycles without them having doubts about me.

"Oh for heavens sake, I'm sorry Kelly. We don't want this to be more taxing than it already is. Take some time and think about this situation in its entirety. Who are you going to trust? We are all human, your family so to speak. We just don't know what these aliens are capable of doing to us. It's possible they may want us for some sort of medical experiments or worse." said Slater. "As I explained, I am a highly skilled scientist, I have done some tests here and without boring you with such technical details I am certain the devices that were inside our bodies, which are presently still inside yours, are solely for the intent to have us under their complete control."

I could see now, how he had been persuading the other humans to join and believe in him. He was using scientific knowledge to baffle them, lead them into doing what he wanted because they were ignorant of the truth. He used their ignorance, their fear and their greed to control them.

"What sort of scientist are you Jacob?"

"When I was taken from Earth, I was developing my skills in the economic sciences." said Slater.

I just starred at him, what the hell kind of answer was that, I thought. Economy? So what! That's got nothing to do with real science. I searched his face in another genuine display of confusion.

"And how is that relevant to you knowing about human physiology?" I asked hoping I didn't sound like I was interrogating him.

"I am an archaeologist actually and I finished medical at Berkeley, top of my class, or at least very close to it. My main interest turned to the economic sciences after I had been working as an archeologist for a number of years. I studied in many reputable institutions around the world, fascinating, the whole thing was really fascinating but the truth of it is there's not much money in it if you don't find the big treasures. What I did find though is that there is money to be found in economy." he gave out a loud, pompous laugh at what he must've thought was a grand joke.

I faked a laugh but found no humor.

"When you said scientist I thought you meant something more…I dunno, science-like, things about biology and chemistry. But then I don't really know anything about archaeology."

"Oh, not to worry Kelly, I have done many scientific studies over the years and have spent a sinful amount of time in laboratories and as I said, I am also licensed to practice medicine. I know all about biology and chemistry."

"I assure you Kelly, he's our man. Jacob here really knows his stuff. He is our town doctor if you will, he's mended broken bones and developed an incredible headache treatment that blows away anything I've ever used before. He's set up a place for treating us when we get sick and does some great scientific type stuff for us there. He knows what he is doing. I am completely sure about that" said Sherman. He was trying to convince himself but his demeanor was far more subdued compared to when he first arrived.

"Your right though Jacob, I need a little time to think about this. It's not that I don't want to trust you, God knows I need to trust someone or I'll go nuts, I just don't know what's going on right now. For all I know you could be an alien in disguise." I said laughing. They didn't share my sense of humor either.

"It's understandable, we don't want to put any pressure on you. Kelly, it sounds to me like you could use some extra help though. We have a fine counselor in our midst. She's really very good and she's helped most of us adjust to this alien environment, psychologically speaking. I am sure she would be happy to make a visit if you'd like." said Slater.

A light-bulb went off, an inner indication of action. Yes, I should see her too. It would be worth it to talk to as many of them as I could in my territory.

"She would come here?" I asked faking again, a desperate plea for aid.

"I'll ask her to come by tomorrow. Forget about those dreadful things inside your body for now and just relax."

"Okay, thank you for being so understanding and kind. Jacob, Sherman. Forgive me for my cowardice, it's just been so difficult, this whole thing." I hung my head down as I spoke mocking a look of despair.

"I know. We are all in this together. You are not alone." said Jacob he reached across the small table and put his hand over mine.

"So what's going on over there?" I asked giving myself an excuse to move my hand to point in the direction of the Quonset.

"It's a general meeting place for us. Some of us have gone into separate groups. Fear divides us up sometimes. We use that facility to make peaceful negotiations, hold meetings on common ground. That way those of us that have broken away from the main group can stay in contact as friends. We don't want to cast any humans out. God knows, we need each other, don't we? There are only a small number of separatists, eventually I think they will join us again, most of them do." answered Jacob. "We meet with and remind them that we are supportive, we are the friendlies and it's a brutal planet were dealing with out there."

"Yes Jacob, it sure is." said Sherman as he stood up. "I think we should get back to our gathering and leave Kelly to think things through. It's been a pleasure meeting you." he held out his hand and I shook it. I walked them both to the front door.

"Remember, we are here for you. I'll send Shannon over tomorrow." said Slater.

"How do I know when to expect her here?" I asked.

"Good question, I don't imagine you have a watch?" said Slater laughing. "None of us have an accurate measure of time but for lack of a better understanding we just say it's noon when that alien sun is over our heads. So we'll say around noon, alright Kelly?"

I nodded and opened the door.

Sherman stepped out quickly and still looking uneasy, waved and turned his back to me.

"Sleep well Kelly. You have friends here now, everything will be alright." said Jacob and gave me a most sincere smile.

"Thank you Jacob." I said.

They walked back toward their meeting hall. I stood at the doorway, watching and breathing in the night air. It was funny, I could see that they were more afraid of being here than I was. They were so willing to spread the fear and call it help, reassurance and unity. They were vainly holding on to what they knew, only hoping to have control over their lives again.

Sacro stood behind me. I welcomed his warmth. The reality of the unconditional friendship that existed with him, Donally and Dante. It mattered nothing that Sacro wasn't human, it was far easier to trust him than it was to trust most of the humans I'd ever known.

"Good work." he said softly.

"You should've seen Shermans' face when I told him about the Devid's. He went pure white." I said as I closed the door. "Slater didn't tell them all the details."

"Slater didn't tell them anything." said Donally, "It's pretty obvious he thinks he knows what's best for everyone."

"I scared him too, he had to convince himself that he was right. I don't think he knows what he's done to them or to himself. Did you hear him? He wants me to go there so he can do it to me to."

"This might be good for us though, if any of those people have any sense at all. The Devid communities have agreed to help again on the condition that the humans give their consent to the union. Maybe some of them will take the time to understand us better." said Dante.

"I don't think Slater is going to rethink his actions. When he has doubts Raleigh is there to push them out. People will die before Raleigh will accept our aid, and even then she is too stubborn to admit she's wrong. I can see her blaming the deaths on something else even though the reality is right in front of her" said Donally.

"But don't forget, this Shannon person is coming over tomorrow, I can work on her too." I said feeling hopeful that I was making a difference.

"Yes, very good Kelly. We do the very best we can, continue to check our own motives and be patient. If they listen and are willing to take care of themselves then they will be alright. Now what about your own doubts Kelly?" asked Sacro. They all looked at me.

"Doubts? What doubts?" I asked defensively.

"The feelings that came up for you while you visited with Jacob and Sherman. I sensed the pull, your curiosity about them. As subconscious as it may have been, you held a thought that they could be right. You wonder if you are the one making a mistake."

I felt cold all over. He was right, I did question them in my mind. I did wonder what if. My strength drained out of my body and I embraced a sense of giving up. I wouldn't defend myself, there was no point, but I felt confused again. I remembered hearing stories of cults on Earth. Strange religious groups that brainwashed people and enslaved them with mind games. There were cautions of these groups all over, people were killing themselves and others in the name of God. I couldn't lie, I was wondering if I was being led into some kind of craziness.

"Yea, your right, okay. I'm all screwed up here."

"Trust your instinct's Kelly." said Dante.

"Instincts? Ha! I don't have instincts. Do you know what kind of a person I am? I never made a right choice for myself in all my years! Sacro, you saw where I got myself, I was a mess, I've always been a mess. It's not you I'm doubting, it's me. Not once have I chosen the right path." I started off yelling but I lost the power behind my outburst and slumped back into a chair.

Donally came towards me. I felt afraid, that because I had doubted them she would do something horrible and painful to me. I shut my eyes and cringed as she approached. I was expecting her to hit me or worse. She pulled up a chair and sat beside me.

"Easy Kelly, just take it easy." she said softly. I opened my eyes.

"I'm not going to hurt you Kelly, you haven't done anything wrong...yet." she laid her hand on my shoulder. "We've all been through this. I went through it, Dante's been through it and all the other people that come here have had their moments of doubt. There won't be any more people coming here but that's not the point. We know this is difficult."

"Questioning what's going on ain't the problem, it's whether or not you use your real instincts for your answers." said Dante.

"That's what I'm saying Dante, I'm screwed for instincts. I drank most of my life away, I did drugs, I lied to everyone about anything, never paid my bills, I don't know what's going on, not even on Earth. If I had no common sense on Earth, why would I have any here?" I asked almost pleadingly for someone to give me an answer.

"Nobody knows what's really happening on Earth, there are too many distractions. Whether are not you make it in an Earth society is not a good measure of success or ability. The point is you do have good instincts for yourself, just learn to use them." said Donally. She seemed to have far more compassion for me than before. "You have to go inside yourself and listen, if you don't hear anything now then wait until you do. Open your eyes and watch what is going on around you and then go inside and listen. Your instincts want to tell you what is good for you. It's been there, always, trust it."

"Not one of us can tell you what to believe, as much as I want your friendship and company. I can do nothing to make you trust me Kelly, you must decide based on your point of view." said Sacro.

"If you decide to go with the others, to live on the colony and all that then that is what you'll do. I won't stop you. But if you do that and join them in the senseless, offensive acts against others on this planet, I'll kill you. I am here to protect those beings that I believe need protection, I made that choice for myself and I've never regretted it." said Donally.

"Have you ever killed anyone?" I asked.

"Yes, yes I have." she offered no further explanation.

"Why?" I prodded.

"I killed three people from the Raleigh group. They had gone into a Sitran settlement during the night. They killed two parent Sitran and tried to take the children back to their colony. I happened to be on security at the settlement that night. I heard the clicking cries of the children, it was clear to me that the offensive humans didn't want to talk, I killed them, all three, to save the lives of the innocent Sitran."

"Why do they do those things? Why did these people want to take the children?" I asked genuinely confused by such violence.

"Because those people see the different life forms as beings that are less than themselves. Less worthy of peace, comfort, love and joy. They see workers, they see the Sitran as a resource. When the Sitran refused the boss-slave relationship, the humans put it down to primitive ignorance. After all, the humans believed they were giving the Sitran a good deal, food, a place to sleep, they didn't seem to notice that the Sitran were living lives that went far beyond survival, they had everything. The humans figured it was a matter of enforcement and the Sitran would learn to behave. They still believe that. Fear lives on Evolution because of that attitude. I have never crossed their boundaries though. I have never gone into their camp and killed anyone in their sleep and I never will."

"Can you do this thing with Shannon? I don't want you going into situations with these people when you're all messed up. You look messed up Kelly." said Dante.

"I don't know how I could ever doubt you. I just don't understand how these people could have their heads so far up their asses. They can't be that stupid, can they?" I asked.

"That's one for your instincts, answer that for yourself, watch them and what they do, really check them out." answered Dante. "I know they keep up a good front but they're all used up inside. Anger, fear and insecurity have taken them all and I don't even think they really know what they're doing or what kind of pain they're causing."

Noises from the equipment room changed the subject. We all moved into the room and went to the colorful display on the monitors. There were people outside my house. We could see the signatures of thirteen different people from the colony, one of which was Sherman Castledown. They were grouped together just beyond the walls of the equipment room. I had a bad feeling. The group broke up and surrounded my house.

Sacro was the first to notice that they appeared to be trying to look in the windows. All the shades were drawn, all except for my bedroom. Thankfully all the windows were locked.

"They are checkin' you out baby." said Dante. He shivered as he said it like he was getting some excitement out of the moment.

"These Seletzium transmissions are also detecting a heightened level of anxiety in some of these people. I am wondering if Sherman told them about the Devids?" Sacro said.

"They certainly don't trust you Kelly, I wonder what they're looking for." said Donally.

"Probably us." Dante noted.

"Nobody leaves this room until they are gone, we don't need the hassle right now." said Donally firmly.

I was tired, not so much physically tired, just sick of the adversity these people were putting me through. I was eager to enjoy the peace and serenity Evolution had to offer. Sacro talked about the days before the crazy humans arrived when anyone could go walking at night without fear. I wanted to go for a walk. I wanted these paranoid crackpots to leave us all alone.

"Don't worry about it Kelly, they get tired quickly, it won't take long." said Donally, that same strange look of compassion shining through her battle ready exterior.

CHAPTER 13

It was my human willpower, the drive for control, that made me doubt the peace of Evolution. The people that chose the colony, ran their lives on that drive. I found out that most of them were professionals at one time or another. The people that made business move or set the trends of society. Not just the trends of the wealthy or powerful but people representing many different cultures. They all had that conquering spirit that seems to be so revered on Earth wherever one happens to be. I suppose it's greed, the idea that if this planet can be this wonderful then it could be that much better if one could harness the resource and sell it all. It wasn't Sacro that manipulated, he offered freedom and strength.

The colonists worked hard at making their deception look good. They were campaigning, sending me promises of prosperity and power, while trying to make the opponent appear evil. A lie is a lie no matter how great it sounds and lies don't hold up in the long run.

"I'm Shannon. Jacob said you needed a little extra human support. I'm here to offer my help." She said with a big, shiny smile. She had the look of a country club woman, born and raised on private school propaganda and pool party politics. Shiny, blonde hair framed her bony face, a face that matched a barbie-like body. I clenched my jaw as I smiled back telling myself to stop making judgments. Opening the door wide, I peered out around her to see if anyone else had accompanied her, but she was alone.

"Yes, yes, I'm Kelly, come in and have a seat. Can I get you anything?" I asked. I felt prepared for the situation however, I was tired of the phony quality that I had to put across. I was phony, they were phony. They had no idea that I was trying to save their lives.

"Do you have any coffee?" she asked.

"No! Do you?" I reacted, a little shocked. I'd forgotten about coffee but the mention of it sparked a craving.

"No, but I have a good substitute for it back at the base, has the same effect."

Was that part of the campaign? My kingdom for a coffee substitute? I rejected my craving. Not once did I find fulfillment out of answering the call of a craving. I would not be lured into her trap with my addictions.

"I have water." I said plainly.

"That would be just marvelous." she said with another bright, shiny smile.

Butterflies in my stomach followed me into the kitchen. Focus, focus, focus, I needed to focus on the task at hand. Dante, Donally and Sacro had stayed the night and assumed their positions in the control room. I felt a faint sense of security coming from Sacro, like I was receiving something from him even though he was in another room.

"There you go, I'm really glad you came by Shannon. It's been really hard for me here. I don't talk to anyone." I said.

"Mmmm, yes. Many of us are at a loss as to understand why we are here. Yes…" she said. The session had begun. She wasn't talking like a normal person. I'd done therapy enough to catch the change from person to professional.

"So how are other people dealing with this?" I asked after munching on some fruit I'd laid out on the coffee table.

"In a variety of ways. How about if you tell me how you're dealing with the changes."

"Well, actually, I feel pretty good overall. A little bit scared I guess."

"What kind of state of mind were you in before you got here. Did you feel scared or maybe hopeless or anything like that?"

"No, not really." I lied. I was a mess when Sacro had picked me up, scared of my own damn shadow but she didn't need to know that. She actually looked surprised by my answer.

"Oh. Hmm, that's a little bit different." she admitted.

"What do you mean?"

"Many of our people are in somewhat compromising situations just before they are taken…but that's not really relevant here anyway." She fiddled around in her bag for a few seconds and pulled out something that looked like a pocket knife with the blade folded in. It had four switches on it.

"Do you mind if I record this conversation?"

"What for?" I felt the butterflies again.

"I want to give you my best possible care Kelly. I want to be able to really hear what your saying. Sometimes I forget the most crucial details, ones that might be vital to your recovery." Another big, shiny smile.

My recovery? She had a program ready and waiting for me. She knew what to do with me before she met me. It wasn't really important to her what I was talking about, her main concern was to fit her theories into my story, like a two-bit fortune teller. If she asked the right questions she could get enough information about me to see my weak spots, then she could come up with something I might buy into. The pay off for her, if she brought me into the colony, was probably a nicer apartment or a higher rank. The psychology of politics was the theme here. Quite an unsophisticated manipulation even by my unrefined standards. But, I also had a plan, and recording the conversation would be good for my intentions. How many others would hear this conversation? I could plant the seeds of skepticism in more than just a couple of them. These people needed to know that their lives were in danger.

They would need to know what to look for before they got too sick to reverse the effects of exposure.

"That would be just fine." I replied with my own big, shiny smile. "I really do appreciate this Shannon, thank you."

"Kelly, it's the least I can do for my family. We need each other more than ever. There are so few of us here. Humans must stick together to survive this. We must stick together, Kelly. You and I and all of us at the base. It's as though we have been chosen to overcome this adversity. We are one glorious, spiritual family set out on a path to conquer the primitive forces in the Universe. I will do anything to help make this easy for you. We are truly alone here and there is no telling what kind of barbaric circumstances can happen out in this new world, a world full of aliens, non-human monsters. It can be scary, but we have the safety of our human collective. Humans always win." She switched on her little recording device. It was all too overwhelming to be real. Her statements of family and unity were said in such an unhinged way.

"That's very touching."

Focus, focus, focus. I could feel Sacro again, subtle but very distinct. I was receiving his encouragement. I had a definite purpose here and nothing else mattered, just get the message out.

"What do you think is your greatest fear about this ordeal Kelly?"

"Oh, there's so much, I don't really know where to start. Okay maybe I do. It's something Jacob talked about, well actually I brought it up because of what the alien man said." I purposely started babbling to get her involved in my drama.

"Kelly, it's alright. Maybe slow down a little and tell me what you and the alien man talked about."

"Yea." I took a deep breath. "When I got here, I had a long talk with a man, well not a real man, not human, but he looks like one. He talked about a lot of things. The thing I remember the most was the talk of the things that were inside me, helping me to stay alive. I was all freaked out, I mean it was just one thing after another…" I proceeded to tell her about the role of the Devid's as Sacro had described it and then went on to the story of Jacob Slater. I told her that I didn't know who to believe and that I felt really stuck in my confusion. Her mouth dropped open on a couple of occasions but she composed herself again and took on that professional look. I yada'd on for what seemed like an hour. She never said a word, just nodded her head from time to time. I had planted the second seed of doubt, the first being in Sherman Castledown. I never did get her last name. She didn't last long after our meeting but she got my point across to the rest of them, for what it was worth.

Shannon left with her recordings promising to come back and proceed with her intensive therapy sessions. She also promised that I would be just fine and I seemed like the type of person who would adjust to all of this and come out on top. Lastly, she carried on in the doorway about what a caring and kind man that Jacob Slater was and that he would never do anything to harm his family. Like Sherman, the only person she was convincing was herself.

My friends came out of the room and joined me in watching her as she walked toward her home.

"She is already sick." said Sacro. "There is not one among them that can help her with what she is about to encounter. Her own body will revolt against her intolerance to true peace."

"And now it's all up to them, ball's in their court, so to speak. You did a great job Kelly. I knew you would, thanks." said Dante, giving me a friendly slap on the back.

CHAPTER 14

I can't truly describe what we found as Donally and I walked through the small group of what Slater called separatists. There were thirteen of them, all dead. They didn't have a clue as to what had happened to them. Why any of them agreed to let Slater remove the Devid's was beyond me. They weren't part of the Raleigh pack. Unfortunately, they trusted Raleigh more than Sacro and that cost them their lives.

I had never actually seen a dead human, only on t.v. and nothing seemed real on t.v., not even the news. Sure I'd seen numerous shots of the various wars and such but never had I stood in the middle of a death camp. Sometimes, I'd watch those education stations that showed the ravages of disease in the third world countries but I had never witnessed the decomposing of bodies or smelled the rotting of their flesh. I wish I could still say that.

Donally began working right away. It didn't seem to touch her as it did me. She was more concerned with the clean up. She wanted to make sure that they were properly disposed of and that the area that they had adopted as their home was cleared away and given back to the natural inhabitants. I couldn't help her, I tried but I couldn't get within ten feet of the corpses. She hauled them along and carried them over to a spot where she lined them up. Three others joined us when she had realized I wasn't going to be of any help to her, the extra support was there within minutes. She didn't ask me to help after she saw the way I reacted. I suppose the puking, gagging, and retching sounds made her aware of my inability in the situation.

One human, named Isaic, one Sitran, who never offered any introduction to me and one other being, an Astorian whose name was Sagan Ra, helped Donally clear the bodies and to my utter horror, burn them in a pile. I moved around the spot trying desperately to get away from the stench of burning flesh. The light breeze seemed to follow me not allowing the comfort of a single fresh breath. I moved back and sat down on a rock, covering my mouth and nose with the collar of my shirt.

A tiny thing came out of a hole in the ground. It looked like an animal but not one that I'd ever seen. It had fur all over it's body, quite mousy looking ears and a chimpish looking face. It was a beautiful little creature in a rodent-like way. It was no bigger than a guinea pig. It looked into my eyes deeply and then looked toward Donally and her crew. It pointed at the campsite and looked at me again. It scurried up to my place on the rock and placed a tiny clawed paw on my hand. I had never had such a meaningful interaction with an animal before. I don't think I ever paid much attention to animals after I lost my childhood dog pal, it hurt so much to lose them that I didn't bother anymore.

After another curious eye contact between me and the creature, it leaped away, back into the ground. A voice came into my awareness.

"It is that you have never been so open to the intelligence of all things living." said Sacro. I heard him as if he were right in front of me but he was not. Sacro had journeyed to the other side of Evolution to meet with his peers, a council of elders is the way Dante put it. He told me he would not be back for a few cycles. I heard him clearly though. It wasn't my memory of his voice but his actual voice, separate and distinct from my own thoughts. It wasn't the same as when I had traveled through space in the protective bubble of the Devids. I had asked about that before. Why could I hear him then but not when I landed on Evolution? It was because of the state of my physical body in space. I had no dense mass in the Devid bubble. I was in the mind of Sacro not only being carried from Earth by the Devids but also by Sacro's thoughts. He had in fact, consumed me with his intelligence and carried me to Evolution on a thought wave. He had permeated every cell in my body and connected me to himself. It was a state that he could not keep for long and when I reached Evolution's atmosphere, he released me and I became wholly myself again, which broke the connection and therefore I could no longer hear him. Not until that wonderful moment when I finally felt and connected with the Unified Field of Evolution. I was receiving him. I was tuning into the flow of Evolution's' telepathy. Dante had told me Sacro would be the first to make it through the haze of my mind. It was his job to break barriers and create links with all who came to be here. It felt incredible and absolutely effortless. I just heard him.

I yelled out to Donally who immediately told me to shut up. I suppose the stink and sight of the bodies had started to get to her. How tough can a person really be? I ran over to her and told her what had happened. She forced a smile out.

"Pretty soon you'll be hearing me and then you'll wish you couldn't." she said jokingly.

"I can't wait, I want to hear you all." I said forgetting that I stood in a putrid, decomposing death site. Forgetting for a moment anyway…I ran away throwing up. Donally told me to go home.

"There have been more deaths." said Dante. He didn't bother to say hello.

I stood at my door, barely awake. The fresh air seeped in around Dante and wrapped me up, I felt like a blooming flower. Dante didn't show the type of emotion one would have when relaying such information. He looked fresh, healthy and very happy, just his ol' radiant, evolved self.

"I've been spying and listening. Some of them are very weak, they can't stop me from hearing them anymore." he continued.

"At the Raleigh camp?" I asked.

"Yup, some of them will be coming here to talk to you. We need to get you out of here for awhile." He pushed passed me and went straight into my bedroom. He was carrying a large bag, something like a duffel bag which he threw on my bed and looked at me expecting me to know what to do.

"O.K., get some of your things together. We're all going to Donally's." He left the room.

Renfrew came to the front door. I took my bag of stuff and climbed in as did Dante and we were on our way. Dante and Renfrew seemed to talk a lot and I was beginning to understand what they were saying from Dante's mental impressions. Renfrew was a very happy being. She didn't have the fear of the humans like the majority of her species. From what I understood, she knew the enemy humans would be gone soon, one way or another and with them the threat to her people. She instructed her people on which humans to stay away from. She encouraged peace with those of us that were willing to cooperate in loving ways. I had made the Sitrans good list according to her. Dante gave me a proud pat on the back and said he told her so. I felt like I had just won a prodigious award.

It was another beautiful day on Evolution, despite the impending doom on the sick humans. For those of us with our Devids, it was heaven. Warm rain fell from purplish clouds. Beams of energy shot out from many sources of life. There was no way of getting used to the ever-changing landscape. It was meant to be appreciated all the time.

We arrived at Donally's house after a long but refreshing ride. I thought seeing her home would give me a chance to get to know her better. I'd imagined displays of weapons and security equipment lining the walls, she was such a warrior-minded person but what I saw was the home of an artist. Amazing pictures and paintings of animals from Earth and Evolution. Small statues of different beings sat on strong stands, they looked as though they were being offered as gifts to the eye. Each article had its own aura and unique presence that filled the house with mingling energies. Donally led us through the front rooms to the side of her house where we came to a larger room with similar displays of artwork, tables and furniture, some meant for human use and some not. Renfrew had gone around the house and met us in a room which was big enough to shelter her comfortably. We sat together and talked. I found out that Donally herself had made much of the artwork in her home which absolutely amazed me. I never would have guessed that she was so artistically talented, not by the way she acted. I was reminded of my judgments that came with me from Earth. Did I stereotype people? Who me? Of course I did. I didn't know anyone on Earth that didn't do some type of categorizing when they met people. What was the one that cut me off from seeing Donally for who she really was? Oh yea, tough, strong, hard people don't care about art. Donally was strategic, not artistic. She was a military-minded person, what would she care about beauty or creative expression? I had ignored the fact that if the enemy humans weren't enemies, she wouldn't be doing any of these acts of security. Experiencing her home also reminded me that level headed, straight to the point people can be very creative. My limitations told me that artists had to be kinda flaky, a little bit off balance and not so stable in the mind, none of which were traits that Donally had within her. I was delighted by my wrongness.

"Why are we here?" I asked. It suddenly occurred to me that if the enemies wanted to see me they wouldn't be able to. "What if they are looking for help? What if they believed everything I told them and they want to see Sacro to get help?"

"It would be nice if that were the case but it's not. Kelly, you are the enemy to them, you did this to them." said Donally.

"Why do you say that? They don't know about me. They know nothing of me."

"No, they don't know a thing about you, so what? It doesn't matter, they've made up their minds about you. The deaths started after they met with you. Jacob was quick to blame you for infecting them. He has established that you are to blame for all of this. He has told his people that he has seen us all together and that we built this plan together to wipe them out. They think we did this to them." said Dante, "I told you, I've been spying."

"They think I did this?"

"Shannon died three cycles after she left your place. Sherman died just after her. They were the first to go and that's why it was easy to link this to you." said Dante.

"But Jacob's not dead, is he?"

"No, he's not dead" answered Donally.

"He was with me, how does he explain that? He was with me and Sherman."

"Jacob baffles them. He gets a little scientific with his explanations and they buy into it. Truth is Slater and Raleigh both know it's not really you. They are scrambling for control over the situation. They understand what you told Jacob was right. But if they can keep the focus on you being the bad guy, then they can gain back control by directing the hate toward us. Keeping the negative attention on you stops the group from thinking for themselves. With their hatred focused on you, they don't need to think just hate. If no one finds out that Jacob was wrong, then no one finds out that Raleigh and Slater are not the great leaders they claimed to be. Slater wants you dead, in his lab. He knows you have your Devid's, he knows you are telling the truth. He believes if he can get inside your body he can extract the Devid's from you and reproduce them. Having done that, he can then go ahead and inject them back into the remaining colonists and be the great hero." explained Dante. He didn't look at all worried about knowing all of this. I felt horrified. No one had ever actively searched me out to kill me. With all that I knew about these people, I was still shocked that they would actually want to kill me.

"They can't get you here Kelly." said Donally. "I would've been dead long ago if they could get through my security."

"What about the others, the people that still have their Devid's?"

"Well, you know they are safely guarded but they aren't really in danger. The Raleigh group is after you. Their minds are on revenge and to seek revenge you need a bad guy, a symbol that represents the one that did this horrible thing to them. They have decided it's you they want to bring in and they want you alive...at first, so they don't jeopardize the functioning of the Devid's. Slater knows very little about them. He's thinking in terms of technology, that Devid's are some kind of nanite so he's not sure if they depend on the main body, which would be you in this case. We know that this isn't the case but he doesn't bother with the reality part of all of this." said Dante with a mixture of amusement and disgust.

"So, your telling me they want to catch me, poke around inside my body to get the Devids out and then kill me?" I asked, just to be sure I was getting all this accurately.

"Yup." answered Dante.

"Oh my God."

Renfrew came closer to me and raised her stalky eye appendages so that she was staring at me eyes to eyes. She talked to me in her language of clicks and hisses. I understood that she was consoling me, letting me know that everyone on Evolution had faced the same awareness about the enemy humans. It was true, they were prepared to kill anyone if they thought it was necessary to further their greedy cause.

As bizarre as her language seemed to me, I could understand her through the new link I had developed with Evolution's Unifying Field.

Such an inexplicable understanding of which I had never felt before. Part of me thought it impossible to actually know what she was saying. Logically, I did not know her language, therefore I could not understand her, that seemed simple, but a deeper sense of me did understand without the burdens of conditioned thought, my deeper sense followed her, went beyond her language and straight to her heart. We were connected and there were no barriers to our understanding. It was calming but I still felt dizzy from the knowledge that someone that I had invited into my home, had placed a death mark on me only to protect himself from humiliation. Jacob Slater knew damn well that I didn't infect his people. The greedy, little man knew how to solve the problem and who was really responsible for it yet he was prepared to defend his lies, to actually end my life, to protect his ego.

The immunity I had acquired from my life on Earth regarding senseless violence, had been steadily wearing off. I did not have the same ho-hum kind of attitude about destruction. This wasn't some unrelated, brutal murder story on the six-o'clock news, soon to be a TV movie where you could just change the channel and forget about the whole thing. No, this was about me and people I'd grown to love. I was particularly fond of the peace of Evolution. The focus of growth and progress rather than money and power, was quite refreshing.

Donally left the room while the rest of us sat in a calming silence. The rain had passed over. The landscape was glistening, clean and magnificent. I knew I was safe but still felt shaken. I looked at Dante and then to Renfrew, my friends. I missed Sacro. Somehow, I knew we would get through this but wondered what was needed to resolve the problem.

Within moments a darker part of me came up out of the depths of my being. I had not sat in peace long before a coldness of insecurity, an inner tremor I'd grown so used to, welled up in my guts. In our stillness the small, dark spot grew. A familiar feeling crept into my calm appreciation. I quietly began to feel skeptical, untrusting of Evolution and God's will for me. Maybe everything would be OK for Dante and the rest of the Universe but God had me pegged as the scapegoat. It was the worst of my emotions, the sick darkness that weighed me down during various points in my life. The darkness that said I had no soul, that I could never be as good or as safe as I wanted to be. My own little inner nightmare of doom.

I'd always thought of it as an inborn trait because I couldn't remember a time when it had not been there for me, telling me I wasn't strong enough to be the person I imagined I wanted to be. It was this horrible inner shadow that led me to drinking and drugs, since I couldn't stand the pain of hearing my own destructive nature tear me apart. I don't remember my early twenties because I was so drunk all the time, I drank to drown out the voice of this horrid darkness, until I couldn't remember if I was even alive. God damn, this stupid shadow. It had followed me to Evolution. Why? I asked myself as I fought off the anxiety. What good would it do me here, to be so afraid of my own shadow? Why did it tell me that it was my fault that these crazy people wanted to kill me? For the same reasons, I thought, it had told me that anytime anyone hurt me or insulted me it was my fault, that I am always the bad guy.

My inner shadow was struggling to take hold of me again. Fighting for the right to dominate my every thought. It told me to never have faith in that thing I called a loving God. It told me to destroy or be destroyed. It told me I would never be part of the good guys team.

My head hurt, my heart sank and I felt myself drifting into a sea of negativity. Wasn't there supposed to be a light in every darkness? I couldn't see light. This wasn't some slight self doubt or a little lack of faith, I had learned to cope with those passing storms. This inner shadow seemed independent of me, as if it had punched a hole through my heart to get inside me. I had no real warning that it was coming, although I'm sure the news of Jacob's plans signaled my weakness.

I began to feel ashamed of myself for ever believing I could help Evolution. What made me think I was so special? Here I sat on a planet, among fantastic aliens and evolved humans, thinking I could make a difference. It was the shadow, with it's heavy, liquid voice, telling me the truth. I was nothing to anyone here. They stayed with me out of pity. I was a burden to all of Evolution and I would be better off surrendering myself to the enemy.

I tried hard but I couldn't speak out through the darkness of my shadow. I couldn't open my mouth to ask for help. As Dante and Renfrew sat in silence resting and relaxing, I was in the grips of utter panic, silent only because I couldn't speak.

The world outside of me was disappearing and the haunting of my inner shadow clouded out the hope I'd felt before, making it seem that the only thing that was really dependable was the negativity. It was like a heavy, lead curtain closing all around me.

"My best friend." the Shadow said to me from deep within. I could see it's dark smile. It wanted me to look through it's eyes again, to see the world through it's heart and mind. The world is different through the heart of a shadow. My friends were not friends anymore not in the grip of this shadow creature. Dante was a childish, arrogant wind bag. Renfrew was a worthless alien freak probably ready to attack and kill humans at any opportunity and Donally was a twisted, war hungry bitch, bent on fighting because she was so afraid to be vulnerable. The Shadow grew strong, became well defined. It told me to see Sacro for what he was, an iconoclastic alien who could not be trusted. All he wanted was control over Earth and it's humans. He was full of lies, he didn't want peace and love, he wanted power. I had no strength to fight off the inner mumbling, this was the worst feeling I'd ever known. My soul was fading into this black hole. God if I could only ask for help, just call out to them but how, I wondered, could anyone help me with this inner battle?

"Kelly? Are you there? I hear you, Kelly?" It wasn't the voice of the Shadow calling me. It came from inside my head, but it wasn't the Shadow.

"Kelly? It's Donally. I can help you, I can hear you. Just see me Kelly, see me in your mind. Make a vision of me and hold onto it. Hold onto me. I am going to pull you out. You have to hold on to your vision of me. Keep it clear."

I felt cold and beaten but I concentrated on Donally. I saw her but I also saw the Shadow looming over both of us. I felt my body sitting in the chair, silent and still. All this was going on inside my mind. I thought I must be cracking up.

"Kelly, this is very real. Concentrate on me." said Donally. I focused on her face.

"Don't think about anything but me, stay aware of me. I am getting rid of this thing. I will make it go away but you must not give it your attention. Hear me Kelly? Stay with me." She seemed to be yelling.

This was not the inner work my therapist taught me. This was all going on inside but independent of me. I did not creatively imagine the battle between Donally and the Shadow thing. It was happening whether I wanted it or not. I felt burglarizes by the dark being. It had broken into me and was trying to take all my valuables. It would have if Donally hadn't been there. I watched the fight between her and this dark matter. It wasn't a physical battle but one of dimension. The shadow worked hard at trying to consume her, a battle of light and dark quite literally. Her weapon was the power of light, to intensify her light levels to illuminate me. If she could turn on every light in my soul the Shadow would have nowhere to hide.

This evil wasn't part of me the way I'd always thought it was. Some hideous, dark part of human nature that everyone human had to deal with, it was the popular psychology of our time. Every therapist told me I had to deal with my dark nature as a part of being human, there were no devils, no demons, no angry Gods, we could blame ourselves for the darkness. No one told me that I had a choice as to whether or not I gave it a home. I unwittingly gave it the penthouse suite in my psyche.

As Donally fought with it, she also helped me understand it. I had not been born with this thing. The Shadow was an invader, an unwelcome guest, a liar and a con-artist. And it was really good at what it did. This one entity had the whole of the human population going on it's lies. All of Earth had succumbed to it's ugliness, had even taken responsibility for it as being part of self. No one questioned that the dark side of humanity was real and endless, something that couldn't be beaten, just dealt with, accepted, lived with. No one claimed that they had found true freedom of the darkness because no one really knew that they could be free of it. This Shadow had indeed persuaded us all that it was at home inside our souls and not once did a human decide against that.

The battle inside me was common place for humans that moved to Evolution. Donally had fought with it many times and won. The souls of Evolution did not welcome the dark visitor and rejected it's evil. But it wouldn't stop trying if it thought there was any chance of success.

At that moment when I was told that there were those that wished to kill me, that there were real people who would take away my body and my life without mercy, I became weak. The feelings of betrayal weakened me, left me with no defense, no will for survival. Although I had always known that the enemies were cruel and strange, I still felt separate from their fight and struggle. As their target, I realized how precious being alive really is. It was betrayal, I was being betrayed by my own kind. Were they not human? Could they not let go of their greed for a moment and try to understand me. No. They wanted me dead, no questions asked. Betrayed.

I could feel the phantom relish in my pain, drinking it as I would of drank whiskey years before. The Shadow was high on my fear of betrayal.

They continued to fight inside me. I went in and out of conscious-ness. Dante, who was made aware of my situation, was holding me. He talked softly and rocked me. Donally yelled for my attention.

"Focus on me Kelly, Focus, FOCUS!" she yelled as she fought the Shadow's distortions. I did what she told me. She grew larger in my vision, until all I could see was her face as if she stood before me with a great light shining around her.

"You won." she whispered and disappeared into the light.

I woke up in a room I was not familiar with. I swung my legs to the floor and stood up only to fall back into bed. I didn't feel very well. My body ached, my mind was foggy and I was really hungry. I knew where I was because I could feel the presence of my friends close to me. I felt like I was in the grips of a terrible hangover. My mouth was dry, the taste was unspeakable. My head pounded, the worst part of it all was the nau-sea, such a sick feeling throughout my body.

"Tolosod can take a lot out of ya' but you'll be just dandy after some rest and good food." said Dante. He stood in the doorway with a tray of food.

"Tolosod?" I grumbled.

"Tolosod." He said plainly and came into the room.

"I remember." I said rubbing my head.

"Oh, you will never forget Tolosod my friend, never forget."

"Probably not." The grim image of the beast of darkness lurked in my dream head.

"Why do I feel this way?"

"Are you kidding? Your lucky your out of bed already. A fair fight with Tolosod is bad enough but when he gets inside you like that…well your lucky kid."

"Where's Donally?" I changed the subject so I wouldn't have to really hear just how lucky I was.

"She's out doing another clean up."

"Who is it?"

"It's part of another separatist group. There used to be six of them, now there are three. We can save the other three."

"So they believe us now?"

"Yes, the remaining separatists do. Sacro is with them. They have agreed to reestablishing a unity with the Devid Communities. They'll be okay."

"Yea, sure they'll be O.K. but can we trust any of them?"

"No, but they have no love for Raleigh. We are keeping them in quarantine until the threat is over. Evolution is a peaceful place but we aren't stupid. No one here puts false hopes on humanity. Those three will have to gain our trust, we're pretty hard to fool." Dante put the tray down on a small table in the corner of the room. I was hungry, really hungry but I also felt ill. The smell of the food was tempting and revolting at the same time.

"Am I really safe Dante?" I asked thinking of the shadow, Tolosod.

"Tolosod is powerful but he knows his limits. You showed him your power even though you were weakened by your surrender to fear, that you had no trouble accepting help from your friends when you needed it." He was proud of me, I could see it shining in his eyes.

"But what the hell is he? Where did he come from?" I asked. Dante looked around the room, picked out a chair and sat down.

"Tolosod is the Devil." he said. I laughed thinking he was joking but he wasn't.

"Oh God! Your serious?".

"Tolosod is what you felt. Darkness most dark, misery, struggle, doubt, fear. You know what I'm saying. He can't manifest though, he's got no power to be completely physical, whole, like you and me. The ol' shit can't make his own body and that's why he enjoys the human race so much. It's an easy hit for him. Humans have an open door to Tolosod because we've been so ignorant to his presence. Everybody else knows when he has made an intrusion and tosses him out for the garbage that he is, quickly and easily. Humans, Earth humans have for some reason, accepted his presence and integrated him into themselves. They claim the Devil for their very own. Haven't you ever heard that stuff about honoring our dark shadow-self, embracing our dark side so that we may be enlightened. Yea, you've heard it, you know the story, you bought into it." said Dante.

"It's like a spirit then?"

"It's really just a concentration of thinking evil. Spirits tend to be denser, the mind of someone who has passed over, not yet taken a new body. Tolosod has never had a body. It's humans that give him his power. Some think he was born on Earth but I don't really know. There have been times that he has mustered up enough strength to create an image for us and always chooses the shape of a human."

"Does he still bother you?"

"Not anymore. He can't get near me. I can spot him lurking before he can get close enough to knock on my inner door. I'm free from his threat personally but I still have to deal with him. Tolosod has manifested himself an army. Raleigh, Slater and the bunch, they worship him although they would never admit to it. Tolosod whispers to them while they sleep, while they dream. He lives inside of each of them like the residue of smoke and without the Devid's protecting their bodies, his presence turns into cancer for them."

"Can't we get Tolosod out of them, like Donally did for me?"

"Did Donally get Tolosod out of you?"

"Yes she did."

"No" he said "No you let Donally help you. Donally and you together became powerful enough to push Tolosod out. He knew he had no home in you anymore. When he saw Donally, Tolosod knew you had crossed the line."

"I crossed the line?"

"Yea, your not alone anymore." You have undone your boundaries, made new ones, the prison walls have crumbled." Dante's expression changed and he stood up. "You don't look like you need anymore of this conversation Kelly. You just rest, let us watch out for you. Eat if you can, I'll be around if you need anything." He left the room.

I looked to the food but fell back to sleep before I could think too much about getting out of the soft, warm bed.

CHAPTER 15

Sacro hugged me and commented on how well I looked. He had been away for so long and even with my new connection to The Unified Field I was not well versed enough to have satisfactory telepathic communication over any long distance. It had not yet become a natural situation for me.

I enjoyed my old senses, my sight, smell and all of that. The sparkle in his eyes gave me a warm feeling of being truly safe and anchored, until he gave me the news of their plans.

"I'm not going into that place!" I yelled. Sacro sat silent. I took a few deep breaths.

"Yes I am going in there, aren't I?" It was no use. I knew by that time that I was a key part of the solution.

What Sacro was presenting was that I go to the colony and talk with Raleigh face to face. I wouldn't be alone, we would all go together but I would lead in the presentation. I'd made my choice while at Donally's, that I would take on the job of being a representative of Evolution on Earth. This was all part of the job. We had to deal with Slater and Raleigh before I could move on. No more time, no more games, no more war. They were dying. It was funny how they resisted us, fought against us with such fervor. All of them convinced that they were protecting their rights in some way. What they were really doing was killing themselves all in the pursuit of conquering the new frontier and without having any understanding for it.

The Devid Communities were ready to cooperate again and waited on the dying humans to allow them entry. Most of the sick ones could be restored back to health, although we were sure to lose a few more before this was through. We, or rather I, would explain this to Raleigh. If she didn't accept our aid then we would have to battle our way out of the little village.

Sacro had met with the others that had agreed to join us as support and extra protection. We were to bring no weapons, which made both Donally and myself a little uneasy. I laughed at myself for thinking it would be easier to talk to Raleigh if I had a gun pointed to her head but I doubt that it would've encouraged much in the way of trust. I don't even know that I cared much about encouraging trust, I didn't want to deal with the situation at all. I had never met with Raleigh face to face, only her presence on the planet could be felt as a cold, dark spot, completely uninviting. Tolosod was with her and I certainly didn't want to meet with him again.

I wondered if I could actually help her. Would she listen to me at all or would she discount anything I had to say based on her fear of me and the others? Deep down, I really didn't want to even try to help her. I was a coward and I wanted to run but I was a coward with the strength of Evolution surrounding me which made all the difference.

We made our plans. I was agreeable, not as tempted as usual to resist my worth in the mission. It took fourteen cycles to fully prepare for the event. Ten people died in that time including two pregnant women, I guess some would say that twelve people died.

I was taken to my home on occasion to run through the tracking equipment. I would gather information on the colony and Renfrew would take me back to Donally's where I spent most of my time. I was never left totally alone.

Sacro taught me how to welcome death. It's not quite as bad as it sounds, death gets a bad wrap with the living. If it's right, death is a wonderful transition. If it's not right then there are problems and confusion can take over which is how the Hell theory began. Sacro explained that the problem with death is that we don't know how to judge it, especially for ourselves. Preparing for death is not like saying 'I want to die' it's more like feeling that everything will still be alright if I do. If I died on the mission, I would still be alright. I didn't need to be afraid of the losses.

After each the lesson I would notice a change in the air around me. A new, shimmering presence in my meditations that vibrated a sense of peace to me that was stronger than life or death and could withstand the traumas of both.

More beings came to Donally's house to join in on the project. I met and talked to a deer from Earth. I made connections with a Whicen that could only see with the sounds it produced. I talked to a woman with wings who was no larger than a dragonfly. And through it all, the peace remained. The meditations made me whole and strong. I stayed close to Dante, Donally and Sacro as they were still my closest, most secure friends. It felt easy to communicate with them. We used our words less and less as I practiced my developing telepathy. Some moments flew by and some dragged on but fourteen cycles did pass. We gathered together on that fifteenth day and faced the enemies of Evolution once and for all.

CHAPTER 16

Members of Coalamine's family guarded me as I walked through the shattered colony. I moved deliberately to the big house where I hoped to find Raleigh and Slater.

Sacro, Donally, Dante and others formed their own protective group but all of them knew that I would be the target if the enemy decided to attack. Slater may have known the truth about me but we were all sure that he would keep that truth to himself.

As I walked through the grounds, the people began to stumble out of the buildings to the left and right of us. I could smell the decay. Disease in many forms had made homes in each of these people. I was horrified and actually lost my balance at the sight of them. All were sick and grief stricken from the death that surrounded them. Not one of them seemed to know that they had anyway out of the Hell that they were in. Raleigh and Slater had kept the solution a secret. These dying people waited on their leaders to take control and save their lives.

Each one of them glared at me with hate and blame so intensely that I felt myself waver under their attention. I could feel the vibrations of disgust emanate from each of their weakened bodies. They yelled harsh words at me, beating me with them as if they thought they could knock me down with the sound of their raspy voices. I blocked the scene out and directed my attention to the big house.

I had spent fourteen cycles preparing for this moment and the simplest of procedures scared me into ignorance. Should I knock on the door? Ring the doorbell? Was there a doorbell? Should I just kick the door down? I saw no doorbell and the door looked far stronger than me so I choose to knock putting some authoritative force into it. She answered the door as if expecting me.

She was much taller than me. I had to look up to make eye contact. Her eyes reminded me of the darkness of Tolosod. She was well dressed, clean, not at all sick looking, like the others. Her hair was cropped close to her head giving her a harsh appearance despite her physical beauty. She looked beyond me and directly at Sacro.

"Hello Kelly." Raleigh said.

"Oh good, you know my name." I felt more afraid than I had anticipated.

"So aren't you here to make some kind of a deal?" she asked. She continued to look at Sacro.

"I am here to help you and your people if you will accept it."

"Come in, we'll talk." she said opening the door wide and stepping back. "Alone."

"We, Dante and I will accompany Kelly." said Sacro. He was suddenly right behind me.

The Kivians of Coalamine's family moved back, making a guard wall between the house and the rest of the colony.

"Very well, but be sure that little traitor stays out of my house." said Raleigh pointing at Donally.

"Donally is very happy to be spared the drama of meeting with you again Margaret." said Sacro.

I went in first and was offered a seat in the huge, luxurious front room. I sat down on the firmest, hardest looking chair I could find. I didn't want to get too comfortable in her living room. Sacro and Dante stood in the doorway and waited for me to begin. I didn't give in to the pressure of the moment. Sitting silently, I calmed myself using my connection to the Unified Field. I had the support that I needed in a matter of seconds.

"Margaret," I said boldly, "I am here to offer you aid in this time of trouble. You and your people are in danger due to the evacuation of your Devids. I'm sure you know about this, but what I think you may not understand is that, these Devids were with you to protect the sensitive human system from some of the harsher elements of Evolution's atmosphere. I know you thought the Devids were some kind of tracking device and I won't lie to you, they do give signals to indicate their presence in the body, but the real purpose of the Human/Devid relationship is for our protection. Your people are dying and we can help you survive, no one needs to die from this point on, if you allow us to help them and yourself."

"Really?" she said without emotion. She took slow steps from the front window to a chair very close to the one that I sat in.

"Margaret, I can help you." I added.

"Why would I need your help? I'm not sick. Look at me Kelly, do I look at all sick to you? Do I really look like I need your help?" She held out her arms as if she was displaying herself to me, then spun herself around until she faced me again.

"Maybe not now but you will get sick, just like the others and you'll die like the others if you don't allow the Devids back into your system." I found a sense of compassion within me that reminded me that perhaps I myself was indeed evolving.

"Jacob informed me of the situation. So will you sacrifice yourself to save me Kelly? Give me your Devids? Or how about Dante?" She turned to him and walked over as if she thought she had some sort of sexual appeal to him. She cupped his chin. "Would you save me Dante?" She mocked the archetypal victim image.

"Raleigh," Dante said removing her hand from his face with a little more force than necessary. "Truth be known, I would kill you myself and spare the Devids the disgusting experience of being inside you." He backed up to put space between them.

"Oh, what a nasty man you are Dante." she laughed defensively.

"No one has to sacrifice anything Margaret. There are Devids just waiting for you to give the OK. There are enough Devids for everyone." I said.

We all heard the terrible moan from upstairs. Sacro and Dante turned toward the stairs. Margaret quickly ran over to block the way. Sacro pushed her aside gently and began the ascent with Dante and I following a few steps behind. Dante could not be alone with Margaret for to long save that he may give in to his desire to rid Evolution of her presence and I because I was still rather afraid of her. She walked deliberately close behind me and I found myself walking sideways up the stairs so that my back would not be to her. She had a cloud of hate around her that gave her the permission to be a literal back stabber.

The moaning continued to grow louder with each step I took. We reached the room where the desperate sounds emanated. He was calling out to us. No longer able to form clear words, he whimpered out what he could. He was not the same person I had met. Even Dante showed his shock. Sacro just approached him gently and placed a hand on his forehead. Jacob Slater held out his swollen hand and Sacro held it. Slater's eyes showed such intense pain that regardless of how awful he might have been, no one could look on him without compassion. Sacro moved closer and held him. Raleigh screeched when she witnessed the soothing effect Sacro had on him.

"Get away from him you sick fuck! You did this to him." she flung herself toward Sacro and hauled him back away from the dying Jacob Slater. Sacro allowed her to do this to a certain degree and was noticeably cautious as he finally pushed her aside.

"No." whispered Jacob. "No, no, no, let him come. It's the only chance I have."

Raleigh just stared down at him. He coughed and she ran to the other side of the bed where she pulled up a large pot and directed Jacob's head into it. His coughing turned to gagging which turned into all out vomiting.

I wanted to leave. We all stood there though and waited patiently while Jacob Slater turned inside out. He knocked himself out with the heaving. Raleigh took the pot away, walked out of the room, came back with it cleaned and placed some wet towels across Jacob's forehead. She cleaned him up and laid him back into a resting position.

"You did this to us." she looked up at Sacro. "You brought us here, you sick fucken alien. What's your plan? To kill the ones you can't brainwash. To use us as an example to the others who may have some doubts about your motives?" her hatred radiated out and engulfed the whole room. "You can't break me Sacro. I am stronger than you. I will never be your slave!"

"Slave, Margaret, who here looks like a slave?" yelled Dante.

"You do Dante. You have no mind left. How can you abandon all that you know? Do you really think that this Evolution bullshit is real? Everything is free, life is wonderful, peace and love for all, la de da, come on Dante. This crackpot just wants to get you going on that shit, he's like an alien dope dealer handed out packages of confidence until your hooked, then he's got all the control. He's got you Dante, you're an idiot." she said with a voice that sounded more like a hissing cat than a human being.

I thought she was going to attack him. Sacro shared my thought and positioned himself firmly between the two. Margaret was losing her fine political demeanor and it was ugly. My hopes of her seeing our side of the story, maybe considering that we were not trying to brainwash the human race, were dissolved. I could see that she would let her people die, she would kill them and herself just to be right. We were prepared for it, mostly.

"What has he told you Margaret?" asked Sacro.

"He's gone mad anyway. It doesn't matter what he says. He's sick, tortured, he'd do anything to get out of the pain he's in. I know what I'm doing." she said quite obviously trying to get a grip over her emotions.

"I think he may of told you the truth. He told you what really happened, that he had made an error." said Sacro.

"And so what? I told you he's delirious. The poor man is dying. He's weak and desperate for relief." Raleigh looked down to the floor with a hint of shame, or so I hoped it was shame I was seeing.

"Yes, he's dying but we can save him. We can help you all." said Dante, his anger had already dissolved and he spoke in compassionate tones.

"Oh I know. You keep telling me, you keep telling me how your going to save everybody…we are not all dead though. We will save ourselves." she said.

Raleigh moved quickly around Slater's bed and out through the door. We heard her shuffling around on the floor below us. Open door. Close door. Back up the stairs. She entered the room again wielding a double-edged sword. It was surreal, so strange that I felt a little dizzy at the sight of her swinging the silver blade back and forth across the width of the room. I was the closest target and unfortunately to stunned to move out of the way in time. The only reason the blow to my arm didn't cut it right off was that she lost her balance midway through the effort. She did however, make complete contact. The pain was beyond me. For one instant, as I felt the metal slice through my skin and muscle, slamming hard into my bone, nothing else existed. Just me and my pain in a never-ending moment of intensity.

I fell away from the sword and felt myself being caught before I hit the creaky bedroom floor. I think I blacked out, but only for a second. I couldn't believe what she had done to me. My hatred for her overcame my pain. It was hatred that flooded my body and gave me the strength to break free from Dante's grip and lunge at her without a moment of thought. Sacro was between us before I could blink and instead of completing my intentions of gripping her neck in a death hold, I slammed hard into him. Raleigh saw this action as an opportunity to strike again.

Dante had her down before she could get the sword above her head. She ripped herself out of his hold and ran out of the room. She was yelling, calling in the troops with the planned code for attack. She wanted this war.

I fell back against a wall. Sacro ripped off the sleeve of my shirt and wrapped it around my arm.

"Oh God, please…I'm so sorry…sorry. Forgive me please." moaned Slater. He was conscious again.

"They don't listen anymore. Please, get away from here, from them. They only want to hurt you, to kill you, they have the weapons. Sacro, I'm sorry, so sorry. I didn't see it before but now I do, I see it, the reality of this place. Please forgive me." Jacob sobbed as he spoke and both Dante and Sacro went to him.

"Jacob, we can save you. Do you trust us?" asked Dante.

"I know now. I'm so sorry. I loved her, that's all, I just loved her and I made a mistake. I made a mistake…please forgive me." he whispered.

"But it's O.K. Jacob. We'll save you…" Sacro cut Dante off.

"Jacob Slater, you are forgiven. We forgive you." he said firmly.

Jacob died on those words, right in front of me, he just died. It wasn't the way I'd seen it in movies. He started heaving again, throwing up. His eyes opened wide, his face went red. It looked as though he might explode but he just died instead. Sacro told us both to stand back as he placed his hands over Jacob's body. They both shook violently as Sacro repeated the word 'Vairochana', until a brilliant light burst out of Jacob's body. The window shattered, a wave of heat moved through the room, came back on itself and withdrew completely out through the window. Sacro swayed back a little bit but regained his balance quickly.

Donally's voice rose up inside our minds. Coalamine and her family joined the call. The action was coming down all around me and all I really wanted to do was to just sit down and forget the whole damn thing. They needed us outside but I didn't want to go. As much passion as I felt for Evolution, it didn't seem to be quite enough to get me moving.

My arm felt funny, no pain, just numb and I couldn't do much with it. I felt no care for Margaret after what she had done to me and those poor pawns of hers that were dying, so be it, let them all die. How many times had I gone through this? Another roller coaster ride of high morals and compassion down to a go fuck yourself attitude.

"Only act when your on top." said Dante. He'd heard me through the field that connected most of us. I was subconsciously calling out for someone to help me find the courage to care, to acknowledge my own pain and move on. Every time I doubted what I knew to be right, I was asking for help. On Evolution, the help was there instantly.

Sacro and Dante left the room but I held back. I made my way around the bed and looked out of the window. They were fighting. The enemy attacked with their crude weapons and as primitive as those weapons were, my side didn't have so much as a club to beat someone off with.

It felt as though I was watching a movie. Perfect sound effects and the aliens looked so real. Just for a moment I pretended that was what was really happening. I was really in a nice little theater. The movie would end with the good guys winning, it would make me feel good and I would go home to my little apartment with the hardwood floors. My daydream bubble burst as I watched the scene. There was real blood and screams of pain. I turned my head and instead of the rows of seats one would see at a real movie house, I saw Jacob, head slung to the side, dead eyes starring at the ceiling. Blood ran from his nostrils and ears.

This wasn't special effects or make up. Jacob was not ever going to get up. If that wasn't enough to snap me back to reality, the throbbing in my arm prodded me into total awareness. I ran out of the room and down the stairs. I needed something before I went out there, some kind of weapon. I searched around the rooms hoping to find something that Raleigh may have left behind. I heard screams and yells from outside. I felt the pain of the others who were being beaten. Making my way to the kitchen area, I grabbed onto a knife that laid in the wash basin. Thankfully, I had no fear of my own to deal with, all I could think of were my friends.

My arm felt like the center of my body with the wound taking all the attention. Feeling weak and tired due to a lose of blood, I was floating through waves of dizziness. I made it to the open doorway with the knife in my hand, ready, fully willing to slash Raleigh's throat. I could do it if I just concentrated on her. A loud voice boomed inside my head.

"Stay out of this Kelly!" It was Sacro.

I looked for him in the angry crowd of humans, animals and aliens. He stood alone and off to the side of the mob and, he was looking at me. I froze in place, unable to act on my desire to kill. I felt off balance. I saw the whole picture in tiny sections. My eyes darting back and forth across the scene. We fought remarkably well considering we had no weapons. Coalamine tossed people aside with her long, powerful arms. The enemy donned knives, clubs, swords and spears. Many of our kind had the advantage of being stronger physically or able to move faster. No one approached Sacro. The enemy humans were getting tired but the battle continued. The advantage the enemies had besides their crude weapons was the fact that they thought they had nothing left to lose. Most of them thought they would die anyway.

Dante moved through the crowd with his little 'now you see me, now you don't' trick. He made it look humorous as he appeared before an enemy, hit them and then disappeared again.

Donally caught my attention with the fierceness in which she fought. She had a surreal strength to her small, feminine body. She threw people aside almost as easily as Coalamine. I could hear her battle cries above the din of the crowd. Her passion was profound. Donally's stunning performance made fighting look like an art form.

What came after was like a dream to me. I wish it had been a dream. In one small moment, one of Raleigh's mindless converts came up behind Donally. I made an effort to call out to her but my energy was low and the noise from the battle was too overwhelming for my little voice. The large man grabbed her and placing his arm around her neck to steady her, he plunged a long, thin knife into her stomach and let her go. There she stood, alone in the crowd, stunned and confused by what had happened. I ran down the front stairs of the house and into the tangle of war. I thought nothing of protecting myself, I even dropped the knife. I managed to catch her before she hit the ground. Two others came to my aid, another large human man whom I'd met before in Sowthren Court and a human woman that I recognized as being part of the enemy collective.

"I'm sorry. I want to help you. We have to get her out of here." she yelled.

I didn't have time to decide whether or not I trusted her. I would split her head open if she made one threatening move. All I wanted to do was save Donally. The man quickly pulled the knife from Donally's belly and dropped it. Her blood poured out of the wound. She didn't make a sound. We carried her away from the fighting mass as Sacro came to us.

"Take her home. I have called on Renfrew, she will take you. I can not leave here yet Kelly." he said.

"Oh, come on Sacro, come with me. She's hurt really bad. I need your help!" I pleaded with him.

"Kelly, you have all the help you need. Take these two with you. Take her home." He picked Donally up and cradled her as though she were a child. She relaxed in his arms, his warmth eased her pain.

Renfrew came quickly and before long we were carrying Donally to her bed. We laid her down. I did what Sacro told me to do which was to stop the bleeding and lay her on her right side. The other two brought sheets of absorbent cloth, bowls of warm and cold water and ointments from Donally's cupboard. Donally was falling in and out of consciousness while I sat by her bed.

"I feel like I'm dying Kelly" she said softly. Her dark eyelids fluttered as she struggled to focus on me.

"No, no, no, it's not that bad Donally. The bleeding has stopped and your going to be alright. It's just painful but you won't die." I said trying to be positive, encouraging and strong. I prayed by her bedside. Selfish prayers to keep her alive.

"Please God keep her breathing. Please God heal her wounds. Please God stop the bleeding. Please God, don't let her die." I repeated these things again and again in my head. I hoped that she couldn't sense the panic that I felt.

The woman and man tended to her physical needs, putting warm blankets around her head, hands and feet, cold, damp cloths on the wound and feeding her small amounts of warmed water.

"Let's leave her here now. I've given her medicines. She will sleep now and I will continue to watch over her." said the man.

I got up from her bedside, walked down the hall into the large sitting room with all the windows, the room where I first met Tolosod. I sat down and started to cry tears of powerlessness. I wanted control over what was happening, but I had none. I felt like a failure. Hadn't I failed in my meeting with Raleigh? I was supposed to go to her and peacefully negotiate a plan to save everyone. I barely said two words before she went on a rampage. Why didn't she try to listen?

I could feel pains in my psyche. More of them were being hurt, maybe even killed. I began to panic bringing up all the what ifs that I could think of. What if Sacro got killed? What if Dante were murdered? What if the enemy won this stupid battle and no one from my side came out alive?

"She's resting. No more bleeding. The pain remedies are working but we will still have to get her to the OmKyente facility." the woman sat down beside me as she spoke.

"Who are you?" I asked through my sobs.

"My name is Tabatha."

"Your one of them."

Her head bowed and she began to cry. "I am so ashamed of myself."

"What the hell were you thinking? Are you nuts? Are you? You must be crazy, this is the most incredible place I've ever seen, why would you go against this?" I screamed out at her until I could feel my face turn red with rage.

It just made her cry harder. She tried to speak but it made no sense. I left her and walked outside to breath in fresh air. Jumbled messages from the Unified Field blazed through me. More hurt, more pain.

"Donally has to live." I said out loud. I repeated it until it sounded like a mantra. I paced frantically in hopes of ridding myself of the intensity that I felt.

"You won't stop her this way" said Tabatha. She was still crying but had more control over her speech.

"You are not dealing with a fair mind. Margaret is sick, she's warped on her imaginary politics. Margaret doesn't give a damn about your deals. If she doesn't have control then it's no deal. Just look at her. What does she care if we all die? She told us that she would protect us and we believed her. We were all so scared and she talked like she knew things. We've stood beside her, worked for her cause but I know now that we mean nothing to her. I know that she lied. I guess it's easy to get people to believe in lies when they're afraid."

"Jacob is dead." I blurted it out in hopes of hurting her with the news.

"I'm going to die to. I'm getting sicker. I can feel my body giving up." she said, not seeming to acknowledge the real meaning of what I had said. Maybe she just didn't care anymore. How many people has she watched die?

"We go through too much." said Tabatha. "I remember a saying I heard as a child, that we learn from our pain. That's really something to tell a kid, why couldn't it have been, we learn through our love." Her eyes were distant.

"You don't have to die."

"I don't care if I do. Maybe it would be a chance to start over again." she responded.

"How's that?"

"I don't know, maybe there's another chance after you live a dreadful life full of wrong turns and bad choices. Maybe God will be good to me and let me have another chance. If I could remember all the stupid mistakes I've made, I wouldn't do them again." she answered.

"You don't have to die to learn from your mistakes."

"I don't think you understand my situation here. I'm getting sicker as we speak. I don't think I have a choice." she said evenly.

The pain in my arm tore my attention away from the conversation. Such pain and so suddenly, it had all come back to me and I felt my knees buckle under my weight. My body's defenses seemed to drain out and I began to feel everything that was wrong. I quivered in the agony of the wound. Tabatha responded immediately by supporting my weight as we went back into Donally's house. She directed me to lie down in a spare bedroom she had noticed while getting supplies for Donally. The man came into the room and together they worked over me.

"You'll have to go into OmKyente too. The humerus has been fractured. No major damage though. We'll fix you up as good as new. I've given you some medication to ease the pain." the man said to me with a gentle smile, easing me into restfulness.

I felt sleepy but struggled against it.

"Tabatha?" I called out.

"Yes, ah…what is your name anyway?"

"Kelly, my name is Kelly. Thank you and when Sacro gets here tell him you're willing. He'll understand and you won't have to die." I said as I lost the struggle to stay conscious.

CHAPTER 17

The fighting broke up when Raleigh and her group withdrew back into their buildings. They'd seemingly planned to retreat if they found themselves losing the battle by locking themselves into one of the larger buildings and waiting for us to leave their compound. No one from our side pursued since we had only been fighting in defense anyway.

I was taken to OmKyente, a healing and research center, where I spent the night in the care of healers. By the next morning, my broken bone was completely fused and the damaged tissue where the sword sliced me was regenerating. The flesh around the wound tingled and actually felt good and whole again, as if I'd had no wound at all.

Donally died before we could get her to OmKyente. Dante and Sacro had come back from the battle and sat by her bed as I had before, tending to her needs but nothing they did worked for her.

There were many injured in the battle but strangely, Donally was the only one from our group that actually died. I thought I may die from the grief that her passing brought me.

"Her soul continues to evolve. You will join me and you will see." Sacro said as I cried.

The ceremonies began when Sacro realized that she would not make it through her wounds. He spent some time with her alone and the next thing I knew, she was dead. Dante, myself and some others were permitted into her room. Her body was laid on her bed on her right side. She'd been wrapped in beautiful gold and green silk blankets. Sacro instructed us. He sat closest to her and began to speak words unfamiliar to me. Dante entered my mind and told me to listen through The Field. I did what he said and immediately encountered a translation that enabled me to understand what Sacro was saying. He was directing her, helping her get somewhere. I could feel her presence with us. I watched expecting her to start moving as her energy filled the room. We sat patiently while Sacro chanted and the daylight drained away. Sacro ended the session and told us we would begin again the following morning.

I spent all of my time in Donally's home, looking over her artwork and reading essays that she had written. Her room had been opened to her friends so they could view her body and pray over it. When I entered the room all I could offer were tears.

"No Kelly, not here, not now. It just makes it harder for her to go the right way." whispered Dante. He had come in just after me on the morning the ceremonies were to begin again.

"The right way?" I sputtered.

"It has been decided that she must go back to Earth." said Dante.

The others came in to join us. We held hands as we listened to Sacro. It was uncomfortable for me. Just too much emotion combined with love and support. It took everything I had to continue holding hands with Dante and the unfamiliar woman next to me. I wanted to run away and I'm sure everyone around me knew it. Nobody seemed to pay any attention to me as I shook. I could feel their prayers, all directed toward Sacro and Donally. Sacro leaned over and moved the covers from her body. He was checking for something. It was shocking to see her there, so dead. I hung my head to avoid the sight.

Four cycles went by. Sacro completed Donally's lesson as he called it and concluded that she was safely on her way to Earth. My grief prevented me from questioning what I didn't understand about the whole thing. I was so numb that I didn't even realize I had any questions. The idea of Donally moving on to Earth didn't penetrate my sadness at all. To me, she was dead and that was it, no more Donally, she just did not exist anymore.

There was a large funeral that ended in the burning of her body. Many of us cried openly and loudly. I couldn't hold back my tears any longer, from the time we left the funeral, I sobbed for what seemed like forever. I didn't think it would ever end. I stayed at home and cried. I went for walks and cried. I cried myself to sleep every night and woke up every morning in a state of shock. Others came to visit and we cried together, except for Sacro, he left shortly after the funeral.

Thankfully, the grief lifted and slow as it was, I began to appreciate sunlight and warm baths. My sobbing subsided. I asked questions about the procedures surrounding Donally's death.

Dante and Coalamine both came to explain the different states of death. They sounded like fairy tale stories to me. I had come to believe in the finality of death. To me, that was it. A life ends in death, there is no more after the body dies. After all, there was nothing that I had ever experienced in my life that prompted me to believe that anything happens after death. I gave the theories of reincarnation and near death experiences to the crackpots of our New Age. Past lives, tarot cards and UFO's all went in the same garbage bin. But then it occurred to me that I was contemplating these ideas on a planet billions of miles from my planet of origin, with an evolved human and an alien. I was living with this crackpot stuff on a daily basis. For some reason I wanted to keep my belief of death sacrosanct. My worlds had changed but my mind hadn't. I held on to what I believed about death for it was all that I had to keep me human. I always knew that one day I would just die and be no more. There would be an end, the end. Humans always died, I was told, it was something we could never, ever escape.

I understood Dante and Coalamine's teachings on an intellectual level but I couldn't accept it as more than a theory for people that needed to believe in something more eternal. Weren't they just trying to make me feel better? Did they actually know that Donally had moved on? What proof was there? They couldn't come up with the proof. I saw her body burn, she didn't exist anymore so what good were all the stories of her going off to Earth other than to help make us feel better? It didn't make me feel better because I didn't believe any of it. I let them talk, maybe they were making themselves feel good and who was I to interfere with that.

It reminded me of the Alcoholics Anonymous meetings I used to go to. Some drunk would come back after the fourth relapse and persuade herself that the relapse was necessary for her growth, that for some odd reason it was good that she relapsed because she was learning something only a good relapse could provide. It was all to make herself feel better. I figured when things got bad it was just natural to want to make up stories that made us feel right about the shit that rained down on us.

Dante caught on to my game. He talked and I listened, my expression that of a child listening to the community librarian tell tales at the Sunday afternoon story time. Finally Dante refused to ignore my lack of faith.

"Don't be an idiot Kelly." he said as we walked about in OmMandantra, a small city dedicated to the healing arts and interspecies communication. After I had my arm checked at OmKyente, we decided to eat and see if we could get any information on when Sacro would be back. My arm had healed perfectly, it was like it had never been damaged at all.

"Oh well, thank you Dante. I needed that pointed out. I wouldn't have known I was being an idiot without your expert observations. Thank you so much." I said sarcastically.

"You, you don't trust me."

"As if I don't trust you." I said with all my defenses up and ready.

"Oh come on Kelly. Your disbelief is as clear as the nose on your face."

"Alright, Dante. Yes, I trust you and no, I don't believe you. It doesn't mean I don't trust you. Donally is dead, that's it, the final scene is over for her. She is gone." I choked up on the words.

"Why are you so sure?" asked Dante.

"Because nobody comes back from being dead. Nobody ever has and nobody ever will." I said firmly.

"O.K. God, whatever you say." I could tell Dante was losing his patience. "Do you know what Sacro is doing right now?"

"No. He didn't really talk to me about it, just that he was going away for awhile." I answered.

"He is helping Donally choose the right body in which to be born. He is with her right now."

"I don't think so Dante."

"What do you mean you don't think so?"

"Why would he do that? It doesn't make any sense. She's dead!"

"I've been explaining this to you, why don't you get it? Why is it so hard for you to see it?" said Dante, more to himself than me.

We walked along together silently in the warmth of the sunshine and the comfort of a cool breeze. Dante seemed to be talking to himself. He didn't use words and kept his thoughts away from me. Suddenly, he stopped walking and turned to me. I stopped, held in place by his enthusiastic gaze.

"There is this thing about us that never dies. No matter how hard we may try, we can't kill ourselves completely. Donally isn't the body, she's the undead nature that animated that body. At the point when her physical body died she had to go somewhere else. Do you understand that?" he said as he grabbed onto my shoulders with each hand and shook me ever so lightly.

"It's not easy." I said.

"So what? It wasn't easy getting you to accept Evolution, but you did it. What's so difficult about accepting your self as more than this?" He pushed against my arm. "This is just crude matter. You must know that you are more than this."

"It's so confusing, you know. It's easier to think that when you die, that's it. Or when someone you know dies it's over for them, they're gone and you just get used to the fact that they're never coming back. Your telling me that they do come back, that I'll be coming back."

"Yes and that bothers you? Most of us take comfort in knowing we get to carry on."

"I don't remember anything beyond what I am right now. Who was I before I became Kelly McGrail?"

"You've never given yourself a reason to remember. What would you do with a memory from one of your former lives? You'd think of it as a fantasy and pay no more attention. How do you know you haven't been doing that already?" said Dante.

I had to give him that. I couldn't argue that I was absolutely sure that I had no memory of a past before I became the me, that is Kelly McGrail. I was sure of it because I didn't believe that I could have such a memory, I never once entertained the thought of having had any other life.

"You'll remember details when you realize the truth of your permanence in the Universe." said Dante. "With awareness and acceptance you get clarity."

"Do you remember? Have you ever known me before?" I was still disbelieving yet willing to change my doubt.

"You can tell me Kelly, when you discover the truth in what I'm saying."

"I miss her though, you know? I miss the way she looks. I even miss her arrogance."

"Well, that's the thing Kelly. That body is truly dead and it's hurts to know we'll never see her that way again. It's hard to lose a body, whether it's your own or someone else's. I miss the way Donally used her body, I'll miss the way she used to communicate with us, but she will manifest herself again and in an even more arrogant fashion." said Dante. "The qualities we loved about her haven't died."

The instability that I felt was fascinating. The whole meaning of life was changing for me as Dante spoke about the thing within that never dies, not just for humans but for everything that contains the spark of life.

Our conversation transformed from verbal communication to the mind to mind talk I had only recently begun to partake in. It was a lot of work though, much more so than just talking and listening. I had to keep a constant beam of attention focused on Dante so that the thoughts of others didn't overwhelm me. He was good at making his presence direct and he reeled in my thoughts with ease. The more he told me of the endlessness of life, the more I could see the truth of what he was saying. My skepticism would return for I always had believed that I would one day die completely, soul and all, not an easy belief to let go of. I had actually been looking forward to the moment when I would no longer exist. In my early days of sobriety I thought of taking my life myself but thankfully, I always got distracted by small glimmers of hope.

Dante went on telling me how Sacro would give Donally aid to slip into her new body and do some fine tuning to it's brainwave patterns so that she could access her memories and carry out her plan, her purpose. Due to her experience, forgetting her past would not be useful to her anymore, she had gained her way up to full recovery. It was rather exciting and I no longer felt as sad that she had died. Why would I if she was not really dead? Of course insecure moments of doubt held their ground but I did trust Dante and the lessons he taught me. I fought to accept the new concepts without discounting the wisdom they held.

I looked around as we walked on, hoping to catch a glimpse of who ever may be with us. During our conversation I noticed the presence of something else, something other than Dante. A quiet dynamism. I knew Dante felt it to and welcomed it but he didn't address it. The quiet presence was very vibrant. I expected that I should see it clearly but still, it appeared to be only Dante and I. An air of gentleness surrounded us.

I gave up trying to figure out who was with us and just accepted it's quality. I think it may have been God that was with us. We didn't talk about it but there was a definite humility that came over Dante, something about him I had not seen before.

"Do you know where she's going? Will we see her again?" I asked out loud.

"Yes, we'll see her again. In fact, it's important that we do. I can't tell you where and when because I don't know. We just need to be aware. Remember little things about her, then you'll recognize her easily." said Dante.

"Won't she recognize us?" I asked.

"If you're still in this body, then yes she will. Who knows Kelly, where you'll be."

That hit me hard. Me, not in this body? It was easier to accept when we were focused on someone else. Grasping onto my body for life was the only way I knew to be alive. Even though we had spent days talking about life beyond death, when it came to applying it to me specifically, it took on that fairy tale hue again.

The season seemed to be changing on Evolution. The skies were darker shades of green. The sun shone differently, a little less intense. It was raining a lot more but it was still warm. I thought of Tabatha for the first time since I awoke to the news of Donally's death. I hadn't seen her since she helped me with my injury after the battle, The Battle of Donally I refer to it now. I wondered if Tabatha was still alive, in the same small body I had met her in, or did she take the same route as Donally? I heard that more of them had died. It seemed to me that they were no longer much of an enemy but more accurately just tired, desperate humans suffering in horrible pain and needing help, just needing a way out of their misery.

Oddly enough, Raleigh had not yet become ill or she showed no signs of it. Many of the remaining colonists were trying to escape but none had been successful. Some called out to form new telepathic links with us, praying for assistance. It was gruesome. Compassion grew for the colonists, people who were once enemies were being easily forgiven for their ignorance. Still, no one could physically reach those that called out, Raleigh had them locked in tight. She spent no time second guessing herself.

Tolosod stood in the shadows, always ready to support her, intensifying the hatred she carried with her and dominating her with dreams of power and the greed she had always lived by.

Some thought that Tolosod had taken her over completely and was the only reason she hadn't succumbed to the exposure of Evolution's atmosphere. Sacro disagreed, he knew Tolosod well, he knew that Tolosod couldn't survive without the hateful soul that existed within Raleigh, he knew they worked together. No other had escaped the colony, no one talked of Tabatha. I quickly came to the conclusion that she had passed away for I thought there would be excited talk about the only one that escaped the murderous troop. There was none.

Dante and I arrived at Dossamer Center, a building named after the first human that came to Evolution. Most of the Earth related work was done here. Research, education, monitoring, studying and communications with Earth inhabitants usually took place in the tall structure.

"I'll be right back" said Dante as he walked toward a tall, yellowish, womanly looking kind of thing. Her skin actually glowed and her hair was white like cotton. I stared at it as I did with every new creature I had encountered. She welcomed him and together they disappeared down the hallway.

I walked over to a small garden situated in the center of the lobby. I read a plaque that stood beside a statue of a young woman.

'*Dossamer Morran. In honor of the love, kindness and compassion she gave and continues to give, we dedicate this monument and support her Enlightenment. May we always remember her example of the promise of Earth's beings, great and small.*'

I'd never heard of her. The statue was so lifelike, it was almost like looking at a real person but it lacked the vibrant natural color of a living being. Dante had told me a bit about her before we got to the building. He spoke very fondly of her explaining that she was one of the first to truly embrace Evolution without fear. She had first been brought to Evolution as a small child of eight years and grew up surrounded by the information of the thousands of species that came to Evolution. At twenty-nine, she had decided to work on Earth to aid all beings in their growth, much like the job I had agreed to take on. She was tireless in her work excluding no one from her compassionate heart.

She was murdered only seven years after returning to her home planet. Burned to death by the people she tried to help. Dante didn't tell me anymore than that but did encourage me to learn more about her from the archives.

The lobby was empty except for me, the garden and the statue. The building itself felt like Earth. I took some comfort in the sight of familiar things even though I'd grown more fond of Evolution. The planet, the nature of Earth, with it's green trees and blue skies, was as beautiful as Evolutions' nature. It was the cultures of Earth, the people that recklessly destroyed the balance that made the horrible differ-ence. I did not miss the societies of my home world only the design of it's environment. The little garden held a piece of Earth within it. A little tropical Earth, the only plant I could name was the Bird of Paradise but I knew all of them were Earth born.

"Shouldn't be long now, he's on his way back." said Dante rather loudly from behind me. My peaceful focus on the flowers burst open with his playful entrance. The question of Tabatha was foremost in my thoughts and I finally released it to Dante.

"Tabatha? She is doing very well actually. Want to go see for yourself?" he asked.

"Well yes, yes I do." I responded delighted at the positive answer.

We left the Earth building, Dossamer Center, and walked back to the healing center that I had been to before, OmKyente.

"Kelly! Hi." said Tabatha beaming with good health. It was so good to see her and in such good shape. Her natural colors radiated from her healing body.

"You were right Kelly. Look at me, I feel terrific."

"Hi Tabatha, you look great." I said.

"Too great to be sittin' around in here." said Dante.

"They said I'd be in here awhile yet, but I don't mind this. It's really good here and peaceful. I haven't felt this relaxed in all of my life." she said happily.

"I have total confidence that they know what they're doing here. When you do decide to leave, we have something set up for you. And oh, we might get some use out of your knowledge of the colony so we can stop the wicked witch. This war thing between us and Raleigh is getting tiresome. She has no more real supporters but she's got a few people locked up with her. We think it's against their will, that's the impression we're getting anyway. Maybe you can help us get them out." said Dante.

"I'd be glad to help." said Tabatha. Her smile diminished considerably. "I'm so sorry about Donally, it's not fair…" I cut her off.

"It's okay actually, she's fine, she'll be alright."

"But I thought…, I was told that…" she stammered.

"I'll tell ya' about it after your outta here. It's a long story." I said.
Dante gave me a pat on the back.

I sat with Tabatha awhile longer. I thought it was time to make a new
friend, not to replace what I felt with Donally but to honor it. The truth
of Dante's words about rebirth sank in as I made connections with
Tabatha. Donally had died so that she could go to Earth and continue
her life there. The day would come when I would see her again. I felt
confident about that. I could look forward to being with her but now
was the time to build relations with new people, new souls. We talked
for hours while Dante left to check out a few things in OmMandantra.

The conversation led to Raleigh as Tabatha wanted to know what was
going on with her friends in the colony. Many of them had died since
she left, so I helped to ease the grief as best I could.

"I feel bad for saying it like this but I wish she were dead." said
Tabatha. I understood her desire.

"I just want her to go away, leave here, go back to Earth." she grumbled.

"She'd just cause more pain there, she needs to be healed right down
to the core. I'm just glad you didn't die. Dante has told me some things
about dying that I never knew before, most of it I still don't understand.
I guess dying isn't what I thought it was, but I'm glad your still you, the
same you that helped me try to save Donally."

She looked a little embarrassed but accepted my gratitude nonetheless.

There was a momentary, awkward silence just before Dante whirl-
winded into the room ready to whisk me off to teach me some new
aspect of Evolution or at least to repeat the things that needed to be
repeated. We said our good-byes to Tabatha. I promised to continue to
visit her and when she was better, to help her adjust to a new home.

It was easy to see what was happening between Dante and I. He was
my teacher. We walked and talked and he taught me things, gave me lessons. Every moment was a tremendous leap of faith for me. All that I
had been through still hadn't prepared me for all that I hadn't been
through. The absolute vastness of the Universe left me stunned. All

those beliefs that I had clung to, all that suffering I put myself through out of ignorance and then to come to this place where I realized that I had so little experience with reality.

My only comfort was that I had with me, a great master to learn from. Dante didn't look like a master or act like a master but like I said, I had little wisdom about reality. He was a child and a sophisticated gentleman all in one. Completely refined and charming while being silly and trivial, a perfect combination of paradoxes. He didn't much like it when I called him master, he'd endure it as a joke and say "The only master you have is within yourself." That in itself was a joke to me.

It was many cycles before Sacro returned. The whole trip took a lot out of him and rest and recuperation was his first priority. I was full of questions but Dante took me aside and explained that Sacro, like any living being, needed time alone. Sacro did however, mention to Dante that he thought I was ready for training, if I wanted the job of Interplanetary Diplomat.

"I thought I was in training." I said.

"You've been learning certainly, but there are some very specific details about being a diplomat that we haven't touched on." answered Dante.

"So when do we start?"

"You want to do this?"

"I think my question answers your question."

"Maybe, but I'm sensing some uncertainty Kelly. You have to be sure you want this for yourself. Are you sure?"

"Yes…,well, no…look, I'm not one hundred percent positive. I don't know enough to be absolutely sure but I want to find out if I can do this. I've got a great deal of faith in this place, in you and Sacro and Donally. I want to be part of this, to be here when people begin to really accept the freedom. Do you think that I ever thought for a moment that I could do something this magnificent? Dante, I'm a drunk, people have called me a hopeless case and here I am now on the brink of changing the world."

"There will be a point where you can't back out of this." said Dante.

"Well you just let me know when that is and ask me again before I go to far."

"Fair enough." said Dante.

CHAPTER 18

The sight of Sacro made my heart sing. I swung the door open and was greeted with his compassionate face, one of which I had not had the pleasure of seeing for way too long.

"How are you Kelly?" he asked lovingly.

"Sacro, I feel great. All this studying, reading, thinking, it tires me out but I love this. I feel so good." I was beaming with purpose. It was all true too. The confidence I gained through the teachings was more than I ever could of hoped for. It was more than good self esteem, it was more than mere self confidence. I felt truly useful beyond my own self interest.

Sacro was there to give me lessons on anxiety control which I thought would be one of my most useful of lessons. We went through all types of situations of the sort that I would be sure to encounter. Most of my time on Earth would be spent in pools of skepticism and harsh judgment. My days of seeking social acceptance were certainly over, most people would laugh at me. I would have no way to prove my claims, no hard evidence, the one thing most humans would be looking for. No magic, no alien technology. I wouldn't even have a spaceship to show them. My mission was to gain trust first and then I could show off the marvels of Evolution once they were willing to see it for themselves.

I would have some support on Earth, Donally was there after all. Sacro assured me that she would recover full memory but that it would take time for her to grow, as it does with all things alive. There were others on Earth that had knowledge of Evolution, others who would help me along the way as I needed it, essentially though, I had to face many people in high places that would see me as a crackpot. Would I have to deal with any anxiety? We spent a lot of time on these lessons.

Sacro had a way of making the most frightful of situations seem easy to handle, he instilled a quality of calmness into me, bringing me up to a place where I believed in my abilities, even trusted myself to be okay regardless of what I was facing. I would have many personalities around me and on Earth, personality usually came before principles.

There were other lessons, all challenging my four major functions, mental, physical, emotional and spiritual. The emotional components, like anxiety control were most difficult for me. I felt more tired after one afternoon of emotional workouts than of two cycles of physical training. If only earth military conditioning were as complete as this, there would be no war, people would be too whole to kill each other, to aware of themselves and the lives around them.

"Your training is going very well Kelly, very well." said Sacro.

"Yea, I think you're right. I haven't been so sure of anything. This is definitely my calling." I responded. I loved being praised by Sacro.

"Dante and I have been discussing an issue regarding your readiness."

"Oh?" I was immediately confused. "Readiness?"

"Yes. I think we can do something now. I think you can do something now, if you are willing, of course." said Sacro. "You know the condition of the colonists. At this point only six remain that have any hope of surviving. So many of them have suffered and died without proper guidance. Too many of them continue to suffer through the mazes of death, alone and confused only because of this union between Raleigh and Tolosod."

"Do you think Raleigh would still be like this if it wasn't for Tolosod?"

"Oh yes, she acts from her own will. Tolosod does not control her, he fuels her. She directs her own decisions but if Tolosod were to be drawn out of her, she would weaken. Tolosod feeds from her negativity. Hate, greed, you know what they are Kelly, all of that exists in Raleigh, she nurtures her hatred. Tolosod thrives on her personality and gives her energy to continue to use it. Separate them and they both lose power. Divided they fall."

"And what's this got to do with me?"

"You can separate them." he answered.

"And I'm supposed to know how to do that?"

"Partially. We have more to teach you, but basically you are ready."

"Funny, I never feel as ready as you always tell me I am." I said sitting down. "I feel like I need a vacation."

"Evolution can be in peace again once Raleigh and Tolosod are separated and safely contained." said Sacro.

"What do you mean by contained?"

"Tolosod is not entirely an evil being as Dante may have implied. If we could hold him in finite space where he only has access to himself, there is a chance for his transformation, an enlightenment. He would be visited by high spirits and Bodhisattva's, ultimately he would face his own Created Self but he would have no access to the weaker beings, the ones that are vulnerable to his hunger for darkness, such as humans. Eventually, he would choose to be enlightened since it is far more rewarding. It is the only hope we have for your Earth."

"What about Raleigh?"

"She would crumble quickly, as I have explained. Separate her from Tolosod and all that is left is human will. She would have no fuel. Her confinement would be that of holding her accountable for her actions. She will suffer the consequences and probably spend many lifetimes paying for her cruelty. It is our hope that she will reach higher levels of awareness as quickly as possible. I have no jurisdiction on her growth, it is her choice how she responds."

"Would she stay here or go back to Earth?"

"Hard to say. We may keep her here. We are bound to the responsibility of stopping her from further harming anyone with her patterns of violence." he answered.

Sacro sat down beside me. The way he looked at me made me notice how serious the situation was, how much he wanted a solution to work.

"Your right, of course, they must be confronted. Is there a specific plan to this?" I asked, resigning myself to the new duty. I knew that I could refuse but to choose that would mean leaving heavy burdens on those that had helped me so much. My fear was not so great that I would turn to cowardice. I would face them for Evolution and Earth.

"Oh yes, there is a plan." answered Sacro.

"Well I hope it's better than the last one." I tried to laugh.

"We have given more energy on this because of the outcome of the last Raleigh encounter. But still, the danger exists."

"Just mention the name Tolosod and I get chills. I know there's danger. I hope I have the courage to defeat him."

"I have no doubt." affirmed Sacro.

"But I do, lots of doubt. I haven't done well with either of them. Tolosod nearly fried my mind and Raleigh almost cut off my arm, if it wasn't for Donally, Tolosod would've killed me, needless to say Sacro, I'm a little bit afraid."

"Be afraid Kelly, you have every right to be afraid but because of what you have been through, you have learned. Courage comes from experience." said Sacro.

"So does fear, I think." I got up and started pacing.

"I know fear has less of a hold on you. I know you are able to respond well to this confrontation." Sacro followed me with his eyes. "It's the only thing left to do. Evolution can be a safe haven again once their union has been destroyed."

"But what about my ambassador job? I still have to do that." The pressure was building inside me. The Devid's became active, lowering my increasing blood pressure.

"I am sure your trips to Earth will be stressful but you would not spend all of your time there. Just think of how you will feel coming back to this house, no locked doors, no money, you have freedom here. You have not yet experienced the total freedom of Evolution. We have been battling Raleigh and her band since before you knew of us. Without Raleigh and Tolosod, Evolution can go back to being the Universal center of serenity and this is your home. It is your safe haven."

"Maybe. If I can break them up." I said while consciously allowing the Devid's to control my bodily functions.

I stared out the window and on seeing the familiar scenery of Evolution from my own front yard, I realized that my love for the place could easily win over all fear. It had the beauty of purity, of a planet well loved, appreciated and taken care of, qualities that earth had lost through the abuses of the growing populations of impetuous cultures. My safe haven, this new world, only one more challenge to my faith and then I could take part in the serenity of Evolution. But was it worth it? Of that I had no doubt. I had tasted the basic structure of this world, it left no bitterness for me to regret. I would've done much more to restore and preserve the freedoms of Evolution's societies. I would've faced greater challenges to release beings from the greed and hatred that I had learned to live with on Earth. I could do it remembering how Donally kept Tolosod away from me, she battled him and won.

"Your training for this new mission will disrupt your regular schedule. You will learn very different skills for this new, temporary position." said Sacro.

"Yea, well never a dull moment, eh? I want to be as ready as possible."

"Battle training is vigorous especially when your set to fight mind to mind combat."

"And Raleigh? What about battling her?"

"Fortunately, that will not be a problem. Raleigh will be incapacitated during your meeting with Tolosod. He has been protecting her body, as we had expected, from the chemicals that threaten her health.

No, protecting is the wrong word, more similar to numbing her to the effects. Devid's protect, Tolosod makes a person unaware. Devid's enable your body to process what you can use naturally and they convert what you cannot handle to accommodate human physiology. They work with you peacefully. Tolosod mimics what they do. Tolosod does not protect though, he actually breaks down the human system so that it is numb. She feels strong and well but when he becomes occupied with you, she will succumb to the exposure. She will become very ill, very quickly. We will be there to attend to her. The first thing that will have to be done with her is to take her to the containment unit for her own safety. The Devid's have declined her, they will not help her so the containment system will also act as an air filter, she will not be able to live outside of it."

"Are you saying that I'll be alone with Tolosod? I didn't handle that well the first time."

"Your strength has increased. Your abilities have doubled."

I took that to be a yes, that I would be alone with Tolosod.

"We have much to do now Kelly." said Sacro. He still looked peaceful and calm which eased off my own feelings of panic.

"I just wish Donally were here."

"In time." Sacro said. "In time."

All diplomatic training had ceased. The battle training was as vigorous as Sacro had promised. Sacro was a master trainer too. He played mind games with me that I didn't think he was capable of. He'd often remind me that his lessons were designed to help me deal with Tolosod's warped state so that I wouldn't confuse the lessons with Sacro's reality and state of being.

I fell into bed most nights, to tired to take off my clothes or turn off the lights. Much of the time I kept my thoughts positive by telling myself that whatever I thought was impossible before this training and confrontation, would seem easy after it was all over. With my success, the diplomatic missions to Earth would be simple. I didn't entertain ideas about failure or at least, I didn't dwell on them. It was more than Raleigh and her wayward followers that I had to protect from the damage Tolosod had done. I learned what it was about people that made them susceptible to his abuses. Should I have been surprised? Ego, plain and simple. The human ego. Tolosod had such a reign over Earth that he could leave people alone for a thousand years and the minds he had infected would continue to spread his vision without a need for his presence. It was easy for Tolosod on Earth. He planted seeds of despair and misery in the fertile soil of ego weakness and the humans themselves would tend to the garden of his will. People would spend lifetimes weeding out joy, love and kindness to allow his pain to grow. No other species, in all of the Universe, did this for him. Not that Tolosod couldn't cause problems in other systems because he did what he could, but never to the point that the species would actually adopt his evil without a fight. In fact, in the whole scheme of things, Tolosod was fairly weak among other beings of his class. It was the connection with humans that made him dangerous. Over centuries he would tend to his flock of humans, enforcing his will through their egos, instilling a sense of pride or honor to the suffering humans put other beings through, leaving his bitter markings on all. Even after his confinement, my home planet would carry out his work. That's why it was me that had to confine him. I had agreed to the job of being the bridge between Earth and Evolution. After ridding Raleigh and Earth of Tolosod's charms, I would be on the front lines of dealing with his mess. I would be the one solving the puzzle that he created. I would need to figure out how he cut out the good pieces of the human heart. Every action has consequences and in order to be able to undo what he had done, I would need to understand his motives for wanting to control the human species. Facing him and challenging him would give me a first hand view on his character, his weakness, his strength and, I hoped, his intent. I had begun the first steps of solving the world's great mystery, the mystery of suffering.

The idea of confrontation started to become more exciting and less nerve racking as the training went on. A true adventure for the once timid Kelly McGrail. Having such a purpose in the fate of humankind gave me a new sense of boldness that had a very comfortable fit. But, of course, as I had taken my cowardice to extremes over my life I found that the pendulum swung both ways.

CHAPTER 19

I rejected all fear as I readied myself to meet Raleigh. I crossed the boundaries of the crumbling colony and could hear moaning and crying from one of the smaller buildings. Raleigh had locked her remaining few followers in and turned them into dying prisoners. Raleigh, however, did manage to keep herself in the luxury of the large house and believed that she would find a cure to save the survivors gaining their undying devotion, and how could a genius be expected to work in anything less than perfect conditions?

Ten of the colonists were still alive but four of those ten were so far gone into the sickness that even the Devid's and all the advanced healing procedures on Evolution could not keep them alive. My connection to their minds was strong and wretched. I used my new skills to control my mind and tune them out. I couldn't hope for success with their tortured voices lingering around my thoughts. Instead, I directed my telepathy to Raleigh. I couldn't read her thoughts but I knew Tolosod would allow her to read me. She would know I was approaching and that was just what I wanted.

Dante, Sacro and three others walked with me, each keeping themselves guarded. They would overcome Raleigh so that I could reach Tolosod who would be called to attention the moment Raleigh felt threatened by our presence. Tolosod wanted me and would come to meet my challenge quickly, what he didn't know was that I was different than before. He had no knowledge of my new position and ability, Sacro made sure that there was extreme security regarding my job in this matter. Tolosod would welcome a fight from a single, helpless human.

I stood squarely at the front of her house and rattled the door with my fist. Up until that point, Sacro, Dante and the others had not been visible to me and I felt a little preternatural chill as they all appeared by my side.

"Margaret Raleigh!" I yelled. "I dare you to face me!" I thought I could hear her laughing from behind the door.

"I challenge you to a duel!" I yelled out louder. I knew she would take to the drama of the moment, that she would bolt out with her arrogance and anger completely intact. Her anger was her undoing and her arrogance made her completely vulnerable.

Although I had allowed her to sense my approach she was not aware that I was not alone. Sacro, Dante and the others masterfully masked themselves to her and Tolosod. She answered my dare by flinging the door open and standing seemingly ready to fight. Dante grabbed her, held her head and arms while two others held her legs. They hauled her off of the porch onto the open space of the compound. She struggled violently, nearly overpowering her restraints. Sacro stepped in and took control over her with an embrace. She fell limp. I suddenly realized why the huge Sharadian that had accompanied us was standing behind me in a readied position. I had invited Tolosod and he accepted my invitation with such incredible force that I was sent flying back into the massive alien's arms.

My physical senses no longer moved me. Tolosod swam before me in the Formless World that he lived in, one in which he thought he was master. He appeared more hideous than when we last met and he looked pleased at sensing my revulsion.

"I've been waiting for you." His voice was hollow and deep. A cold sound coming from a black hole.

"No, I've led you here Tolosod. I'm in control regardless of what you think. It's over for you, you are finished." I said.

He responded by laughing at me, thundering, humorless laughter that sent a chill through my psyche.

"Your worse than stupid." his voice boomed.

I felt my mind twist, he had begun his attack. Everything in my soul turned gray. Tolosod tried to rip through me, to engulf me as he had so many others. I let myself open. From deep within me, an energy formed, my energy built with faith, desire and love. I let it build. It spread through to the point that I could no longer see or feel the darkness that was Tolosod, and then I let it go. The force of my released power was too much for him. I felt him grasping at the edges of my mind, clawing desperately against the intensity of my blow. He wasn't expecting it.

I broke free from him and he flew back into the cloudy nothingness that surrounded us. I would not have the benefit of shocking him with my power again. I sent out search probes from my mind to locate his presence since I couldn't afford a surprise attack coming from him. I knew he was powerful but if I could face him head on I'd have a good chance of winning. I had the support I needed to beat him. All Tolosod had was himself. If I could make him taste his fear, just for a moment, he would fall apart.

My mental investigation succeeded. He was circling me, believing I was oblivious to his new location. The power of my energy had scorched him but he was able to get his own shields up as defense. He called on his dark energy to protect him. I turned to the direction I thought he was in but saw nothing. I backed away trying to lure him out beyond the hazy obstacles.

Vibrations, mists, beams of light and dark filled the world of the formless. Rays of energy turned empty space into a constantly changing maze. I kept my focus secure on Tolosod, my random thoughts guarded and my purpose clear. I made it a point to let him know only what I wanted him to know, that I was sure of my ability to win this game with him. His disbelief that I could ever succeed in winning out over him would aid me in luring him into his jail cell. He thought he was fighting the weak soul that I was when we first met but I could sense his slight disorientation with the powerful blow I had dealt him. He followed me, still circling, shrugging off the fear that threatened him. I brought the power up again, let it surge through my body. Focused directly at him, I let the bolt of energy go again making sure it was a clear shot. It was. It tore through his cloak of deception and hit him straight on. He fell back and mingled with my power phasing him in and out of dimension. My energy, made of the light of Evolution, cleared through the darkness that was Tolosod like he didn't exist. The force of the blow rocked through the Formless World sending a shock wave of vibration that knocked me down. I deflected as much of it as I could with the intangible stuff that floated around me. Even though I stood on nothing, I felt myself fall. I landed on a concentration of vibrations. I could see Tolosod fighting the residue of the blast I sent him. Shocks of current snaked over his strange body. I gained my balance as he roared out a curse in anger casting out another wave of disturbance. I glimpsed his fear but noticed how quickly it turned to violent anger. He transformed himself from a creature most horrible to one much worse. I felt sick at the sight of him. My vision blurred and my strength wavered.

"You are weak!" screamed Tolosod, so deafening that I fell again.

A terrible sensation surged through me. Tolosod's anger was so enormous that I feared it was too much for me to bear. I couldn't move. Tolosod did nothing more than show his true self to me and that was enough to immobilize me, send me screaming to stop the pain of being in his presence. How could I beat that? What did I have that could make him cower as I was then?

In my struggle to get up, I realized that I had known Tolosod for a long time. That I had been one of his puppets on Earth. I recognized him in a way that I hadn't before. Did he not follow me from one failure to the next, telling me I was truly taking my place in the big picture as a useless human designed only to teach others what happens when your not paying attention? He was there with me, encouraging me to hate myself every time I tried something new. He was there, holding me down, choking the enthusiasm out of me to the point where I couldn't face the world with my dreams. He was there whispering inside me, bitter criticisms to heighten the effects of failure. Tolosod was there when I started to drink, holding the bottle up to me, disguising it's poison in a blanket of courage. It was Tolosod that touched up the hazy LSD trips with moments of well being and teasing me with illusions of enlightenment. And it was Tolosod that persisted in showing me how untrustworthy most people were, driving me away from accepting anyone's love, twisting the intentions of others into betrayal and rejection. He taught me to fear life itself, he taught me to regret the fact that I existed. The darkness that had always surrounded me had been Tolosod.

Sacro had broken the bond between Tolosod and my soul. In the moment that I touched Sacro's hand, he had wrapped me in the warmth of integrity. He showed me what it was to be a complete being, not to allow myself to be divided by what I experienced. It was in those cracks of my heartache and indecision that Tolosod could enter and turn every small crevice into a canyon. Even though I realized all of this, I felt myself withdraw from Tolosod, still unable to fight the power of his frightening rage.

The authority he had held over me was too much. Sacro had protected me all the time I was on Evolution but as I faced Tolosod alone I felt no power of my own, no integrity. My psyche was dividing up into warring parts again, each undermining the efforts of the other. One splinter of me betrayed another. No longer was Tolosod the only enemy, the battle had turned further inward.

I lay, huddled in the Great Nothing Of The Formless World unable to move as Tolosod approached. My eyes focused on his face. A twisted, ugly face that moved closer and closer. With each step, his face grew and changed. It became a mirror and as he hovered over me I saw my face in his. None of the good things about me were reflected. I saw a tired, beaten thing, I saw myself as Tolosod, Tolosod as me. The familiar sense of failure enveloped me. A cold, dark feeling, oddly comforting and enticing. I let myself rest in it believing that I really belonged there after all, that once again I had taken my rightful place in the game of fate. Tolosod laughed over me. His dark, wet voice penetrated my head. I feared he would bore a hole through my mind that would never heal.

"What made such a puny little shit like you think you could beat me?" he said and laughed hysterically.

CHAPTER 20

What had made me think I could ever beat him? Part of me wanted to cower and placate him, assure him that I meant no harm and that I'd been terribly mistaken and would do anything for him if he just didn't hurt me. I had no mask to hide these thoughts, he picked them out easily. I felt myself tremble with shock that I could even be in such a position as this.

Tolosod's shadow grew over me blocking out the hazy light. I could see only his silloutte. The true demon stood before me and all I could do was whimper.

"What scares you?" his dark voice reached into me. He wanted to have my fears, pick them out and devour me with them. I fought him hard, imagining what he could do to me if he knew even one of my fears. I guarded myself fiercely to keep him from reaching inside me.

"No worries Kelly, I'll give them back, one by one I'll stuff your stupid fears down your throat so you choke on them" he laughed morbidly.

My struggle was futile, I was just too weak. He plucked each of my horrors out, one by one and presented them to me in full color.

First, the beetles came. I remember the first time I learned that such large insects existed. The rhinoceros beetle I think it was called. I was ten years old when I saw a show on television about these things. Just the sight of them scared me senseless. They infiltrated my sleeping dreams, became the monsters they never were in real life. My night-time dream beetles grew to be as large as a house cat and came after me as I opened the kitchen cupboards. I usually woke up screaming as they dug their hideous claws into my face, neck and shoulders. Tolosod took my nightmare and made it real. The beetles were falling out of his tattered robes. They fell to a ground that wasn't there and scrambled toward me growing larger with every little step they took. Hundreds of them, clicking and clacking with their pincher horns. Tolosod cackled hysterically like a crazy witch.

"Only I can control this Kelly. You can't stop it. Sacro can't stop it. Who has the power now Kelly McFrail? Who has all the power?" he bellowed and raised his arms up in a gesture of triumph.

I wanted to speak, to retaliate in some way but silent screams formed in my throat and got stuck there, choking me.

"Sacro can't help you." he said in a teasing tone. The grotesque beetles came upon me. I kicked them away. I had gone beyond panic.

"Where is he, Kelly? Where is Sacro, where is your angel of mercy now?" he asked with more antagonizing laughter.

Then came the little frogs. The little poison frogs from South America. Cute little things really. I'd first learned of them on a school field trip to the zoo. We were studying the classifications of living things. One touch could kill, not a bite or a sting but a single touch, a light brush against the skin and it's all over. We were told that one little frog could kill a hundred people but that wasn't what was so frightening to me, it was the way in which the victims would die. Witnesses reported that once someone touched these frogs they would start to shake, slowly at first then uncontrollably until they reached all out convulsions. Their eyes would role around in their heads and mucus would spew out from their eyes, nose, ears and mouth. They would try to scream, to run from their own bodies, some actually screaming out that they were on fire inside. Finally they would die in shock, their hair turned white from the horrible death experience. The teacher told us the story in a kind of "around the campfire" fashion. He thought it was a pretty neat story but I went home with the complete makings for a phobia that I could never shake.

And there they were dropping out of the folds of Tolosod's filthy cloak. Little poison frogs and huge hideous beetles determined to devour me. I looked toward Tolosod, to frightened to make a sound. All I could do was close my eyes and wait for death. Soon the frogs would be upon me and I would die.

Tolosod's booming laughter startled me to open my eyes again. The frogs and beetles were suddenly gone but he stood there in full view. The light was at an angle where I could see him very clearly, too clearly. He looked disgustingly human, the worst of what humans could be. I could see every hideous, evil crime ever thought of by the expression on his face. His eyes were wide and white and in the center were black pits of darkness. If eyes were really the windows to the soul, it was easy to see that his was living in Hell. Long, greasy strands of light colored hair dangled over his face, his shoulders and down to his waist.

That's when I noticed something large gliding in from behind him. The sharks.

Great White Sharks swimming evenly through the air. There were three of them approaching from behind Tolosod. One would have been enough. The terror that jolted through my spirit threatened to kill me. I would certainly die of fright before those creatures could sink their enormous teeth into my thin flesh. The beetles and frogs suddenly seemed more like pleasant companions as I watched the massive shark bodies coast toward me. That was my greatest fear, not to die but to be mangled unforgivingly by such a creature as this. A creature who thought nothing unusual of it's violent nature. An incredible animal that no other could top in the art of killing. No one could stop those teeth from their course once the beast released them, the victims could only pray for a quick death. My only defensive was to turn my back and run the other way, at least I wouldn't see it coming. As I turned and began to run, I hit a wall, one that I couldn't see but felt as if it were solid rock. I reached out and smashed my knuckles on the hard surface.

"Have you ever felt trapped, Kelly? Like you've been buried alive and there's no one to rescue you?" I heard his voice inside my head.

I felt something press toward me, backing me into the transparent barrier that I had just turned away from. It pushed in on me hard and unforgiving. I moved to my right and immediately hit a third barrier. I inched to my left only to find that I had been boxed in. The sharks moved toward me with their graceful, torpedo like bodies until they were inches from me, circling around me. I would've crumpled to the ground but the invisible box I was in kept me upright. I could not escape.

"Not many people can say they really know what it feels like to be buried alive." he snickered, "But then not many people ever live through that kind of thing."

I felt the crypt-like box tip over and I fell hard on my face. I tried to turn upward but there was no room. He was finding fears in me that I didn't even know I had. I heard an echo of his laughter coming from somewhere both inside and outside of the box. I could feel my senses unravel, my mental balance veered off to the side of lunacy as I realized the seriousness of the situation that I was in. This was not a dream. Tolosod hated me to the point that killing me would make him feel good. He was torturing me and enjoying every moment of it.

There I lay, face down in a box, so closed in that I couldn't even move my arms from my sides as this horrid monster stood somewhere nearby, probing my mind and laughing at the agony that I felt. I couldn't hold onto myself anymore. My mind finally twisted up into insanity and my body convulsed with rage and panic. I couldn't bare the feeling of being so closed in. I found myself praying the sharks would take me quickly but somehow I knew they were no threat to me anymore.

"I wonder how long it would take you to die in there." Tolosod whispered into my head. "No food, no water, no light. How agonizingly long?" his words boomed all around me, his voice caused me pain.

I had no defense, nothing to fight back with. I was lost in the dark box, lost in my thoughts of suffering, lost in the cold grip of death. I would go completely mad before I would die. I continued to thrash around in the box until I tasted blood. Through my bitter thrashing I had smashed my head. Blood came from my nose and other undetermined places. I had no form of coherent thought, my mind had gone into overload. Fortunately, my heart and my instinct remained in tact.

Somehow my heart made a link to Sacro and called out to him for help. As the blood flowed out of my nose, I felt myself losing my very will to live and the conviction that I could save my world from this monster.

Softly and without notice, Sacro touched me and said, "Find the light."

At least it was contact. I first thought maybe I had just made it up, an audible hallucination, some cool aspect of the human body to ease the horror of torture but it calmed me down and kept me from hurting myself any further. I looked around me as much as I could but I saw no light, not even the illusion of light.

"There is no light Sacro." I whimpered out loud. I could've just given myself up to death right then and there. Turn off and forget that I had ever existed, but Sacro had other plans for me and he prodded me again.

"Find the light." he spoke.

There was no light to see.

"Kelly, forget your eyes, let go of what surrounds you and see your light. Tolosod can not battle with that."

With my eyes closed I found myself traveling toward my Self. There was some spot in the center of what is me that was like a diamond reflecting the most brilliant sun. It was beautiful and real, more real than the regular me. This deep, white glow of light inside of me rejected the deception of darkness and although I could still feel the confining walls around me, I became very calm and lucid. At that moment, I felt as if I were two beings. In the light I saw myself as the better part of me, the me I always thought I could be but never committed myself to. For that instant, I believed in my own Self and truly knew what it meant to be me.

"Be what you are in that light." said Sacro.

The clear light spread open and gathered me in a firm embrace forcing oneness upon me. The two "me" beings integrated within the great authority of the light. I had, for all I could understand, been introduced and married to my Self in a single, powerful moment. I was no longer desperate with claustrophobia. I could see around the walls of the box Tolosod had encased me in. I could see through the mist to the place where he stood, the evil entity that had given me so much pain, so much to fear. With the new power from my light body, I presented myself to him. He stepped back with apparent shock but easily overcame his dismay and swung at me. His arm burst through me and he spun around growling with fury. I moved toward him with a controlled and confident stride.

"It's over Tolosod. I have evolved, you can't beat me but I can help you, I will help you. That's why I'm here. Just give it up Tolosod." I said evenly.

He exploded with tremendous rage. Running at me with all his force, he attempted to throw his darkness over me like a heavy, wet blanket. He shriveled back as he made contact, as if I had burned him. He groaned with the sudden realization that I had become more powerful than him. He was more than shocked at his lack of control.

The already distorted figure of Tolosod agonized in panic, changing his appearance to match his truth. He was defeated for the first time in thousands of years and it was quite obvious he didn't know how to handle it.

A chamber of color came out of the nothingness that surrounded us, a sure sign that I had won. Magnificent, clear lights of red, orange, yellow, green, blue, purple and white danced together. What was so beautiful to me was horrifying to Tolosod. He knew what was happening.

The chamber of light was where he would face himself directly, no humans to hide in or play games with, just Tolosod with Tolosod.

I felt no pity for him as the chamber grew over him, encasing his wretched soul like a spider spins a web around it's prey. He screamed, pleaded, clawed and when he realized there was no way of getting out, he cursed, threatening and condemned. Nothing could or would stop the process. It didn't take long, once he felt his fear, to give up the struggle. He was powerless to resist the pull of the chamber and he would remain powerless until he understood what true power was, for as much as he had controlled humans he had also alienated the rest of the Universe. No human loved him despite his embrace and he knew nothing of loving another, or himself. There was no power without love, he would learn that eventually.

A flash of light to my left presented an image of Sacro, like a hologram. I felt tired, disconnected and a need to rescue myself. I wanted my body or rather my body needed me. I had to get myself out of the box. As a being of pure light, the connection to time and space was fading, if I was to make it back to material reality I would have to act quickly. I went back to the trap my body lay in and touched it. It fell apart exposing my battered shell of a body. I could see it would hurt to be back in there, I had done some major damage in the panic to get out. Sacro sensed that my desire to get back into the bleeding body was very low and he urged me to move quickly. It looked so uncomfortable, sort of disgusting. With all the effort that I could pray for I broke into it again and fell into darkness.

CHAPTER 21

We celebrated. Such happiness was good for my soul since my body felt so beaten. I could see, from the state of the others, that I didn't fully appreciate the magnitude of ridding humanity of Tolosod's presence. I didn't know what life would be like without him. All I knew about my species had been traits born from the influence of his sick mind.

Evolution was radiant with the joy of welcoming the human race back to the Universal team. The process of peace could once again grow in our hearts and minds. No longer would we be the lonely planet, the ones who questioned why we seemed to be the only ones. Earth would soon be able to open it's cosmic doors and welcome reality.

Margaret Raleigh had been treated and was being held in her own private environment controlled room. She held onto her ideas that somehow we were the bad guys, the ones who should be locked up, punished, persecuted or dead. Confined to this shielded compartment near Sowthren Court she was offered food, shelter, clothing, all her basic needs plus a little bit more. She took everything given to her but swore at her attendants, even spit at them and voiced her extremely negative opinions on the different types of aliens that passed through to help her feel more comfortable. It would take some time for her to deal with her hatred. She was offered the chance to go back to Earth but refused quickly saying the only reason we wanted to send her back was to kill her on the way there. No way would she be at Sacro's mercy again. Margaret was filled with revenge and plans of taking over. Her feeble thoughts leaked out all around her and were open to everyone. Her control had left with Tolosod and she had no idea how to guard her thoughts. She was still very sick but Evolution had the time necessary for her healing. I couldn't see her becoming anything different but Sacro felt confident that she would learn to love herself and others.

I wanted to join the Universal party, instead I was taken to Om Mandantra's healing center. My body was so tired and worn by the fight, even though most of it took place within my psyche, all that I'd been through manifested fully on my physical body. I had finished the toughest challenge I had ever faced, and I had come out on top. I could sleep satisfied and secure despite my wounds.

Tabatha had stopped by to see me, she was leaving just as I was going in. She looked well, healthy and best of all, happy but she didn't stay with me for very long. It was easy to see that I needed rest, so most of those that came by to see me, left quickly. The calmness I felt was profound and aided my recovery.

* * * * * * * *

"I hope you had a good rest Kelly." said Dante.

Sacro, Dante and Coalamine sat around me in the front room of my house. It was great to be home, windows wide open, bright light shining in. The doors needed no locks and all the tracking equipment was gone. We talked about converting the room into a music room or art studio, a place where I could practice a hobby. I had to find a hobby now that I had a room for it.

Many cycles had passed since Tolosod and Raleigh were defeated. I was strong and alive again, ready for more training. I appreciated my role in the whole scheme of things. I looked forward to the work because it seemed to be something I could really love doing on a daily basis. I had always wanted to do something where I traveled and this was more than I could of hoped for. I was the Diplomatic Representative of Evolution—Earth Project, that was my official title.

"Are you ready to begin your work?" asked Sacro.

"I'm really ready. I'm looking forward to my first Earth mission. It's amazing what an effect Tolosod must have had on me. I don't feel afraid of going back to Earth anymore. There is nothing within me telling me I can't do this. I want to help heal the planet that raised me, I'm ready."

"Good Kelly, that's perfect. We need to go over some of the plans. We are in the process of changing Earth in some dramatic ways, very dramatic ways. There are things you need to know before you leave here. You won't be any good to anyone if you don't know what the plan is." said Dante, looking more serious than usual.

"Okay, what is it?" I asked.

Coalamine was completely disinterested in our conversation and wandered around my house, inspecting it's contents as one would in a museum. She had an interest in Earth cultures and wanted to understand the many species of Earth. My house was a good place to explore the 'Common North American Human' as she put it. I was at ease with her snooping. I welcomed her curiosity.

"Do you see how different Dante is from you and other humans?" asked Sacro pulling me away from my observation of Coalamine.

I nodded.

"We are going to make him seem normal in your world."

I didn't understand and allowed my confusion to show.

"It's time for Evolution to take over again. We're better builders than most humans, we have more experience. The humans of Earth have had control for thousands of years but they have abandon much of the responsibility that is needed to nurture a world. Understandably so with Tolosod running rampant through the collective consciousness, his time is over and ours has come. Earth needs a few options and a few friends. Earth has called on us for that help." said Dante.

I settled down in my seat and prepared myself to listen to what I knew would be a very deep discussion.

"So what exactly are we talking about here?" I asked. "And how do I fit in?"

"Just some basic renovations to reestablish the order of things on Earth. In order to do that though, we have to move a few things around and incorporate some new features."

"New features, eh? What exactly does that mean Dante?" I asked seeing that Dante's serious expression had given way to his usual playful but mysterious one.

"We have two new planets to introduce, Sparth and Eemaude. Both are ready for colonization. Sparth already has much of the wildlife in place. The difficult thing is neither planet is in the same solar system as Earth which makes it hard for us to make this easy for humans. Humans don't take to changes easily, you know that. Simple changes freak them out and these aren't simple changes. It's got to be done though or Earth won't survive."

"Earth would, most definitely die without our intervention. The death of Earth as a planet is not such a bad thing in itself, we have witnessed the deaths of millions of willing planets. Earth is not willing, it does not wish to die and has requested this expansion. We can provide the means but timing is very important. Earth is based on time and space, it has needs that it has to maintain in order to continue it's physical manifestation. The energy that is Earth has to have it's needs met at the exact time and place. There is nothing more standing in our way, other than the consequences of Tolosod's reign over the human race. The job you are to do or undo as it now stands, is the destructive effect of the creation of human ignorance and Tolosod's reign." said

Sacro. "You need to fix what Tolosod has effectively broken, the human spirit."

I thought for a moment, trying to decide what I believed the human spirit to be. What was it I had to fix?

"It's just a connection between soul, mind and body. Those three factors are spirit and Earth humans have been living without it for centuries, many centuries. Without that spirit bond, the individual is fragmented and at war with themselves all the time. They are unaware and vulnerable to focusing only on physical needs. Ah, but you'll learn so much from the work we are about to do." said Dante, taking questions from my mind and replacing them with answers.

They went on explaining what needed to be done in order for Earth to get it's specific needs met. We didn't really have a lot of Earth time to meet these goals. By the year 2012 seventy percent of the world's human population would be moved, divided up and transported to the two offspring planets of Sparth and Eemaude. The thirty percent of humans that remained on Earth would undergo several physical changes. I asked about the other life forms but Sacro told me it wasn't my job. The animals didn't need to be persuaded, they didn't resist Evolution only the humans did. As in any single job well done, there were many doing their part to achieve success. I was to keep my skills directed on the humans and then only the humans of Earth. The two new planets were not my concern. It would take all my attention to help prepare people for the changes that were to take place. I would undergo the changes as well as the thirty percent of the population that was to stay on Earth, the others would be moved and carry on in a slower process of growth and change.

The people that stayed on Earth would need a lot of encouragement since everything they'd ever known was to be reorganized. Evolution was to be accelerated and the human body would go through a series of shifts not over a period of years but of months.

Earth, as a planetary body, could not stand another human population explosion. People had become destructive parasites in Earth's delicate system. Only the genius of Evolution could turn the relationship between Earth and humans into the symbiotic one it was originally meant to be.

The reproductive cycles would change. Human gestation would last approximately ten years allowing the fetus to evolve before birth to accommodate the changes in physical structure. The longer prenatal development would also create a far more thought provoking process when it came to the decision to have children. Any couple looking at ten years of pregnancy would have to think on it more than once and mistakes had greater consequences than with a nine-month gestation period. The age of sexual maturity would be increased to the forty to fifty year period.

"Are you nuts! Nobody is going to want to have kids at forty, especially when it takes ten years for the pregnancy. Who's gonna raise the kid? The parents will be dead by the time…" I blurted out but was interrupted by Dante.

"Take it easy and keep listening, we aren't done yet. A forty-year-old person is nothun' but a youth."

He went on to explain that a human life-span would be increased to two hundred and fifty years. Of course there would be those who lived longer and those not quite as long but on the average we could see two hundred as a pretty early retirement age.

"We are giving the human race more time to mature. The rate of intellectual development will be comparable, in some cases increased and there will be a much larger capacity to understand spiritual matters. What you call the paranormal will be easier to comprehend, your minds will have new senses to work with." said Sacro.

"But why live longer if we don't really die? What is the point?" I asked.

"Less trauma to the individual. The death and birth cycle can happen so quickly that the being is left without understanding what they have experienced. For some beings, nine years is enough but humans don't adapt well to the changes. They forget themselves over a period of lives or even from one life to the next. The purpose of living is lost. It becomes pointless to have more than one body since so much of the experience has to be repeated over and over in each existence. We want to give each human being a definite chance to feel what they are, who they are and embrace themselves. Earth has become a stuck point for many souls, a place where the distractions overwhelm the true goal. Do you know what the true goal is Kelly?"

"There's got to be more than one true goal, there's so many different people in the world. Everybody has different goals." I answered.

"There you have it. You do not remember what the true goal is. The true goal is to experience."

"Experience?" I had no idea what that meant. The simplicity was too complicated for me to understand.

"Experience who you are, that is the goal. Experience who you are and experience what you become through creation. You are always creating yourself, it's time to experience what you have created. Humans have given into ignorance, they now ignore themselves to pursue things outside their own skin. We understand that Tolosod hindered the functions of the human body, that he severed the connections of body, mind and soul but as I have said, with Tolosod removed the adjustments can be made to restore the human being to sanity. Earth can again be a place of experience, a playground of physical wonder. Also consider this…humans are not the only beings on Earth. You can be sure that every soul that takes on a human body has also experienced a dog's life, a mouse, a slug. All the bits and pieces that make Earth what it is, is connected by memory but if humans have forgotten their connections to the dog's life, then Earth can not survive.

What do you think would happen Kelly, if your brain suddenly forgot what your liver was doing? Your body would break down. Each atom that exists in your brain has at one time or another, existed in your liver so it must remember what it used to do as an atom of the liver in order to understand and aid it in doing what it needs to do for the good of the whole organism."

I saw Dante and Coalamine out of the corner of my eye as I listened to Sacro. Dante was giving his interpretation of a bit of artwork on my corner table. I felt flattered that Coalamine stopped and inquired about it since I had made the thing myself. A little clay dog, my attempt to honor my first love, my dog—Jonesy, who had died when I was fifteen. She'd been with me all of my life at that point and when she died I went numb. Who had she become after she left me? Would I ever know her again? It seemed that it was very likely that I would or did.

"You do not need to remember everything now. The greatest fun of the whole physical experience is remembering who you are over time." said Sacro. He clapped his hands and stood up.

"The lesson is done for today." he said and walked to the open window.

The sparkle in his eyes revealed his intense love for the sight of Evolution. I watched him looking over the land in front of my house. He looked free and happy, happier than I'd ever seen anyone look, it was so genuine and pure, unmarred of any worry or fear.

I breathed deeply and basked in the aura of Sacro's peace.

CHAPTER 22

"The time has come." said Sacro and indeed it had. I was ready and waiting to go back to the world from which I came. My leg bounced up and down in a nervous reaction to the anxiety of having to travel back to all that I had left behind, all that I had been before Evolution.

Dante, Sacro and I sat together at a small, outdoor café, inside the Dome of Sowthren Court. The sun beamed through the Dome's outer shell and I welcomed the energy it provided me. I needed all the support I could get for the long journey I was about to embark upon.

"Everything is ready. Nothin' to do but get there." said Dante with a sigh, a sigh of acceptance regarding the change that was about to take place.

The three of us walked leisurely out of Sowthren Court. I let my gaze mingle over the sparkling lake and the clean pathways filled with aliens doing whatever they needed to do, not at all concerned that I was about to travel billions of miles through space to change the function of an entire planet.

Our pace quickened as we left the domed city and walked through the drab tunnel that led to the compound. There wasn't much to mingle over in the dull, gray concourse.

We didn't stop, just walked straight through and out into the fresh air of Evolution. It was about an hour's walk to the lift off point, the place where I would be adjusted to the demands of space travel and sent off.

Everything had been arranged for me including accommodations and a large supply of money to keep me out of any great need. Sacro was well aware of the problems I'd face and adding poverty to the equation was hardly a recipe for success. Unfortunately, money was power on Earth whether I liked it or not and Sacro set me up so that gaining that influence over others wouldn't be a problem.

I choose to walk even though Renfrew had offered her services, because I wanted to bask in the beauty of Evolution, take in all that I could handle so that I would not forget the purpose of my cause.

Earth could one day, be as radiant as this place and I would help it get there, I thought to myself as I looked over the landscape. I picked up a small stone and tossed it into a large puddle along the side of the pathway we walked on. Ripples danced across the water and waves of energy fluttered from all angles. One day people on Earth would be able to see the sparkling colors that comes from a stone in motion and the aura of life that encases even the smallest of living creatures.

"You are aware of the fact that many people will want you dead, kill you themselves, they would." said Dante. It was the first time he spoke in a long while. He walked very close along my right side.

"Yes, I've been made aware of all the risks. I know what I'm doing, you trained me yourself so what are you worrying about?" as I spoke, Dante put his arm around my shoulder and brought me closer to him. It was strange, different than his usual show of affection.

"No amount of training can prepare you, not really, not with humans. They are so, you know, unpredictable and so full of hate, just blind hate." he said with a distant expression.

"Tolosod is gone though. They won't be so bad without Tolosod." I said with an ever present hope that somehow humanity would prove to be a positive force in the Universe.

"Sure, they won't be so bad without him. Yea, they'll recover some of their dignity but for now Tolosod's influence continues to mask their reality.

I do worry about you Kelly, I don't want you to get into any trouble that you can't get out of, you know what I'm saying?" I nodded, a bit confused by his sudden hesitancy regarding my departure.

"Your still naive about human nature and that bothers me, really bothers me. Never assume anyone is on your side. Too many of those people don't want anything to do with the changes you're going to bring with you. Kelly, you present the greatest challenge the human race has ever faced. They are not gonna like it or you." Dante went on with his warnings all of which I'd heard and understood in my lengthy training.

I looked to Sacro, who walked calmly on my left side, somewhat further from me than Dante. He smiled and sent me a mental message just between him and me—let him talk. I nodded and looked back to Dante, beautiful Dante, who wanted nothing more than to protect me from all things dangerous and devious on Earth. We knew all too well that there were more than a few risks for me to face, and I would have to be successful with or without their help.

We approached the launch site, an area much different from the one where I had landed. This was more of a station where ships landed and people from other worlds prepared for their own space journeys. Never before had I seen so many different modes of travel and I was excited by the display of technology.

Many types of space crafts were lined up, like cars in a parking lot. Some were beautiful with sharp colors and sleek lines, others looked as if they'd seen more action than was good for them.

Dante stopped his rambling and took in the animated scene of the busy spaceport, a place that was always active on Evolution.

We walked into the massive, sprawling center and I was, as usual, stunned by the sight of diversity. Not only in the types of beings but also in their methods of travel. Ships were used, as I had seen outside but there were also compartments where people entered then just disappeared.

"There is one type for each species capable of this type of travel." Sacro said. He pointed to the transporters, as he called them. Each one had signs and symbols attached to them, guiding the user to the right one.

"God, they're real. Why can't I use one of those? Wouldn't it be easier, faster?" I asked hoping that I would get the chance to use what had been total science fiction to me just moments before.

"You could use one but you'd end up dead before you got there. Our physiology won't take it, not enough cohesion in our physical structure, you'd break down just fine but you'd have a hard time coming back together, your body would anyway." answered Dante.

"Yea, alright. I'll just stick to the long way then." I said nervously and continued to watch as others found their designated pods and disappeared.

Dante pulled me along with him, his arm still around my shoulder, still holding me closer than usual. I let him lead me, it allowed me the chance to look at everything without worrying about bumping into things.

Sacro swerved to the left and was gone before I could say anything.

"Where'd he go?" I asked.

"Take care of some business, what else? He'll be back. Let's sit over there, you can watch ships take off from there." he said pointing to a deck that jutted out from the main traffic flow of intergalactic travelers.

We were the only two beings in the whole observation lounge. The lighting was provided by the sun shining through the window that overlooked the docking area, M-68. There wasn't much movement in

M-68 save for a couple of human looking technicians puttering around underneath a largish, yellow ship, one of the sleek looking ones.

Dante and I sat next to each other in front of the window. I was quietly in awe of the surroundings and the view. It took me awhile to notice that Dante was looking at me, staring at me, not saying anything with his mouth or his mind, he was holding back his thoughts. I reached out with my own tendrils of thought only to find his guarding wall of privacy set up like a no trespassing sign. I continued to stare but my focus on the sights of the docking bay broke apart as I wondered what Dante was doing. He looked nervous and confused, something I'd never seen in him. It made me feel nervous and I glanced at him hoping the eye contact would break up the tension or at least make him look away. My glance was meant to be quick, just a show of discomfort but as my glance met his gaze, I became locked in it, I couldn't look away.

Blood rushed to my face and I felt the flush in my cheeks. Something was different, not just with him but with me. My peripheral vision faded and for just a few seconds, he seemed to be the only thing in the Universe, the very center of the Universe. He smiled and my heart pounded harder than it had when I first met him.

"What's going on?" I said in a whisper.

"Your swooning?" he said trying to answer me but sounding instead like his own question.

"Swooning? Dante I…"

"Kelly I love you" he said cutting me off. He reached for my hand and held it between both of his.

My vision blurred a little and I looked away from him hoping to get some feeling of stability going. I focused on the shiny, yellow ship now being moved to a different spot.

Tears formed in my eyes and when I blinked they fell over the edge of my eyelids and onto my still hot cheeks. He wiped them away.

"I'm sorry Kelly, I didn't think you'd react this way. It's just…"

"You love me?" I cut him off this time. "What does that mean, you love me? Are you talking love, love or just love, like I love you buddy?" I was still trying hard to focus on the yellow ship to avoid any random eye contact. I didn't want to be looking at him when he answered me.

"I mean the big love, the all capital letters love. I love you Kelly McGrail." he spoke firmly.

My tears were misleading, I knew he thought I was upset with him, unhappy about the new development but I was stunned with joy. I took my hand away from his and slapped him across the arm, not wanting to hurt him just not knowing how else to deal with the mixture of emotion I was feeling. I'm leaving and he's telling me he loves me I thought to myself, making sure he wasn't able to view the contents of my mind. I'm going a gizzilion miles away from here and this beautiful man tells me he loves me as we are practically waving goodbye.

I loved him too but I'd never admitted it to myself let alone spoke anything of it to him. His very presence made me quiver but I didn't give it too much thought and I never thought for a second that he had those feelings for me.

"When did this happen?" I asked, the tears had stopped but my eyes were burning with the anticipation of more to come.

"I'm not really sure. I didn't mean to upset you, it's just that I couldn't bear to let you go without telling you. It didn't seem so important that you knew until now. Kelly..." he stopped after saying my name and looked as if he didn't know what else to say. He moved back a bit obviously guarding himself from another slap.

"I'm not gonna hit you." Oh, how I wanted to kiss him. I kept looking at the yellow ship, fearing that if I were to look at Dante I might jump on him in an uncontrollable fit of passion. With his admission of love for me out in the open, my resolve to keep him out of my fantasies had completely broken down and washed away. Nevertheless, I sat rigid in my seat, staring straight ahead, my skin bristled with goose-bumps. I thought if he touched me again, I'd go through the roof.

"So, you feel the same?" he asked hesitantly.

I had not been able to guard my thoughts well and he picked up on my vibrating mind. I stuttered, tried to reply but nothing decent came out of my mouth. I forced myself to sit back and take a few deep breaths and as I did Dante did the same. We both stared at the yellow ship that was now moving slowly away from us, out into the open where, I presumed it would be taking off.

"Yes" I said finally. I wanted to say more, like how much I wanted to cancel my trip so I could spend the next couple of weeks with him, alone in my house, mostly in my bedroom, now that the creature of passion had been released between us. I wanted to tell him that even though I'd never believed in love at first sight, I was willing to make an exception for him, that I knew that I wanted him from the very first moment that I'd seen him appear before me out of thin air. Instead, I just said yes again to reinforce the first one.

Dante let out a heavy sigh and turned to me. His delight entered me like vibrations from a sweet song. He touched my arm and I melted a little and as I turned to him our eyes met again. He leaned into the gaze and taking the cue, I met him halfway until our lips touched. My body stiffened and I almost backed away but the sensation only lasted for a second. Both of us let go of our reserve and opened our hearts to each other.

CHAPTER 23

When Sacro found us, we were both sitting quietly, holding hands and looking out at the empty docking bay. He stood quietly but then burst into laughter at the obviously dazed quality we were both displaying.

"I see you handled things Dante. I am so pleased for both of you." he said through his smiles.

Both of us turned to him rather slowly and regained enough of ourselves to acknowledge his presence. I blinked to fast. I wanted to ask Sacro if I was dreaming but thought how stupid that would sound and put it out of my mind, of course I wasn't dreaming. I didn't know what I was supposed to do. I wondered if I was still expected to get up and leave, travel back to Earth alone knowing that a man I had thought was too good to be true had declared his love to me.

Tears welled up in my eyes again but I held them back.

Dante pulled me up out of the chair and hugged me with more of the compassionate manner that I was used to getting from him. I hugged him back hard and took relief from his strong body.

"I have to go now." I meant it as a question but it came out as a statement of my decision. It wasn't up to them whether I went or not or when I went, it was all up to me. I couldn't see myself leaving Dante but I knew I had committed myself to this Earth journey and I was in it for the long haul.

Sacro and Dante looked at each other with conspiritory glances. They were obviously communicating without me.

"What's going on?" I asked, my brow furrowed over my eyelids in a concerned gesture.

"I will wait for you by chamber number six. That is where you will be beginning your journey, you see? Right over there." he pointed to the direction of the chamber I would soon enter and began walking toward it. He gave Dante a hearty pat on the back as he passed.

I turned to Dante holding back a powerful urge to kiss him again.

"It's like this Kelly, I want to come with you. Not right now but in a couple of weeks. I wasn't sure before but now I know and I don't want to be away from you for too long."

I couldn't stop the smile from spreading across my face. I got an image of the first time I'd seen Dante do that child-like dance he did around Sacro and I as we walked. I wanted to dance.

"I don't want to be apart either. Not even for a couple of weeks but yea, if it has to be this way. I want you to be there with me. We'll be a team, save our planet together." I jumped a little with the excitement.

"It's done then. You go and get set up and I'll be there. I'm so happy Kelly. You've made me so incredibly happy." Dante pulled me closer until I only had to turn my head slightly to invite another glorious kiss, to which, of course I did without hesitation.

Moments later, I was in Chamber six, alone and awaiting the changes the Devid's were to perform on my body so that I could endure space travel and speeds incalculable by Earth standards.

Sacro remained connected to me telepathically, the same way he had when I came to Evolution. His subtle presence was calming and necessary.

A burst of light forced me to close my eyes. My body swayed as a gust of hot air blew up from beneath me. I lost my balance but it didn't matter because the Devid's had control over all of my physical functioning.

I let them have me, completely trusting their extraordinary abilities to get me to the place I once called home.

* * * * * * * *

The sun was rising in a spectacular display of reds, pinks and purples. The blue sky held only a few gleaming white clouds. I opened my bedroom window and breathed in the familiar spring air. Life had adjusted itself to the season. Flowers bloomed and the smell of the blossoms on the tress was heavenly. I bathed in the mundane beauty of my old neighborhood.

I'd arrived quietly in the early morning, almost exactly the same spot from which Sacro had taken me. He had taken care of everything while I'd been away. Paid rent, bills and all outstanding debts. I had a clean slate, nothing to worry over other than changing the focus of the whole human population on Earth. Six billion people to work harmoniously with over the course of the next twelve years, what was there to worry over?

I wouldn't be staying in the little apartment, in fact I wasn't really going to be staying anywhere for too long. My new job meant incessant travel, always on the go. I did however, want to stay there for a day or two, clearing out some closets and getting rid of old things.

A co-worker, a friend from Evolution would be meeting with me to organize my efforts with the others who worked for Evolution's cause. I looked forward to meeting my new friends but I was enjoying the moments alone in my old place, fondling remnants of a life I'd never know again, cherishing anything good I could take out of it and forgiving myself for all the hardships I'd endured. It was actually good to be home even though I knew it wasn't really my home anymore. Evolution was my home. Sacro and Dante were my home. The incredible things I'd learned were my home and ultimately, the new being I'd grown into was my home. The changes in me were real. My mind, body, all of me was growing and one day I knew I'd have more in common with Dante's level of existence than with the one I'd become used to as I was growing up.

All of humanity would have to feel this, I thought as I looked out of my apartment's front room window. All people would have to accept the reality of the new understanding of Evolution, that it was to happen to us whether we agreed to it or not.

The wise, accepting individuals would reap such tremendous rewards but I knew that out of the whole six billion individuals of humankind, only a few thousand would really give themselves to the process. Survival of the humble was the name of this game. My greatest hope was simply that I would have enough of a trusting presence to get people to listen and try to understand the nature of my work.

An entire day passed with me staring out the windows, watching the streets, the cars, the people passing by unaware of my spying. I watched the cycle of the day, content to observe without trying to change any of it.

The sun and the streets cleared and I thanked the Universe for providing me with such a serene and peaceful day.

With all the lights turned off, I slipped into my comfortable bed, secretly saying goodbye to it and my life as I had known it. I closed my eyes slowly, knowing full well that when I opened them I would begin the delicate work of changing the world.

About the Author

Jennifer MacDonald lives with her husband, son, six cats, a rabbit, a dog and eight fish in Calgary, Canada.

Printed in the United States
1187800004B/263